# THE BLADES OF CORDOBA

# THE BLADES OF CORDOBA

*by*

Terence Kelly

**Dales Large Print Books**
Long Preston, North Yorkshire,
England.

British Library Cataloguing in Publication Data.

---

Kelly, Terence
   The Blades of Cordoba.

   A catalogue record for this book is
   available from the British Library

   ISBN 1-85389-811-2 pbk

First published in Great Britain by Robert Hale Ltd., 1981

Dales Large Print is an imprint of
Library Magna Books Ltd.
Printed and bound in Great Britain by
T.J. International Ltd., Cornwall, PL28 8RW.
2756489 4

# AUTHOR'S NOTE

Whilst this is a work of fiction it is based upon many years spent in the Caribbean during which my wife and I were most graciously received into their homes by planters such as Harry Blades. All of the characters are intended to be fictional but it is, I suppose, impossible to avoid similarity entirely. Should any of those who have been kind to us see something of themselves in Harry Blades, I hope they will not feel offended—Uncle Harry is a good man and quite typical of many good men who were planters through the smaller and larger islands whom I met in those enthralling years. So far as any other characters are concerned, however, any similarity to anyone living or dead is entirely coincidental.

To Mike and Sue
who also knew the Caribbean

# One

They were dressed alike, Inspector Hastings and Harry Blades, in khaki shirts and shorts—but Harry's, neat enough, were limper, faded, the glaze of ironing less arrogant. Hastings, a strong man who carried himself superbly, jet black of face, grim of expression, stood stiffly beside the table on which he'd put down cap and cane; he made Harry, seated, look old and tired—as well he might, a man of seventy after a hard day in the canefields. But now, waiting for Paul, his nephew, to come in from the platform which ran the length of Norfolk Hall and from which almost all of the thousands of acres of Norfolk's sugar fields were visible, there was relief on his face—even the wry, mischievous smile of a man with a quiet sense of humour at once guilty and pleased at having an unpleasant business interrupted. And when Paul came in there was joy in the way he greeted him.

'Hallo, Uncle Harry,' Paul said with almost equal pleasure. 'Good evening, Inspector.'

'Good evening, Sir.'

11

'Help yourself to a drink, Paul,' Harry said.

That was an instruction—Hastings was to have his say. Paul nodded and as he crossed the beautiful sitting-room which once had been merely Norfolk's entrance hall he could hear the policeman going on but in a tone which admitted defeat.

'We know it was Ryle.'

'How d'you know?'

'We've spoken to his wife.'

'But that's not evidence, is it?'

'No.' And, after a moment. 'We can't prove it, sir. Not without your co-operation.' There was reproof but neither appeal nor lessening of respect.

'I'm sorry,' Paul heard his uncle answer. 'I can't help you, Hastings.'

'You discharged Ryle two days ago. He's been with you more than five years and he's the fourth-generation Ryle to work at Norfolk. A week before you discharged him there was a cane fire at Ely Pen.'

'There are other reasons,' Harry said, 'for firing men.'

'After four generations, sir?'

'If,' Harry said, 'I had evidence which helped convict Ryle he'd get ten years, wouldn't he?'

'Yes.'

'Don't you think that's too stiff a punishment?'

'My opinions don't come into it, sir.'

'The law on cane fires here's too harsh,' said Harry. 'I'm sorry.'

The policeman turned to Paul. 'You know George Ryle, sir?'

Paul nodded.

'Then,' said Hastings, picking up his cap and cane, 'I should be grateful, sir, if you could persuade Mr Blades to tell us anything he knows.' He turned back to Harry Blades. 'And meanwhile I should advise you, sir, to lock up the house at night.'

Harry shook his head. 'I'm sorry to add to your problems, Hastings, but it's a tradition at Norfolk Hall that it is never locked.' He crossed to the bell-push and came back, holding out a sun-stained hand. 'No hard feelings?'

'You don't make it any easier for us.'

Harry dropped the hand, unshaken. 'I'm sorry,' he replied.

Alexander came into the room; an old man too, but immaculate in white, with brass buttons which would have done a guardsman justice.

'Inspector Hastings is just leaving,' Harry said.

When they were alone, Paul said: 'Did Ryle start that fire?'

'Yes.'

'Then why not tell Hastings?'

'For the reason I gave him. Ryle's been punished enough.'

'He won't forgive you just because you're shielding him.'

'No,' Harry agreed. 'But that's nothing to do with Ryle, Paul, that's to do with life. The more you shield a man, the more he's likely to end up hating you. But the fact a man hates you isn't any reason for doing something you don't think is right.'

'I don't find that a very telling argument.'

'No,' said Harry, smiling. 'I don't suppose I did when I was your age.'

Regarding Paul more or less as his son, he found it difficult not to lecture, not to advise, not even, sometimes, to patronize. He was aware of these faults and made resolutions to avoid them—but they were always creeping into their conversation.

So he dropped the subject and taking Paul by the arm, said: 'It's good to see you, Paul. I wish you'd come more often. Let's go outside—it's a wonderful evening.'

It was indeed—suddenly cool with a sky almost without cloud hazing pink towards Palmira to the west and the black kling-kling birds passing by in resolute tail-heavy troops as they always did at such time of the evening and a magic gentleness on everything. Below, as brightness faded, the fields of sugar cane were soft, stretching on and on, and far and wide towards the

14

unseen road running from French Bay to Pilotte, while, beyond the road, margining the long, deep, white sand beach, the thick belt of coconut palms was blackening to a myriad spiders hoisted up on poles.

'Best time of the day,' said Paul.

Not when you're old, thought Harry; when you're old the morning is the best time of the day. But he thought this without sadness for life had taught him to be philosophical, and he kept it to himself because he was not a man to look for sympathy.

They sat, side by side, in white-painted, chunky, wooden flat-armed chairs with holes cut in them big enough to take the heavy tumblers men who sweated from an hour after dawn through to dusk needed for their evening drinks. They were, for uncle and nephew, very unalike. Harry was stocky and of less than average height with bright blue eyes which, and especially when he was at ease with friends, could be very merry, with a mass of soft white hair and a face crazed with wrinkles and sunburnt teak. But Paul, who took after his grandfather, Matthew, was naturally dark, tall and thin, intense and with a sophistication which was attractive to the women of Coral Gardens where he worked.

It was Harry who broke their silence: 'Well, Paul?'

15

'I'm seeing Daniel Fonseca tomorrow,' Paul answered rather tersely.

'And?'

'Well it has to be Norfolk, doesn't it?'

'You don't have to speak to him about it.'

'When he's got all those shares in Coral Gardens?'

'Oh rass, man!' Harry began to object— but then changed his mind. 'I'd better,' he said, chuckling, 'get myself a drink.'

He went along the platform to the trolley Alexander had wheeled out under the yellow buzz-off bulb by the sitting-room door. Paul stared at the sky whose last pastels were just fading into the blue of night. The air was still. The sea breeze had died; in moments the cool air of the mountains backing Norfolk would flow down the hillside like water, creaking the palms to life, stirring the leaves of the immortelles, the mangoes, cottons, cassias. In moments the bullfrogs and the cicadas in their millions would croak and rasp and then there would be no more real silence until dawn. In only minutes the first few stars pricking the sky would have multiplied to challenge the myriads of fireflies which would glitter in the bushes. But apart from them, the stars and the fireflies, and the yellow buzz-off bulbs, and the light filtering from the house, there would be darkness all around, and the hillside would be black except for the single light which marked Copra Valley, the shabby house where Paul's other uncle, Harry's younger brother, Malcolm, drank away the evening.

Paul was embarrassed and irritated that he should be—for Norfolk Hall and all its acres belonged to him with Harry merely holding a lifetime tenancy. His grandfather, Matthew, had willed it that way: to Harry, his elder son, Norfolk; to Malcolm, Copra Valley. But only for their lifetimes.

So Paul had every right to discuss Norfolk with Daniel. But emotion said that Norfolk should belong outright to Harry—and although Paul Blades loved Norfolk, Harry Blades loved Norfolk more.

Harry came back. 'How's Coral Gardens, Paul?'

'Full.'

'H'm,' said Harry.

'Oh, come off it Uncle Harry, it's not as bad as that. Come and see for yourself Stay a couple of nights.'

'You'll have,' responded Harry, 'to get rid of that damn level crossing before you see me in the place.'

The 'level crossing' was a weighted pole painted red and white which barred the way into the golf course and cottage colony. Beside its weighted end was a small hut accommodating two policemen who raised it only after motorists had proved themselves guests, or been recognized as cottage owners or company employees. Paul was no more enthusiastic about the pole than Harry—but the cottage owners had been adamant. We, they said, are bringing in our good dollars; putting them into bricks and mortar; and inside the bricks and mortar will be our expensive furnishings, liquor, paintings, jewellery. We're entitled to protect them. And we're entitled to our privacy. Take it or leave it—no guard room, no Coral Gardens. And Cordoba, persuaded of the magic profits tourism would usher in, had not merely yielded but even out of its meagre constabulary arranged to have two on duty, day and night.

'Don't known how you can stick the damn place,' Harry was going on cheerfully. 'Worst thing that ever happened to us.'

'Oh come off it,' said Paul, who loved Harry too much to be annoyed. 'That's a bit of an exaggeration.'

'Not a blast! Think of the effect of it on the natives...'

'Who never see it!'

'Hear about it, though. Think about

18

it, Paul. What's he need—the average Cordoban? A tin roof. Kerosene. A decent Sunday suit. Pretty dresses for his kids. Food in his belly. And a few dollars for the rum shop.'

'For people who've got all they need...'

'They spend their time grumbling? 's a Cordoban disease. Their prerogative. But Cordoba works. It does, you know. Of course it must be difficult for your lot to believe, but islands like Cordoba are best left alone. So long as we don't get too swell-headed—want our own airline and all that nonsense, we'll manage. Not very well by other people's standards, maybe, but well enough by our own.'

In spite of all his resolutions, he was laying down the law again. But he was going to finish. He came to stand beside Paul who had gone to the platform's edge. It was full night now, the sky a bowl of stars ending only where it met the sea, the air warm and perfumed. The only sound exceptional to any tropic night was that of a distant bus heading towards them from the direction of French Bay, itself invisible but its headlights raking unevenly between the trunks of trees, lighting up the undergrowth, occasionally glinting the sea to life.

'Would you change all this?' he asked.

Paul watched the bus now come into

sight, threading its way through the intermittent screen of trees, its roof girt with a necklace of coloured bulbs like a Christmas tree. He listened to the quite unnecessary blaring of its hooter. Would he change it? Change what had remained unchanged for centuries? If he had the power to sell Norfolk off to Daniel Fonseca and he used that power, everything would be changed. The road the bus driver had entirely to himself would become a double carriageway, a busy road cold with sodium lights. The wall of darkness which was not really darkness but shades of night, would be punctured by the lights of hotel bedrooms, dining areas, night clubs and car parks. The crumpled hills which drew sharp lines against the sky would be speckled by the buzz-off bulbs and the pool and burglar lights of villas which followed a tourist development as swiftly as does a rash, disease. The silence, which like the night was not so much silence as a background, steady, unremitting, so unchanging as to be heard only when listened to—that silence would be queerly overlaid by the sounds which tourism brought, mock calypsoes and the rest. And the hooting of a bus would be no longer an event which drew attention, a joyous shout of sheer exuberance, but merely one of a continuing series of statements which strung together would proclaim Cordoba had become another country.

Would he change it? Take the responsibility of bringing a new Cordoba into being?

Harry read his thoughts.

'A lot of beach, three miles, isn't it Paul?' he said. 'Could take a lot of hotels I daresay. And the lower land. Pretty flat. Probably not difficult to turn into a golf course?'

'Ideal,' Paul admitted.

'You've thought about it?'

Paul shrugged his broad but bony shoulders.

'Vaguely,' he agreed.

'Only vaguely?'

'Yes. Not much point in doing more than that when you'd never agree to part with any of it.'

'Not a square foot,' Harry said quietly. 'Not a yard of beach.'

'So you see...' Paul's voice was dry. 'I've been protected.'

'But you'd find it exciting, wouldn't you?'

'Of course.'

'And *would* you do it?'

'I don't know, Uncle Harry. Honestly I don't know. One side of me wants to keep things as they are. The other...' He left it unsaid.

21

'And you'd be rich. The world your oyster.'

'The world's not interested you. Norfolk's been enough.'

'More than enough, Paul. It's been my world. And Sophie's.'

After Harry had gone to change for dinner, Sophie, his wife, came out— wearing a full length, old-fashioned dress of oyster silk.

Paul found her absurd—a second Miss Havisham presiding over huge, empty, echoing Norfolk Hall as if nothing had changed. As if the carriages still drew up beneath the curving double staircase leading to the platform and all of Cordoba's gentry thronged its lofty rooms. But as well as absurd, he found her tragic—for Sophie Blades was an arthritic cripple with a body as gnarled as a branch of a pimento tree while her fingers stuck out rigidly in all directions like a dead hand projecting from a shallow grave.

'Good evening, Paul!'

Her voice, rasping and triumphant, led him back through the years. As a child she had terrified him. He had never found the way to come to terms with her. He wondered, as he had a hundred times before, how Harry managed to stay patient and considerate. How, even, he managed to remain so balanced. His respect for

Harry was huge in many ways but probably in no ways more than this.

He stood. 'Good evening, Aunt Sophie. How are you?'

'As you see me. Fetch me a brandy.'

She banged her hands, which were crowded with rings, on the rims of her wheelchair and spinning them impressively, sped back out of sight into the house. By the time he was at the trolley pouring her drink she was in her usual corner, watching him. Her eyes were very strange, the skin stained beneath, the irises brown darkening towards the pupils but with a thin blue rim round them where they met discoloured whites. And they were malignant eyes, unwavering, holding a contempt so all encompassing as to embrace even her own affliction. Knowing eyes—looking into them one had the sense of being taken back in time to the days when the first Blades came to Norfolk as if in some magical way she had managed to assimilate all the whole brood had learned.

He poured her brandy and put it on a small table within her reach. She banged a wheel with her wrist and her jewels winked in the candelabra's light.

'Sit here,' she ordered. 'Where I can see you. What have you come to Norfolk for?'

'I'm seeing Daniel Fonseca tomorrow.'

'It's so far from Coral Gardens you have to break the journey?'

'No. But it's obvious what Daniel wants to talk about.'

'And you wanting to soften up Uncle Harry?'

'No. It's the least I can do to let him know.'

'He'll hear of it anyway.'

'Yes. And I'd rather he heard it first from me.'

'H'm.'

Sophie drank a little of her brandy. This was a purposeful action, a distressing and yet a compelling thing to watch. Her fingers would never move again—to raise a glass she had to grasp it, vice-like, between her wrists and thus lift it to her mouth. And while she did this she was watching to make sure that she was watched—you were obliged to share her discomfort. And the drinking itself was a messy, noisy business—and a dangerous looking one. It was all you could do to resist hurrying to her aid. All the advantages were with Sophie when she drank a glass of brandy. And she used them.

'Daniel, eh,' she said suddenly, rattling the glass back on the table. 'How much him offering?' This was another ploy, lapsing into brilliant mimicry of the market women.

'There's no guarantee...'

'Stuff!' she interrupted. 'What else can he want with you?' She considered, then changed direction. 'Hear tell he's changed his politics.'

'Daniel?'

'That he's started living in Bertie Sasso's pocket.'

'I haven't heard that.'

'He's got Sasso's daughter working for him, hasn't he?'

'Has he?'

'Bertie Sasso!' The contempt was withering. 'Bertie Sasso for Chief Minister!'

'He'll get in.'

'Chief Minister!' She put back her head and cackled. 'Lawd God him start as yard boy an' now them "peak him Mass Sasso! Mass Sasso"!' She exploded with laughter, stopped abruptly and then said cruelly: 'If he does it'll be his wife who got him there. The ugliest woman in Cordoba!'

Paul was nettled. 'He married her,' he reacted curtly.

'Because she was the whitest he could get. And she married him because she was so ugly only a nigger would have her for company. I was at school with her, you know. At Hendriks. And afterwards

25

she went back to teach. It was all she could do.'

'She still teaches at Hendriks. And she doesn't need to,' Paul said coldly. 'Not married to the man who's going to be the most important in Cordoba.'

'She had money,' Sophie said, destroying her earlier argument without compunction. 'He couldn't keep his pink palms off it.'

'Who couldn't keep his pink palms off what?' said Harry, entering, and looking far less efficient in a shapeless white tuxedo.

'Bertie Sasso off Alice Williams' money.'

'Oh go on with you,' said Harry cheerfully. 'He's a very decent fellow. And when he gets in, which he will, he'll do a damn sight more for Cordoba than Costa's ever done.'

'You know his daughter's working for Dan'l?'

'No,' said Harry. 'I didn't. But does it signify?'

'With Dan'l changing sides?'

'How can Daniel Fonseca change sides,' said Harry, chuckling, 'when he's always on both sides at once?'

# Two

Almost everything that happens in St James happens around Victoria Square into which the town's principal artery, King Street, descending ramrod straight and downhill from a smaller square on which is perched the Parish Church, enters and dies. The harbour is nearby but only glimpsed through the bars that give the covered market, crammed with old women selling everything imaginable, the feeling of an open prison. The buses, garishly gay in colours that announce their routes, line one side of the iron-railinged square in which a stone Queen Victoria (herself be-railinged) cumbered with the orb of office stares with unblinking disapproval at the hurly-burly going on. It is all heat, clamour, colour and stink. Coconut water-sellers knock off tops of coconuts with terrifying machetes with the disdain of a housewife slicing cucumbers; drunks thrown out of rum shops lurch along cracked and sagging pavements scattering the nervous and prudent into gutters squalid with trodden mango, pau pau, ugly, ackee; precocious children with close curled hair and eyes as big as footballs beg, grinning, more it seems for the fun of it than in any hope; mothers with eight and a half month bellies waddle along leaning backwards at dangerous angles and ebony beauties, obviously unaware that one day they will do the same, pass with a disdain and grace to make a ballet master swoon with envy; old crones with feet-tied chickens squat cross-legged—black faces in shapeless shouts of colour and wizened little men, like nuts, with rimless spectacles, clever eyes and zipped-up briefcases scurry towards the Court. The stench is awful with rotting codfish joining sweat and the pervasive warm smell of rum to overcome the cloying scent of frangipani; the noise is shattering: shouts, cackles, curses, blaring horns, jingling bells, squealing tyres, thumping drums, hoots from some ship on the roads.

Daniel Fonseca's office is in Victoria Square, a converted warehouse, its ground floor of yellow London stock bricks brought out as ballast, its upper part clapboarded and searing white. Inside it strikes icy cold. There is a continuous counter with a gate and behind it two dozen girls in white blouses and blue skirts or men in white shirts and black trousers. There is a waiting area with magazines. It is all very modern and surprising.

A girl with slightly oriental eyes, coarse black hair, high cheekbones, of quite unusual beauty, led Paul Blades through. In Daniel's office there was as well another man he had met before but had no idea he was going to see that morning. This was Solomon Kornblath, better known as Solly, who was renting a cottage at Coral Gardens and was a soft, genial, multi-millionaire who smelt of talc and toilet water.

'Good morning, Blades,' said Solly cheerfully.

'Good morning, Mr Kornblath,' Paul replied. 'This is a surprise.'

'I hope to surprise you further,' Kornblath responded as if speaking about a fairly unimportant matter. 'I want to give you two million pounds for Norfolk.'

'You can't be serious!' exclaimed Paul, bewildered.

'My dear boy, of course I'm serious. It's a very good property.'

'But...' Paul struggled to collect himself. 'I couldn't... Well I couldn't sell it to you, anyway. Mr Fonseca must have explained that to you.'

'Oh, I'm sure you could,' said Kornblath encouragingly. 'Show him, Fonseca.'

Paul had never imagined the day would come when he would hear Daniel so addressed without objecting. He watched,

29

disbelieving, as Daniel, without the least flicker of expression on his aloofly handsome face, rose to his feet, crossed a room so sparsely furnished as to echo its owner's personality, and collected from off a drawing chest an expensively produced and very large book bound in blue.

'Open it, Blades,' suggested Kornblath gaily.

Paul examined the book while Daniel sat watching expressionlessly from across his desk and Kornblath benignly from his armchair.

'It's impossible!' Paul burst out at what he'd studied. 'Impossible! It could never happen!'

Kornblath chuckled. 'You don't think so?'

'No,' said Paul. 'I don't.' He appealed to Daniel. Kornblath was beyond him. 'What's all this about?'

'New St James.'

Daniel's voice was effective because it was so quiet you had to listen carefully to hear what he said.

'But... Is the Government going to agree with what's in this?'

'There've been discussions.'

'They must have been bloody secret.'

'They were.'

'But... Why tell me anyway? Norfolk's

not in that brochure.'

'Mr Kornblath wants to buy it too.'

'Too! You don't mean that... What the hell's it going to cost? *This* thing, I mean?'

'Three or four hundred million of your dollars,' Kornblath said. 'Maybe half a billion.' He spoke as if he'd prefer the half a billion.

'I can't believe it,' Paul said. 'I just can't believe it.'

'Never mind,' said Kornblath soothingly. 'Pen, Fonseca.'

Daniel found him one. Felt-tipped. Kornblath unscrewed it and let the cover fall to the floor and, hoisting himself out of his chair, crossed to the photographed montage of the island of Cordoba which entirely filled one end wall.

'Blades,' he commanded. 'I wonder if you'd mind?'

Paul joined him.

'What's the extent of Norfolk?'

Paul traced it with his fingertip.

'About that?' To Paul's horror Solly Kornblath quite ruined the montage.

'That more than covers it,' he managed, staring at the thick black ellipse within which, amongst the grey and lighter greys, the cicatrice of Norfolk's beach glared white.

'Two million pounds then?' Kornblath

spoke as if all was settled and the rest pure bonus. 'And if it interests you, shares on ground floor terms in the major project and a seat on the Board of the local Company.'

The girl was standing by the gate, pulling it back against her skirt. 'You must be Bertie Sasso's daughter,' Paul said.

'Yes, Mr Blades. Dorothea Sasso.'

'If you've nothing better to do, come and have a drink.'

She nodded. 'There's a couple of things I've got to finish. The Inn?'

He shrugged. 'All right.'

'I'll be fifteen minutes, Mr Blades.'

She was prompt, pushing the hinge-rusted gate to the tired parched garden, standing in the hard sunshine looking for him, giving life to the seedy indifferent place, making the young Cardobans swivel on their stools at the claptrap bamboo bar and show their dazzling teeth. She looked, he thought, exactly like an air hostess.

When she saw him, half hidden by a screen of vines at a table under the projecting balcony of the upper floor, she came across, her high heels clicking on the broken concrete path. The eyes of the young Cordobans followed her all the way.

'I hope I didn't keep you waiting, Mr Blades.'

He was in no mood for irony. 'What would you like to drink?' he said.

'A Coke.'

He ordered it and another beer. 'So you're Bertie Sasso's dauthter?'

'Yes, Mr Blades.'

'And work for Daniel Fonseca.'

'That's right.'

'You must know all about this New St James business.' And, when she nodded: 'It's nonsense, of course.'

'Is it, Mr Blades?'

'Well, of course it is. New deep-water harbour. International airport. Hotels. Racecourse. Stadium. Shopping centres. Office blocks. Where do they think this is? Puerto Rico! And how's it going to work? The finance, for example. Tell me that?'

She laughed: 'Don't be so damn foolish, man.'

'Well, you work for him.'

'It's above my head. Way above my head.'

He was suddenly suspicious. 'They have to have been working hand in glove with Costa.'

She was faintly amused. 'Naturally,' she said. 'How else would anyone get anything done in Cordoba these days?'

'And *you* knew.'

'Now what,' said Dorothea, 'do you exactly mean by that? Does Daniel tell me? Don't be so damn foolish, man. I type his letters and hear parts of conversations. But I don't sit in the Chief Minister's office, do I?'

'But your father...'

'What has Daddy got to do with it?'

'He only leads the opposition party...'

'He only leads the opposition party! And what is that supposed to mean? You think Vernon Costa sends him copies of his secret meetings?'

'But your father simply has to know. It just isn't possible to keep a thing this big a secret in Cordoba.'

'Did *you* know?'

'I'm at Coral Gardens.'

'You don't get the paper there? You think if it was common knowledge the *Star* wouldn't know about it?'

He grasped her wrist.

'But they will know, won't they?' he accused her. 'It'll be in tomorrow's paper won't it?'

She looked at his hand. 'You'll be starting talk, Mr Blades,' she said.

'I daresay.'

'I have a point of view,' she reminded him.

He removed his hand, 'It *will* be in the *Star* tomorrow, won't it? However carefully you keep a thing like this under wraps, the time comes when to get it moving you have to take them off. And once they start talking to outsiders...'

'They haven't talked to outsiders, Mr Blades. They've just talked to you.'

'Well,' he said. 'I don't know why they waste their time. Daniel knows damn well Uncle Harry'll never sell an acre of Norfolk and that there's nothing I can do to make him.'

'Is that so?' She was obviously surprised.

'You didn't know?'

'Why should I, man?'

'Everybody knows.'

'You think *they* know?' She waved a slender hand towards the Cordobans at the bar who had all changed the direction of their seating so as to be able to look at her. 'You think that waiter knows? You think that old woman...' She waved again at the dusty, blinding street. 'You think she knows?'

'Well he won't,' said Paul ignoring all of this. 'Not one single acre.'

'But I thought Norfolk belonged to you.' And, after he'd explained, she said: 'But surely, Mr Blades, when your uncle realizes what this means to you...'

'He'll also realize what it means to Cordoba. This place, for example!' And he banged the tin table with his fist. 'It'll

35

be gone! This is where they're going to have the stadium! You know what they're going to leave?' He began a catalogue. 'The Parish Church. Victoria Square...'

'I've seen the brochure, Mr Blades.'

Her crispness silenced him. 'Let's talk about something else,' she said. 'Like Coral Gardens.'

'What about it?'

'I've never been there.'

'Why should you want to?'

She cast a meaningful glance which threw 'The Inn' into focus. It was a place he rarely used and he was, of a sudden, uncomfortable. There might be little enough choice in St James, but at least there was better than this decaying building with its tin tables and tired banana trees.

'We'll go up to the Darien!' he said.

The last thing she wanted was to run into a gaggle of adolescents. Possibilities were stirring in her mind.

'I don't want to go to the Darien,' she said.

'You have to eat.'

'I can have a sandwich here. Or do without. I don't mind either way.' And she added mischievously: 'Of course if you'd said Coral Gardens, that might have been quite another matter.'

'Come over any time you like,' he said carelessly.

'When are you going back?'

'This evening.' He stood. 'What do you want to eat?'

His going gave her time to think. When he came back she said: 'I'm going to take you up on that invitation.'

'Oh?' He spoke with little interest. 'When?'

She smiled at him, standing above her, tall, broad, spare and straight, holding a cold beer beaded with moisture in one hand and a cold Coke in the other.

'This evening,' she said. 'Can I come back with you this evening?'

'No.'

'Why not?'

'It happens to be the Cane Cutters Ball.'

She had genuinely forgotten the Cane Cutters Ball which was the big annual shindig at Coral Gardens by means of which the stockholders pre-empted, or at least diluted, opposition to the colony. Everything raised, a considerable sum, was given to the local French Bay Hospital. She felt a growing excitement.

'That's why I'd like to go this evening,' she answered coolly.

He laughed. 'My dear Miss Sasso, it's not that simple. To start with there's a waiting list for tickets...'

'Who makes the selection?'

'The committee.'

'On your advice?'

'You're very well informed.'

'It's obvious, man.'

'Anyway,' he said, still not taking the suggestion seriously. 'I'm on parade. I wouldn't have the time to give you the attention you deserved.'

The touch of irony pleased her. She was making progress.

'You think I'd be a wallflower?'

'You might be surprised.'

She was quite shocked: 'You don't mean it!'

'There's a good sprinkling from south of the Mason-Dixon line.'

'But these days...no, I don't believe it.' But then, realizing the golden opportunity he had inadvertently handed her and which she had all but passed up: 'Oh, I see.'

He flushed. 'You don't see at all,' he snapped angrily. 'I was thinking of you.'

'You mean it *wouldn't* worry you?' And at his slight hesitation. 'Give it to me straight, man.' She stressed the West Indian accent as West Indians often do when they want to make a point.

'All right,' he said. 'All right. Come.' And the irony was back. 'It is after all the Cane Cutters Ball...'

'When royalty throws open its doors?'

'Something like that. Although to be fair...'

'Let's not bother about being fair. Being fair doesn't interest me, Mr Blades. It's going to the Cane Cutters Ball I'm interested in. And you didn't give it to me straight. Will it worry you taking me?'

'No. Not in the least. But it'll worry some of those who employ me.'

'Because if I come with you tonight they'll be thinking maybe you'll ask me to come tomorrow as well and then you'd stop being one of them and become one of us?'

'You'll have to make your own arrangements for getting back,' he said. 'It goes on for ever.'

'I've an aunt who lives in French Bay,' she lied.

# Three

Cordoba is a symmetrical island rather less than forty miles long and less than half that width with a high central ridge, known as The Saddle, which rises at its ends to high peaks, called respectively Grijalva and Morne Fleury both of which fall directly to the sea. St James, under the lee of Grijalva is in the south-east corner, French Bay diagonally opposite under Morne Fleury. There are two further townships: Pilotte, which is close by Norfolk, and Smithstown, even smaller, which lies like St James on the south side of The Saddle and is directly opposite French Bay. Thus Cordoba is divided into two halves both of which are distinctly different from each other for the trade winds, heavy with moisture, pour down their torrents on the northern hillsides and there is nothing left for the other side which is dry, almost desert like. But north of The Saddle, Cordoba is tropically beautiful, soft with almost unbroken plantations of coconut, banana and sugar cane, its sea brilliant turquoise and sapphire, its skies, except for an hour or so either side of night, made interesting by swiftly changing clouds which by casting moving shadows on the ocean give it life.

There is a road of sorts from St James to French Bay via Smithstown but it is little used and most traffic goes by way of Grijalva Gap, through Pilotte, then, passing Norfolk and the Juliens' estate of Palmira, on to French Bay and Coral Gardens. It is a dull road at first through cactus-ridden hills out of which have been carved the homesteads of St James' better-to-do, but once these are left behind, it corkscrews beside a very deep gully flung with huge boulders yet, except in times of heavy rain, carrying only a trickle of water barely sufficient for the country people to wash their clothes in.

At the top there is a dramatic change. One is of a sudden driving through a Gothic archway of bamboo, a cool nave of yellow, green and bistre before this, as it were, thrusts one into the open and a vista of quite remarkable beauty, a land of forest greens of a myriad shades and textures, which tumble down in buttresses and valleys towards the lower, more even, seemingly manicured margin of plantation land bordered by the sea.

Cordoba is a small island but not so small that even from this high vantage point the whole of its northern coast is visible, there are too many folds running upwards towards The Saddle to make this possible—but one can see perhaps half of it and certainly the whole of Norfolk and Palmira.

Paul, driving Dorothea across to Coral Gardens, after an afternoon through which he had had time to start putting things a little more into perspective and also to recall just how extraordinarily attractive a young woman Dorothea Sasso was, now conscious of the closeness of her body, her shoulder touching his own in the confines of his M.G., made a sudden decision. As they neared the end of the bamboo tunnel suddenly, without explanation, he turned the car off the road at a place where a gap in the bamboo wall formed, as it were, a transept.

'Something to show you,' he said laconically.

He led the way, their feet hissing through snuff-coloured fallen bamboo leaves until the trees thinned to individual clumps which, beginning with close-knit bases, soared high in outward spreading curves, trembling and swaying delicately, lacing the sky and casting a cobweb of shadows over them. These then yielded to a surprising flat patch of limestone rock which, ending abruptly in an awesome drop, exposed a fantastic view.

'There,' said Paul, pointing. 'Norfolk Hall!'

Dorothea's eyes followed his pointing finger and at length picked out, several thousand feet below and seemingly almost on the margin of the sea, a tiny oblong of pewter which was the cedar shingled roof with its colour burnt out by the blazing sun. Her eyes held it thoughtfully.

'And there's Cuevas,' she heard him say.

The sugar factory was easier to spot—a small silver oblong flashing back the sun and a single chimney yielding a thread of smoke. Close by it was a neat line, brown one side, green the other; Dorothea understood the meaning of that line: it marked the point where harvesting had reached.

'And that's where Malcolm lives!'

He was giving her no time to study anything he pointed out; his spirits were, she realized, too quickened, too kindled by the day's excitement to rest for long on anything. It was a vital day in his life. And a vital day in her own as well—such as might never come again.

'Where?' she said.

She couldn't pick out the house. All she could see in the area to which he was pointing was a sort of bright broken yellowness which was the sun reflecting off wind stirred over-lapping fronds of coconut palms.

'Where?' she said again. 'I can't see it, Paul.' And deliberately she leant against him as if better to follow his pointing finger. She knew that by now she had fired his physical interest, that she was now something more than the mere sounding-board she had been in that first half-hour. She had met him at an important moment when on the one hand he was possessed by a sudden sense of authority born of the realization that huge power was almost in his grasp, while on the other frustrated by the knowledge that the decisions which could give him that power lay in the hands of older and more experienced men. He must be feeling, she told herself, desperately alone, needing reassurance. But she was young and men found her beautiful and one thing she had learnt was that sex could be a most effective weapon when men were uncertain and confused. And so she had prepared herself for him both to stress her youth and sex. She had chosen tight white slacks and a gay short sleeved shirt of black and white hoops low and clinging on her boyish hips. She had brushed and brushed her hair until it was a helmet of burnished black, urchin fringed, swept just above her ears to fall softly on her back and shoulders.

She was, she knew, at her best, young, desirable, tempting. So she moved that much closer so that her shoulder touched his arm and at once, as if he had needed only this breath of encouragement, his arm was around her waist, pulling her against his side, and then his hand moving up on to her breast.

She eased herself free, almost at once, but not in such a way as to embarrass him or deny herself.

'No, Paul,' she said. 'No. Not now. Not here.'

She spoke very practically, making it absolutely clear that he could make love to her in a better place. She made it sound to him as if she was gripped by the same, sudden desires as he was. And it was convincing because it was true. The incredible possibilities which until only a few hours before had never crossed her mind were a separate thing, and a more important thing, than a sudden urge for sex—but the urge was there all the same. She was of a race capable of great depths of sexual passion, ardent in love, quite without inhibition, and the very *difference* of this as a place for making love stirred her imagination. This, she realized, was a place he had brought women to before—and very impressive too. On a constricted island where the facilities for sex were hard to come by, where girls did not have rooms and few young men apartments, where parental control (in effort anyway) remained Victorian, making love could end up a most unsatisfactory business managed somehow in the backs of motor cars. How much more telling it was to wave a hand across a few thousand acres than turn up hooting in a Ford—which was about the maximum most young Cordobans had to offer the girls they intended to seduce.

Even the rock itself, its very harshness, caused lust to flame in her. The heat of it beneath her flesh, the pain of its ridges, its hardness which would emphasize the thrust of his penis into her—these thoughts set her body trembling. She was forced to pull herself away from him more fiercely than she had intended. Now! her body told her. Why not now! Suddenly. Unplanned. Here. In this incredible place. What does it really matter?

But it did matter.

All through the dragging afternoon she had considered the wonderful chance accident had offered her. On the walk back from The Inn through the sordid, searing, shabby streets; in Daniel Fonseca's general office, looking at the men and girls around her and considering the limits of their futures; through the heart thumping minutes waiting for him to fetch her and wondering if he'd changed his mind—through all this time she had thought of nothing else and hopes had solidified into rock-hard decision. Paul Blades would marry her and she would see that, somehow, he would sell Norfolk off to Kornblath. Theirs could be the world. They would exchange this incarcerating, annihilating, petty island for it. Through the sale of Norfolk and Norfolk Hall. Her eyes searched for and found the house again and clung to it. She knew if she yielded then she would have thrown away her chance. In the aftermath, in that awful aftermath, that period of reaction steeped in self-accusation, the hours ahead instead of as now all excitement and expectation would hold nothing but regret and they would share one ghastly evening through which he would side with the criticism, spoken or unspoken, of the ruling clique of Coral Gardens.

'Not here,' she said.

'Dorothea...'

'Please, Paul.' And when he still tried to take her in his arms, she backed away. 'No,' she said. 'Don't touch me!' She walked away from him, to the, farthest extremity of the slab of rock. 'My cigarettes are in the car,' she said. 'Go and get them.'

When he came back she said: 'What do you have at Coral Gardens? A room?'

'No. A cottage.'

'You could smuggle me into it?'

'Yes.'

'Wouldn't that be better?'

'I suppose so.' She recognized the sulky tone which she had heard sufficiently often to know what could follow it and that she must be very careful. 'Light me one, will you?' she said.

What was, at the moment anyway, the important thing to him was, she realized, not sex but the wish to conquer her, the masculine desire to put power to the test—something she had known in men before and had invariably annoyed her. She was not an instrument for satisfying vanity and her own desire for sex was anyway too demanding. But this was not some casual, unimportant young man who might or might not satisfy her needs but one who could take her into an entirely different world. At the right time and place he could do what he wanted with her and she mustn't risk him brooding in the interval.

'Paul?' she said.

'Well?'

'I don't have any aunt at French Bay. If you can't arrange anything at Coral

48

Gardens, I can stay at the Windsor. Could you run me back on Monday?'

Nothing could be more plain—her body offered to him through the long weekend without strings of public recognition.

'If that's what you want...'

'It's exactly what I want.' She moved closer to him. 'I want sex as much as you do. It's what I've been thinking about all through the afternoon and on the way up here. And it's what I want to go on thinking about all through the evening. Then I want it to happen. Properly. Isn't that better?' She noticed the fingers holding his cigarette were trembling. She put her lips softly against his cheek and let them brush it lightly and whispered. 'It'll be worth waiting for, I promise you.'

Then, swiftly, she moved away from him and, going unhesitatingly to the edge of the stone platform where the land fell away so steeply, sat on it, dangling her legs, turning her head, laughing up at him, patting the stone.

'Now,' she said briskly, when somewhat reluctantly he had joined her and they were sitting side by side, 'show me where this house that Malcolm...you call him Malcolm? Not Uncle Malcolm?'

'Just Malcolm.'

'But it's Uncle Harry...' She hummed a few bars. 'Poor Uncle Harry, wanted to be a missionary...' Her voice was musical and seductive. 'Always Uncle Harry?'

Her smile was mischievous, her determination to lighten the mood between them beginning to have effect. She noted with relief the lessening of his tautness. I can manage him, she told herself. There are going to be difficult moments, but I can manage him. It did not occur to her that with a man like Paul Blades things could be thrust into the background and yet remain as strong as ever; that he had made a conscious decision to take all the present offered and worry about the future later.

'Yes,' he replied with a faint smile. 'It's traditional.'

'There's a lot of tradition down there, I daresay?' She waved her hand across all of Norfolk.

'Steeped in it.'

'Is Malcolm traditional?'

'Malcolm is a drunk.'

'Is that why he didn't come into the important part of Norfolk?'

'No. He became a drunk because all he got was the scraps of it. Uncle Harry's the older.'

'What's he like, Malcolm?' She had thrown her cigarette away, her hand was on his knee, her calf against his.

'The local Errol Flynn.'

'But surely, Paul...'

'There's twenty years difference between him and Uncle Harry and he's got the constitution of an ox.'

'What's he like? To look at? Like you?'

'No.'

'What about your father? Did he die before your grandfather?'

'He was drowned.' He stared at the sea. 'Out there. With my mother. They were on a fishing expedition and a sudden squall capsized the boat.'

He felt the momentary lessening of pressure as she half lifted her hand off his knee with the surprise of it; then the hand was back again, firm, warm, a reminder of what was promised him. He felt differently towards her; more intimate than he had before. A sense of well-being flowed into him. He became more the man the women of Coral Gardens thought highly of. The confidence which the shattering events of the last few hours had badly shaken was back.

'So who brought you up?'

'Matthew Blades.'

'Your grandfather?'

'Yes. But I never called him that. He was always Matthew Blades.'

'Another tradition?'

He chuckled. 'Right. Matthew Blades. Uncle Harry. Malcolm.'

'What about you?'

'I'm no legend.'

'But you're going to be, Paul, aren't you? And more than them. Because you'll be a legend beyond this bloody little island.'

'All the way from Florida Keys to Port of Spain.'

'Who said that?'

'Friend Kornblath.'

'Yes,' she commented. 'It didn't sound quite like Daniel.'

# Four

'There are some things...' Charlotte began...

'There are no things,' Kornblath interrupted, managing to inject menace into his tone without the geniality leaving his eyes. 'That was the...' he paused. 'Shall we say...' and he chuckled. 'The specification?'

Charlotte shrugged. She knew when she was beaten.

'Good,' went on Solly in a businesslike tone. 'Now—I'm not paying five thousand dollars for my own direct benefit. Understand?'

Charlotte nodded, listening carefully.

'Four gentlemen,' he told her, 'will shortly be arriving. One is my architect who is a happily married man and will admire your beautiful body as an artist. His name, by the way, is Martin Tod. The second is my surveyor whose name is Gordon Hamilton. I'm afraid he will leer at you whenever he thinks no one is looking but I promise you you won't be troubled by him. The third is Sir Christopher McCallin who has his own cottage...' Solly waved an airy hand to somewhere beyond the pool, the lawn and the hibiscus hedge. 'The fourth is Mr Errol Rose who is the Minister of Finance in Cordoba. It is for Mr Rose's benefit I have paid my five thousand dollars.'

'Is he black?'

'A little charred,' admitted Solly. 'Does it matter?'

Charlotte shook a head of titian hair drawn back and upwards exposing ears and forehead and falling luxuriously all over her shoulders.

'I guess not,' she said.

'But one likes to know.'

'Right.'

'Well now you do, my dear.'

He allowed his eyes the luxury of travelling over her bikinied body. It was superb. Long golden limbs, gently moulded stomach, flat bones at hips, slim waist, unblemished skin. Her body was better than her eyes which were rather small.

'I have to tell you,' he said, with a faint tinge of regret, 'that by all accounts, Mr Rose is a man of considerable imagination.'

Three of Solly's four men were walking Norfolk's beach. One was short and broad with merry eyes and a face etched with creases. This was the architect, Martin Tod. He carried his shoes in his hand, the bottoms of his trousers were rolled

54

up and he was walking in the edge of the tiny surf.

The other two were up the beach a little, trudging with more difficulty through the sand which was very white, and very soft. They had met many times before. One was Gordon Hamilton who had pale blue lifeless eyes and pale white lifeless skin and, except when with underlings, an air of overtrying; the other was Sir Christopher McCallin, Managing Director of Agricultural Life Assurance Company who was bigly built, a man of power with a mauve face. McCallin had already formed his own opinion of Norfolk's beach but would have walked its entire three miles had this been necessary rather than discuss it with Hamilton whom he heartily disliked. Hamilton, fully conscious of this dislike and aware he would do best by keeping silent was unable to do so.

'Certainly a wonderful beach,' he puffed.

'Yes.'

'Need a lot of drainage though. And probably swarming with mosquitoes. Or sand-fly. I remember...'

He went off into a rambling discourse about another beach in Barbados Kornblath had considered, in the middle of which McCallin interrupted brutally by stopping in his tracks, leaving Hamilton a pace or two ahead, and calling: 'Mr Tod!'

55

'Yes?' Tod called back from the water's edge.

'Do we need go any further? It all looks much the same to me.'

'No, I don't think so.'

'Nothing else you want to find out?'

'No,' said Tod. 'I was just enjoying paddling.'

'Cordoba,' said Errol Rose, 'hopes the day will never dawn when our people will forget the helpfulness of the United States towards them. Those...and sadly there are those...who speak against that great nation do us nothing but disservice.' He fixed the opposition benches with a disapproving gaze. 'We are not hermit crabs with shells into which we can crawl at the hint of danger. We are not moray eels living in holes from which we can dart to take what we need and then withdraw again. We are not chicken hawks who can soar the sky with all the world below our prey. The Right Honourable Member for Palmetto Bay has extolled the virtues of what he calls independence and is in reality isolation. For if we do not encourage, we discourage and if we discourage we find ourselves alone! That is what in fact the Right Honourable Member proposes. That we stand alone! Turn our backs on all who wish to invest, to buy, to visit. We don't need your investment here—we don't need investment! We don't want your trade—we don't need trade! We don't want your visitors—we don't need your visitors! We are Cordobans! Thank you for your interest but, no, we stand alone. Well then...'

And, most effectively, Errol Rose allowed his notes to slip from his fingers and flutter at his feet while he challenged across the Chamber's floor the Member for Palmetto Bay, the Right Honourable Herbert Shawbury Sasso, leader of the P.N.P. (The People's National Party).

'Well then,' he ended, 'let us speed our most Honourable and Eloquent Member on his way into the wilderness—for that is what his independence is. And let us do so with kindness, not wishing to accompany him, but sending him on his way with the words of a better man than any of us echoing in his ears: 'Let him that thinketh he standeth alone take heed less he fall.'

And to not inconsiderable applause the Right Honourable Member for St James East, the Minister of Finance, Errol Granville Dexter Rose resumed his seat. And then, bending to pick up his notes, took the opportunity of glancing at his watch and reassuring himself as to the time. There was more he could have said, and indeed would have liked to say, but he had an appointment with a lady.

And Bertie Sasso sniffed something in the wind—else why, he asked himself, had Costa's C.D.P. (the Cordoban Democratic Party) with its in-built steamrollering majority made such a fuss over a superficially not too important affair to do with the granting of tax holidays in certain selected and unlikely fields? He sniffed...and smelt...and wondered...

# Five

It was Martin Tod who drew Kornblath's attention to Dorothea Sasso.

'Look at that girl, Solly! What a raving beauty!'

Solly had looked.

Paul had just led Dorothea out from the obscurity of a small rear table on to the dance floor. Solly's table was ringside; if he could not have been given a ringside table he would not have been there at all.

He had not disagreed with Tod. His bright blue eyes lingered lovingly on Dorothea's body which was merely emphasized by the scarlet dress plunging to the hollow of her back, its simplicity relieved only by thin *diamanté* shoulder straps. Charlotte on his right (destined for Errol Rose the other side of her) had been resistible, this girl was not.

'Who's that girl?' he asked of the Cordoban. 'The one dancing with Blades?'

Rose reduced the pressure on Charlotte's knee. It took him a moment or two to pick out Dorothea. When he did his eyes, rather protruding eyes protected by heavy lids under almost non-existent eyebrows, sharpened.

'That's Sasso's daughter,' he said, startled.

'Sasso?'

'Leader of the Opposition.' He said it automatically, his fish eyes still on Dorothea. He was a tall, gaunt man with a beaky nose, pointed ears and short curly hair which had receded like the tide to about halfway up a sloping forehead.

'The P.N.P.,' Hamilton said helpfully, 'People's National Party.'

Kornblath dismissed Hamilton with a brief, impatient wave of podgy and perfectly manicured hand.

'What's their relationship? She and Blades?'

'I didn't know they had one,' said Rose who was as intrigued but for different reasons. 'You haven't met her before, Mr Kornblath?'

Solly stared at Dorothea, eyes rising from sinuous swaying body to lovely face. He thought perhaps he had seen the girl before.

'You know,' he said. 'I think I have.'

'She's Daniel Fonseca's secretary.'

'Ah,' said Solly Kornblath.

The whole table's interest was now engaged.

'I'm surprised she's here,' said Lady

60

McCallin tactlessly.

'Why shouldn't she be?' argued Sir Christopher who had his back rather to the floor and no intention of admitting to any such humdrum failing as common curiosity.

'Well,' said Edith McCallin confusingly, 'it isn't usual.' She was a rather vague, good-natured woman who had retained her prettiness. She had never imagined being titled and secretly wished she weren't. She would much rather have lived in a village and been a prop to the Women's Institute.

Tod, who liked her, said helpfully: 'It's a small island, Edith. I imagine Mr Fonseca isn't all that bothered.'

'They're very pretty these Cordoban ladies, aren't they?' Lady McCallin responded brightly. 'I wonder one of them didn't catch you, Mr Rose.'

'Mr Rose is married, Edith.'

'I'm afraid my wife is indisposed,' the Minister said.

'Oh, dear. Nothing serious, I hope?'

'A little migraine. It attacks her from time to time.'

'How inconvenient.'

Tod caught Charlotte's eye. Very occasionally Charlotte found a man attractive. She liked his screwed-up eyes and the barely perceptible closing of one she read correctly as a wink and more importantly his acceptance of her as a person. She didn't like Hamilton who had adopted a supercilious attitude which wouldn't have held him back a moment if he but had the chance and she didn't like McCallin whose stony glance had told her his contempt was total.

'What's she taking for it, Mr Rose?' she said pushing his hand off her lower thigh while managing to show a brilliant smile with layers of ice in it. 'I thought I read somewhere they'd found a cure.'

'It's finished, you know,' Dorothea said.

'They may start again.'

'Not for a while.'

The other couples had left the floor and were dispersing to their separate tables, each with its candle-glow. The band was floodlit and cunning glows lit up their background of planted banana trees. Otherwise there was only starlight.

'Come on,' Dorothea said. 'Everyone will be watching us.'

He led her off the floor reluctantly, holding her hand and halfway back to his table impulsively changed direction. Momentarily she resisted then allowed herself to be almost pulled by him, his back to her, as he threaded his way between tables. She heard someone, an

American, call his name.

The dance floor was tiles forming an area which by day served as sun-bathing base. The sand came right up to it so that the moment they passed the last tables it was under their feet. It was a deep-sand beach enclosed by two horns of rock on which cottages were built but whose lights could be seen only where they filtered through the planting which gave them privacy.

The beach was empty, a palm or two creaked gently, the surf was little more than a sigh and they could hear the curious hollow sound of broken coral remnants rolling over and over where the sea-bed had not been raked. A tethered raft, fifty feet out, rocked enough to break and rebreak the clear horizon.

He led her along the beach, the soft sand pulling at their feet. He moved with the determination of a man who knows what he intends to do and intends to force compliance by that determination. At an arbitrarily chosen spot he stopped abruptly and took her in his arms. She made no resistance, melting her body into his and meeting his mouth with hers. They kissed hard and fiercely without tenderness thrusting against each other, her hand on his head pulling it down, his exploring her body naked beneath the scarlet sheath. But then, suddenly sensing the onset of his lust, Dorothea, pushed him from her angrily.

'Not like that!' she cried.

'What...'

'You'll come. And then...'

'My cottage then!'

'No. Not now.'

'When?'

'Later. When you don't have to go back to that mob.'

'You'll change your mind...'

'Oh, God no, man. I want you inside me. I want to feel it...'

It was not false. Her blood was afire, her body moist, her pulses hammering. But she knew. It would have been over in an instant. Their senses flayed by the waiting, their dancing, the passion of their kiss, were at explosion point. The first thrust of his penis into her would have ended it. And then what?—Gritty sand, creased clothes, redressing, the uncomfortable silent retracement of their steps and all the rest of it.

'Man,' she said. 'Listen to me. I never wanted it so much. But when you give it me, I want it all the time. I don't want it interrupted. You think *I* don't want it now? That I didn't want it on that rock this afternoon? But it wouldn't be anything. I'd come if you as much as touched me. It would be over before it started. Maybe before it started. You think I'm giving you a hard time. I'm giving myself a hard time too. I'm shaking all over inside. It hurts. I've never felt like this before. I never wanted anyone like I want you. It's fantastic. I want to feel you inside me. I'd like it now. Just for a moment. So that we could go back there...' She nodded towards the glow of lights and the beat of music '...and I could remember what it was like. Having you in me. Just for a moment. That would do. I'd feel it in me all through the evening. That would be fantastic. But that isn't what would happen.'

She paused.

'When do you do the auction thing?'

'In about an hour.'

'Is there anything you have to do after that?'

'I don't have to do the auction.'

'Yes you do. I want you to... I feel better now. I can wait. Now, I can even touch you. There!' She leaned forward and kissed him lightly.

And she laughed.

'Don't be angry with me, Paul,' she said. 'Be nice. I'm going to be awfully nice to you when the auction's over. You'll never have realized how nice having sex can be.'

Martin Tod was not surprised (and was delighted) when Kornblath left the table and went across to Paul and Dorothea—nor was he surprised when Kornblath brought them back in triumph. He usually got his way. And if Tod wondered why they were so easily persuaded, it was not for long for after making the introductions, Solly added: 'I've offered this young man two million pounds for the estate his uncle's squatting on.' This, of course, brought responses which put Kornblath in even better humour. Edith McCallin said, 'Goodness me!' and although Charlotte managed to keep silent, her small eyes were of a sudden even smaller.

'Take this chair, my dear,' said Solly to Dorothea meantime, 'I'll organize another for Mr Blades.' And he called very loudly to a waiter a table or two distant to bring two chairs and then, filling a glass with champagne, held it up and said jovially. 'Your health, my dear. So good of you to join us.'

Paul, meanwhile, rather out of things, was kept out of things by the waiter being instructed on arrival with the chairs to put one of them between Lady McCallin and Hamilton while Kornblath (with great *élan* which ensured everyone nearby giving up their conversations to watch what was going on) lifted the other high in the air, plonked it down between Dorothea and Charlotte, and squeezed his ample bulk between them.

'Rose tells me,' he said, reaching for a new cigar, 'that your father's hoping to be Cordoba's next Prime Minister.'

'Chief Minister, actually,' said Dorothea.

'Normally,' said Solly, lighting his cigar, 'I object to being corrected, but you, my dear, can do it as often as you like.'

When the time came for Paul to act as auctioneer, Solly said to Dorothea: 'We don't want to listen to any of this nonsense do we? There's plenty of champagne in the bar.'

She rose obediently.

'After you, my dear,' said Solly.

'I don't know where it is.'

'Ah!' He took her arm in his soft and cosy hand. 'Then I must show you, mustn't I?'

The bar, a pink and Regency-striped affair, was empty but for the barman.

'Champagne!' shouted Solly. 'Dom Perignon!' And taking his hand from Dorothea's elbow he slipped it round her waist to guide her to a table. 'Well, my dear,' he said sitting down, 'this is very nice. Now you must tell me all about yourself, because I want to get to know you.'

His eyes, she saw, were very blue and his skin soft and pink, like those of men who scarcely need to shave. Had she known nothing of him, she might easily have taken him for a well-fed priest out of uniform, a jolly priest who couldn't for a moment bring himself to believe that God would condemn sinners to eternal flames but would, instead, chastise them mildly and send them back to earth in another body for a second try. She noted that his forehead was dewed with sweat, that his rather oversize tie had slipped and that he smelt like a pampered baby.

'Why,' she said, 'do you want to know me?'

'You realize I'm in love with you?' he said.

'Don't be ridiculous!'

'I am not in the habit of being ridiculous.'

Dorothea could no more miss than Charlotte had been able to miss this ability Kornblath had for remaining genial while being menacing. His voice was gentle, even teasing and his eyes stayed mild. But the threat was there all the same.

'I'm sure you're not.' She managed lightness. 'But really, man!...' (she had considered 'Mr Kornblath' and abandoned it) '...After one dance and half an hour's conversation!'

'I was in love with you before we danced or spoke,' Kornblath responded benignly. 'Watching you dance with young Blades was all that was necessary. You are the most beautiful woman I have ever met. I am prepared to take you back to England and establish you in a flat. I will make a settlement on you which will enable you to live the life of a wealthy woman independently of anything else I may give you. This does not mean I want to marry you, or that there is ever any hope I will. My demands on your time will not be overwhelming and you will find my sexual needs neither outrageous nor perverted. From time to time I should want you to come on a trip with me and of course I shall expect reasonable access to you in your flat. But aside from that your life will be your own and I am not so foolish as to imagine you wouldn't have lovers of your own age. Now,' he chuckled, and put a soft hand on her knee. 'I think you must agree I am making you a most generous proposition.'

'Very,' said Dorothea dryly.

At that moment the waiter arrived with the champagne, giving Dorothea a few moments to reflect. She was aware how she was balanced on a tightrope. She accepted Kornblath's offer as quite genuine and was a little surprised she could do so. She had never met anyone like him in her life, she had never left Cordoba; but on the other hand she was not for nothing, Bertie and Alice Sasso's daughter. She knew instinctively that she was sitting beside a man who, because of his staggering wealth and history of success, hardly questioned his right to have and do as he pleased. In his eyes, and in fact, she was a coloured girl of modest background from a small and unimportant island. She had caught his eye and, on a whim, he was offering her the world. And it was tempting. If she hadn't met Paul she was not at all sure she mightn't have thought long and hard.

But, astonishingly, she had a choice and she knew which she preferred—the problem was that if she turned down Kornblath, she might scupper Paul.

When the waiter had gone, Kornblath probed gently: 'You were sitting with young Blades.'

'Yes.' She lied: 'He's an old friend of mine.'

'A friend?'

'We're going to get married, Mr Kornblath.'

It seemed neither to surprise nor bother him.

'Then he'll have told you already about that two million?'

'Of course.'

70

'Suppose I withdrew my offer?'

'I'd marry him just the same.'

He chuckled. 'I don't have to have Norfolk, you know. That's quite a small thing.'

'Compared with New St James?'

'Ah!' He looked at her rather differently.

'It really will happen?' Dorothea asked.

'It will happen.'

'But who on earth's going to rent the offices, fill the hotels...'

The soft hand was back upon her knee. 'Pretty girls like you shouldn't trouble your heads about such things.'

'If it didn't happen,' said Dorothea, ignoring his hand, 'would you still want Norfolk?'

'I wouldn't touch it with a bargepole.'

That explained much. If New St James came into being and somehow there was enough demand to fill the offices, then Norfolk would be very desirable indeed. A three-mile beach little more than an hour's drive from a bustling metropolis would attract other developers apart from Solly Kornblath. One day even two million might seem cheap.

She began to feel a little more secure.

'But others would,' she pointed out. 'Once New St James had happened.'

'My dear,' he said. 'New St James will happen but it will take a long time to happen. For two or three years there will be nothing but dredging out a deep water harbour and things like that. These dreary things...they're called the infrastructure—roads, drains, electricity, water...they take a long time to put in. If Blades doesn't accept my offer he'll have to wait a long time for another one. And remember, I shall know everything that happens. I shall be in contact with the planners all the time.'

'If there was an election now,' Dorothea pointed out. 'Costa would be slung out on his ear and my father would become Chief Minister.'

He nodded agreeably, not in the least put out.

'Now why do you think Costa has been so willing to co-operate?' His smile was at its kindliest. 'For that very reason. But in two years time? In two years time Cordoba will be having such a boom as it has never known. The world will have woken up to what is happening. Banks, insurance companies, hotel operators, manufacturers will be queueing up to be here. Money will be pouring in, labour will be in demand... My dear Miss Sasso I think your father can forget his political ambitions. Costa will be returned with such a majority that he'll be virtually a dictator here... So...' His blue eyes twinkled. 'Shall we summarize the situation?'

'No, I don't think that's necessary, Mr Kornblath.'

'Mr Kornblath? Does that mean you reject my proposition?'

'It means I need time to think about it.'

Solly sipped a little champagne, regarding her benignly over the glass rim.

'I do not, you know,' he said, 'object to your being married. If you had told me you were already married I should still have put my proposition.'

'Apart from the two million pounds,' she said, 'Paul tells me you've offered him a job.'

'A directorship. He could be useful. But he is not essential. You don't, I take it, plan living here when Blades has got his money.'

'Would you?'

'That is quite another matter.'

She shook her dark and lovely head. 'No, it's not. How many of that lot in there would live here?'

'Very few. None possibly. And you feel you're one of them already?'

'I intend to be.'

'Then accept my offer.'

'And have you change your mind tomorrow?'

'I'm not in the habit of doing that.'

'You might get tired of me.'

'I think that most unlikely.'

'But it's possible. And it's not a risk I'm prepared to take. At least married to Paul Blades I shall have Norfolk behind me.'

'For what it may be worth.'

'You really would stop him selling it to anyone else?' He nodded, cheerfully; she shrugged and took a tremendous risk. 'Well it's a problem, isn't it. Whatever happens, whatever else I may do later, I am going to marry Paul Blades. So if we have anything to talk about we have to start from there.' She smoked for a long moment, watching him all the time, aware he was thinking of her less sexually than before, that winning the struggle itself was now of at least equal importance. He was not a man who could stomach leaving meetings empty-handed.

'In any case,' she said, 'you won't get Norfolk without my help. Harry Blades, Paul's uncle...'

'Has a lifetime tenancy. I have bought out many lifetime tenants.'

'Not like Uncle Harry.' She used the title deliberately, claiming more than she was entitled to. 'You could never buy him out. No one could. The only person who could persuade him to sell is Paul and Paul hasn't the strength to do it on his own.'

'I was quite impressed with him this morning.'

'Determination, then,' she said. 'Ruthlessness. Call it anything you like.'

'Ah,' he said. 'But you have these things.'

'Yes.'

'All right then,' Solly said. 'You can have six months.'

'What does that mean?'

'That's the time I'm going to give you to get me Norfolk. If I haven't signed a contract for it in six months, I won't be bothering with it.'

'And the other proposition?'

A boneless hand reached out, like a cushion round her arm.

'I shall be sending you,' he chuckled, 'the key of a Mayfair flat and a first class one way air ticket to London for a specific flight—probably the day after the six months has expired. My chauffeur will be waiting to meet you at London Airport. If you don't arrive you can consider that proposition withdrawn as well and I hope you'll treat yourself to the luxury of lighting your cigarette with the ticket rather than cashing it in which you'll be entitled to. In the meantime if you let me know the day you and young Blades get married, I'll send you a wedding present.'

# Six

The several cottages owned by Coral Gardens as a company rather than those far more luxurious owned individually, were all exactly the same and identified by names of trees, that which Kornblath was renting being 'Spathodea' which, translated, meant African Tulip Tree, or, more colloquially, 'Flame of the Forest'. Further to make the point each cottage garden had been planted with an example of the species which bore its name and in each sitting-room was a framed print of its flowers accompanied by detailed information on the tree itself—the Committee had felt that doing these things might impart a sense, even if transient, of special ownership to those fortunate people whose application to rent had been sifted and approved.

'Spathodea', like its fellows 'Cassia', 'Jacaranda', and so on, was not in fact one cottage but two—the first being the major residence and the second, at a little distance from the kitchen quarters, a separate building consisting of two-bedroom and bathroom-suites sharing a communal patio. The idea was that an important tenant, such as Kornblath, might be able to invite guests without losing personal privacy or, alternatively, out of season each building could be separately let and serviced by the communal kitchen.

In the present case Kornblath occupied the principal bedroom, Martin Tod and Hamilton the spare rooms in the main cottage and Errol Rose and Charlotte Amalie were each allotted one of the interconnecting suites in the annexe. Apart from bedrooms and so on there was also of course a sitting-room to which Kornblath, having returned Dorothea, on his arm, to his table, retired, having instructed Tod and Hamilton to join him for a conference on Norfolk's possibilities. McCallin, meanwhile, invited Rose and Charlotte Amalie for nightcaps on his patio.

Errol Rose was a clever man, the cleverest by far in Costa's cabinet and ambitious to supersede him. The son of one of the island's lawyers he had been educated at public school in England and McGill's in Canada where he had been nicknamed 'The Black Crow' not unreasonably—because he was after all black and he did, with his heavy-lidded eyes, his enormous Roman-style nose and his particularly protuberant cheekbones in a fleshless face, look very much like a crow. But he hadn't liked the nickname which had made him unsure and perhaps contributed to his unusual sexual tastes. Probably it was only his burning wish to be Chief Minister which had saved him from the disaster which his appetites threatened and up to now he had managed to discipline himself well enough to indulge them only when off the island.

Kornblath had learnt of them after an evening in a favourite night club to which he had taken Rose following a satisfactory meeting when the New St James idea had been broached. The night club owner, an old friend of Solly's, had been able to provide the Minister with a companion he was unable to resist who was not shy of subsequently recounting exactly what had happened to her. It would have been unfair to Rose to ascribe the final decision to proceed with the New St James idea as having been influenced by Kornblath's capacity to gratify the Minister's eccentricities—for if his party was to be returned again to office, something very dramatic had to be done, so low had the popularity of the Cordoban Democratic Party sunk. But even if wheels of governments, however rusty, usually grind to their objectives in the end, the process is often achieved more smoothly when the wheels have been oiled. Perhaps it is best to leave it there. At all events it was how it had been left between Kornblath and Rose: 'Spathodea' was to be available whenever the Minister felt the need of relaxation and Solly would provide all other required facilities.

Sir Christopher McCallin knew of the understanding reached. He would rather not have known (but Solly was hardly the man to withhold such information from him) and he thoroughly disapproved— McCallin disapproved of many things which Kornblath did but he possessed sufficient strength of purpose never to allow personal attitudes to deflect him when it came to business and they had managed a mutually beneficial commercial relationship for years, one which had survived greater strains than mere procurement. Sir Christopher could also lay claim to another enviable quality—that of being able to hold ambivalent attitudes with little trouble. Whilst despising Errol Rose for his sexual urges he respected him for those political. And so he detained him, and in the process Charlotte, for quite some time over coffee and brandies on his patio discussing the commercial and financial structure of Cordoba where he hoped to make a killing. But after an hour or so, (by which time the Minister had ceased to contribute to the conversation by much more than infrequent monosyllabic replies to positive questions, while his rather disturbing eyes had begun to flicker with increasing regularity over the glossy skin and tumbling titian hair of Miss Amalie), after this time McCallin admitted tiredness and covered the Minister's retreat from his still quite innocent wife by suggesting it was perhaps not impossible as Kornblath's meeting had been going on some time, he might be glad to have his secretary back.

After the auction there was limboing on the beach. Paul and Dorothea were at the back of the ring of cottagers and guests surrounding the limbo team which consisted of two men and three girls, the men naked but for ragged pedal pushers, the girls in boa bras and pants and multi-coloured skirts which were no more than pieces of material tied in knots about their waists and their ends held up. The limbo, which was being done on a board laid on a flattened area of sand, was nearing its crescendo with the pole resting on the necks of beer bottles. The flares were blazing pennants in the steady night breeze off the land and shadowed the faces of the watchers. Behind the limboers, the band, its backs towards the sea tore into the music with triumphant fury: 'Limbo! Limbo! Limbo like me! Limbo all night and limbo all day! Limbo Limbo like me!' The principal dancer tall, black, sinewy, narrow-hipped, arms out, hands up, swayed and thrust, approaching the pole, backing away from it, savagely graceful, contemptuous of the impossibility facing him. In a few moments the singing would die, the drums would louden, the dancer would attack the pole, leaning back, and back, and back, bending from the knees, lower and lower and lower, carrying himself somehow on his long thigh muscles and his toes. Then when he was low enough his hands would grasp his calves and he would shuffle forwards on the inside of his feet, his body parallel to and an inch below the pole, his chin all but rattling it off its beer bottles, only his head above its level. Then would come the climax and his head would weave, his body shuffle, knees wide and pointing through his pedal pushers as if to split them, arm muscles whipcord, shoulders hunched, and somehow he would pass beneath the pole to rise triumphant, glazed with sweat, the girls and his male partner shimmying around him in jubilation.

Then it would be the turn of the guests to try. Hours of laughter, drinking, *bonhomie*, would have weakened reserve, dispersed uncertainty. Dignity would be forgotten. Pot-bellied tycoons and painted matrons would vie with the handful of slim and young to pass beneath a pole three feet above the sand and fail. No one would mind, no one would look ridiculous. The shuff of the sea would be drowned by the shrieks of laughter, the scent of night jasmine would drift unnoticed, the billions of bright stars be forgotten. The Ball would become a party...

'Let's go, Paul,' Dorothea said to him quietly. 'Let's go now while no one will notice.'

She was concerned—there was a set to his face she didn't like. She was relieved when he answered at once, if briefly: 'All right.'

He led her away from the limboers and their audience. Sand gave way to grass beneath their feet and the grass gave way to a walk of fig trees, tall sinewy trees illuminated by hidden lights and mysterious with liana and long trailing vines. It was a romantic place but he ignored the romance of it, not speaking, walking at such a pace that it was all she could do to keep up with him. Her concern grew to alarm but she resisted cross-examining him, aware that all her plans could founder on one remark.

They came out of the fig-tree walk into

the starlight where they passed another couple scuffing their feet in the dry stiffness of fallen almond leaves and then to her surprise and dismay she found it led them to the car park.

It took a supreme effort now not to speak, not to object, not to explain.

No words passed between them until the pole had been raised to let them out of Coral Gardens. Then Dorothea said:

'If you want to know, he's offered me a flat in London and given me six months to decide. I told him "no" because I was marrying you. That didn't worry him. He told me I've got those six months to help you persuade your uncle to let go of Norfolk after which his offer'll be withdrawn and he'll use his influence to see that no one else gets government approval to develop Norfolk. He won't change his mind. I think that about sums it up.'

'You didn't have to go with him at all.'

The coldness of his tone said everything. He was a proud man, insulted and betrayed.

'Of course I had to go with him,' she said.

'You were a different person when you came back.'

That had not occurred to her.

83

'Probably I was,' she said. 'Just as I was a different person when I left The Inn with you from the one you met in Daniel Fonseca's office.'

'Suppose,' he said accusingly, 'I *don't* manage to persuade Uncle Harry? What do you do when the six months is up? Accept his offer?'

'You think I deserve that question, man!' She was angered herself. But she controlled her anger. Too much was at stake. 'I'd deserve it,' she went on quickly before he might have replied, 'if the answer was to be yes.'

A long silence fell between them. Ahead, picked out by their headlights, could be seen the first shacks of French Bay. In the beams night insects whirled and sparked in unbelievable profusion. The sea was hidden from them by the sea grape.

When at length he spoke his voice was practical.

'You mean,' he said, 'that he both wants me to marry you and you to be his mistress?'

'Yes.'

'Incredible.'

'No,' she said, matching his tone. 'I don't think so. To men with family ties, married women make much safer mistresses. And much less troublesome ones.'

'But if I don't marry you?'

'Oh he'll have me just the same. It's just not what he'd prefer.'

'It doesn't occur to you he'll simply forget all about it when he leaves Cordoba?'

'Which he does tomorrow.' This was a minor triumph. 'No,' she went on, then asked factually: 'Are you angry I told him I was going to marry you?'

'No,' he answered. This was genuine. He found to his surprise that he wasn't angry over that. They might not have known each other for twenty-four hours but much had been concertinaed in the space.

Now they were passing through French Bay—a petrol station on the right, closed, unlit. Garish yellow pumps lettered in red picked up in the headlights. A small Chinese supermarket on the left, barred and shuttered against thieves. A bony dog, long thin and sharp, teeth in some gutter object not leaving its prize but head turned defensively as they passed. Harsh, formless shops with concrete overhangs, cracked uneven pavements, tin-roofed huts, some with wooden balconies, some carried on lumps of stone, mud alleyways. All silent, all asleep. Then they were through the town, headlights raking through palm trees surprising a secret sea, picking up the eyes of a mongoose, twin diamonds gone as quickly. On either hand a million fireflies, ahead the whirling motes.

'I meant everything I told you earlier, Paul,' Dorothea said.

'But I have to marry you first.'

'No, man. You don't have to marry me at all. But I think it would be better.'

'For whom?'

'Oh, man, don't be such a fool!' She was near losing control. 'Do you want to throw it all away? I tell you he means what he says. Maybe it would have been better if I hadn't come to Coral Gardens. But I did and if you needed me before, you need me more than ever now.' She could not resist it. '"If you no done cross riber no t'row 'way you 'tick".'

'In other words, I've got to marry you.'

'No. But it would be much more better if you did.' She saw they were almost on the opening which led to the Windsor. 'We turn up here,' she said.

'I know.'

He spun the M.G.'s wheel and they passed into plantation land with tall, artificially planted palms under which white, horned Indian cattle grazed.

Dorothea's heart was thumping because the moment of decision was almost on them. There was only this long straight drive to the hotel. He was being unreasonable but that was hardly the point. What mattered was that pride

86

was gripping him like a vice and she was by no means sure she had the power to release him from it. In the stubbornness she had failed to take into account lay total destruction of all her hopes. If he left her at the door of her hotel he would never make any approach to her again. She knew that nothing she could say would budge him from his present attitude; only in her body lay any hope. If somehow she could persuade him to her bedroom, all would still be well. But could she? At the moment the idea might even seem insulting to him—he might see himself contemptible yielding to temptation with a vivid picture still in his mind of her being led back with Kornblath's fat arm around her waist.

They came to the end of the planted pastureland and ran through a belt of bush. Directly ahead, on its knoll, luminous in the starlight, stood the pile which was the Windsor Hotel. Not a light shone from it—it looked abandoned and impersonal. Where the bush ended there was a cattle grid over which they rattled, a narrow grid so that the rattle came twice, front wheels, then back wheels, brusque to the silence of the night. The road turned here, a metalled road nowadays but always for a long time some sort of road for what was now the Windsor Hotel had once been a plantation house and carriages had drawn up here in front of the handsome portico which provided both shelter to ground floor stoep and veranda to bedrooms up above.

Dorothea felt the car begin to slow. 'Not here,' she told him quickly. 'Run it in the car park at the back.'

He shrugged as if to say what did it matter, but, changing gear again, swept the M.G. round into the car park. Now the house was to their right, all but hidden by a massive mango tree while to their left the land fell to the sea. Behind and to one side reared the conical mound of Morne Fleury and backing them, overshadowing the house, the ridge which was Cordoba's spine. With each of them obsessed by the turmoil of their minds, neither noticed any of this. Paul sat stiffly, clearly determined to say nothing more, to have her get out of the car, then turn it and drive back to Coral Gardens out of her life for good. She felt quite desperate. Nothing, she knew, that she could say would do anything but exacerbate the situation; but to do what he was in effect bidding her to do was quite unthinkable. In the end she relied on instinct. She opened the door on her side briskly, slipped from the car and slammed the door unconcernedly. She stood for a moment waiting and when Paul neither looked at her nor made any movement to switch off the engine, called: 'Oh, come on, man,' with light impatience and headed for the house, her footsteps clacking away from him loud on the concrete paving.

Many, many times in the years ahead Paul Blades was to ask himself how it had come about that after making such a final decision to be done with Dorothea, he should, at the critical moment have discarded that decision. How different everything would have been.

But he did not, as he had resolved, let the car into gear and be off so smartly that by the time she reached her room all that would have remained of her brief affair would have been a pair of rear lights winking in the distance. Had she tried to stop him, had she pleaded, argued, he would have been off in splendid satisfaction. But she did none of these things and he was not to know her mind. He took the offhand slamming of the car door, the impatient 'Come on, man,' the brisk clacking of her footsteps at face value. In the turmoil of a mind battered by so much emotion in so short a space of time, he read in her actions that she simply had not understood that he was ditching her. And the very pride which had come so near to ruining all of Dorothea Sasso's plans now hastened to her rescue. He would not be humiliated in this manner by a little coloured trollop. He slammed his door twice as hard as she'd slammed hers and followed her.

Her bedroom was an almost perfect cube and everything was white. Match-boarded ceiling, walls, jalousied veranda doors, dressing-table, chest of drawers, chair, bedcover and mosquito net—all was white. Only the wooden floor was not white—the wooden floor and Dorothea in her scarlet dress and her flesh the warm colour of the skin of almonds.

The jalousied doors were open, hooked back and in the most businesslike way she unhooked them and pulled them to. She turned to face him. He hadn't spoken—he required her full attention... What he had to say to her would be brief; she must miss none of it.

But none of it was said. As Dorothea turned to face him her hands moved swiftly reaching up to the *diamanté* straps and slipping them off her shoulders. The dress, released, fell like a blood splash to the floor and she was beneath the dress quite nude. Her body was, simply, perfect—her breasts firm and high, her buttocks taut, her wrists and ankles tiny. She put her hand up higher, to her head, did something, shook her hair and it cascaded down her back. Even before it had settled she was moving

90

towards the bed, lifting up the mosquito netting. He saw her body through it, shaded by its thickness and then she was lying on her back looking up at him, a beautiful young animal naked in a cage.

Paul Blades had slept with many women but he had never known such a night of lovemaking. It was a dwelling in sex. No woman of a *seraglio* ever sought to please her noble more than Dorothea sought to please Paul that night. There was no quick burst of sudden passion as would have highlighted their loving on rock platform or beach—in its place was a dwelling in sex in which it was hers rather than his body which dominated. She kept in check her own languorous yet vigorous sexuality and except that she used her mouth continually on him she rejected experimentation. She sought to make of their two bodies a single body and she succeeded. Never before had it seemed to Paul his being was centred so totally in his penis which was taken by her in hand, in mouth, in body and used. Her hands were deft, now hard, now gentle, her mouth was certain and unhurried; her body possessed of muscles she had learnt to use in the way which gives to man the greatest of all pleasure in the sexual act. The whole effect was to make of the night something quite magical and most extraordinarily soothing. It was not, as earlier he had imagined, a night of thrashing about in lust—instead she drew his orgasms from him slowly in the most devastating and exhaustive manner only, after a pause to murmur, fondle, doze, to nurse desire back into him again.

She did not pretend and he knew she held herself in check. This her whispers and her body told him was to be his night; she had promised it to him and she would keep her promise; she had hurt his pride and she would give it back to him again in full. And in the end when she had drawn from him, from some deep inner place he had not known existed, the last he could give to her the contentment of his totally exhausted body was all the more unforgettable because of its contrast with the jagged troughs and pinnacles which had filled the day. He lay on the cool sheets, with her beside him gently stroking his spent and impotent flesh, idly watching the few fireflies darting around the room, idly listening to the chorus of cicadas and bullfrogs which by their millions shrieked the night away, knowing a sense of having been lifted up and carried away from strife to some cool place where there was only sanity and peace. And so he fell asleep.

But Dorothea lay awake. Her principal

affection was of satisfaction mingled with rationalized regret. Her own sexuality was unsatisfied. So many times she had been on the verge of casting reserve and control aside, of allowing her body the free rein it had demanded. But there would be time enough for that. When next she came to him, it would be new to him. There would be in that, no disadvantage. It would highlight the huge sacrifice she had made for him tonight.

She turned to look at him. In the first glimmer of the sudden tropic dawn she could just make out his features. Spare he might be, but he was a handsome man and there was strength in him. He was a man, she considered almost idly, with whom she could so easily have fallen in love, with whom in moments she had already half fancied herself in love. What she had first assumed as weakness she now realized was something else—an uncertainty compounded of position without power, fighting fierce family pride. When the initial steps were over, when the struggle was behind them, when Norfolk was theirs, he would be a man who could hold his own in any company. Together they would make a couple so formidable as few would match. In the meantime—in the meantime she could manage him. She was sure of that. He needed someone badly, he had been alone too long. He had lacked a goal. His sexual life would have been unsatisfactory. He had been a man, like many, living in a vacuum. She would fill that vacuum and, by doing so, become indispensable.

She slid quietly away from him and covered his body gently with a sheet against the cool of dawn. She put on a dressing-gown and went out quietly to the veranda to watch the dawn come up. The world ahead of her, the bush, the pastureland, was still grey with night but already the birds were chattering. Above, a fret of clouds was laced with gold. In moments only the sun would rise angrily out of the sea. She turned her head to watch its rise. She had had no sleep and her eyes were stained with tiredness; her body brought so near to climaxes and then denied them was uneasy and rebellious. But it didn't matter. She had all her life for making love and sleep. And in the meantime there was much to do.

# Seven

Paul was to remember that weekend spent at the Windsor Hotel as one of the happiest and most hopeful of his life.

He was woken by a Dorothea who after a couple of hours of thought knew exactly the manner to adopt. She woke him gaily, like a bride, and dragooned him into swimming with her naked in the pool which, with the hotel, an unsuccessful old-fashioned place, all but empty, they had to themselves and which was enclosed by a thick hedge of Chinese Hat. They breakfasted, hugely, on their veranda, feeding the banana quits with sugar. They drove down to Coral Gardens and while Paul packed a suitcase, Dorothea equipped herself in the boutique. They ignored a peremptory note from the Management for Paul to present himself at noon, returned to the Windsor, and, now in trunks and bikini, spent the balance of the morning by the pool, swimming, lying in the sun, murmuring to each other and idly watching the humming birds and yellow creepers feeding from the Chinese Hat. They lunched lightly, made love, and slept all afternoon. In the evening the hotel

95

was quite busy with some local people from French Bay, a party from Coral Gardens and a Canadian couple who appeared magically from nowhere and took them for man and wife.

They did not dissuade them—they had by now in any case decided to get married. Yesterday they had met; today they had decided to marry. It did not seem strange, nor even rushed—it was simply unimaginable that there was any alternative. He was hopelessly in love with her and assumed she was in love with him. Responding to the magic and gaiety of the day, he was at his most likeable and self-assured. He saw the future secure and exciting and was blithely confident that now with Dorothea as his wife, Norfolk would fall into his lap. Riding a cloud of dreams all the more self-delusive by an airiness from lack of sleep and too much making love, he gave no thought to problems, the possibility of failure or the penalties of success.

And Dorothea? It would not have been possible in a word to describe her feelings. She would both have her way and yet not have her way—would succeed in life beyond the wildest dreams of yesterday and yet be compromising. She would be envied through the length and breadth of Cordoba and the marriage would be popular and hugely strengthen her parents' political hopes. And none of this depended on Kornblath—he could change his mind and still, at the very least, she would be Norfolk's mistress. By any standards she would be marrying well. Marrying a man who was white but for a trace, and for all that there was no real colour problem in Cordoba outside Coral Gardens, that counted. Marrying a man who was, by Cordoba's standards, rich; who was well-made, good-looking, personable; a man who if impulsive rather than considered would show kindness and consideration.

It was these final qualities which, on reflection somewhat bothered Dorothea. She could not but compare Paul Blades with Solly Kornblath who with his soft hands and flabby body should have repelled her, did in a way, and yet was fascinating. Or with Martin Tod with whom she had had but a single dance but would always remember because of his air of relaxed self-confidence, the tough hardness of his stocky body and the sense that here was a man who did things, a man who moved around, whom it would not surprise you in the least suddenly to bump into in some exclusive club or luxury hotel in some outlandish part of the world to which some accident had taken you.

Her horizons had spread so staggeringly

within the past few hours that she could visualize a life spent with men like Tod or Kornblath—men locked in gigantic enterprises in which they played a vital part. Paul was not involved as they were—they needed him not for what he could do but for what he had, and that given, not won. And in any case she was quite persuaded that without her help Paul would never find the way to meet Tod and Kornblath's needs—that his very kindness and consideration would be an obstacle.

Kindness and consideration are not qualities the young particularly admire—if of advantage to them they take them for granted, if of disadvantage construe them as weakness. Nor do the young when they compare those on the early rungs of success in life with those who have arrived bother their heads too much about what the successful themselves were like on those early rungs. Paul suffered by comparison and by the knowledge in Dorothea's mind that she could with her body control his actions as she could never have controlled those of Tod or Kornblath. So, dizzy though the heights she might reach through him might be, yet there were, she saw, higher peaks attainable.

The news burst on Cordoba on the Sunday.

The paper was delivered to the Windsor late, well after breakfast, and they had been by the pool, just the two of them the Canadian couple having departed as mysteriously as they had arrived. It was only when Paul had gone to Dorothea's bedroom to fetch something for her he had seen it, one of a small pile on the reception desk.

The banner headline said everything:

'CORDOBA TO BE TAX FREE HAVEN'

He scanned the first few lines then hurried with the paper back to Dorothea. She had been lying on a mattress, arms stretched out ahead of her and head between them, her hair wet from swimming, her eyes lazy, her body drinking in the sun, relaxed. But she heard the urgency of his steps and was at once alert, pushing upwards on one hand, half raising and twisting her body, looking at him.

'It's in!' she cried triumphantly.

'Yes.'

'What's it say?'

'I haven't read it yet. Not properly. We're going tax free.'

'What! I don't believe it, man! Give it to me!'

She was on her feet, swift, lithe, eager.

'Just a minute.'

He was reading quickly, holding the paper in both hands against the steady breeze.

'Don't hog it, Paul!' Her tone was almost angry. 'If you won't give it, read it!'

'All right.'

He went back to the beginning:

'In a surprise speech on television last night,' he read, 'the Prime Minister announced that the Government will shortly be putting before the House a Bill which if passed will give Cordoba tax free status in the same way as Bermuda and the Bahamas are tax free. Income tax and almost all other forms of direct taxation will be phased out over a period of five years and death duties and capital gains tax will be abolished. The shortfall in revenue will in the first instance be made good by increases in indirect taxation but it is intended that these will be steadily reduced as a result of the huge inflow of investment from abroad which will follow this decision.

'So far as overseas companies investing in Cordoba are concerned these tax advantages will apply immediately upon the passing of the necessary legislation.

'Bracketted with this Bill will be another which will grant to a consortium of overseas investors in partnership with the

100

Government the otherwise exclusive right massively to redevelop St James. It seems that a study of the possibilities has been going on for quite some time and the Government hopes shortly to be able to put before the people of Cordoba detailed proposals under this heading but it is known that these proposals will include the provision of a deep water harbour, oil terminal installations...'

Paul came to the end of the page from which he was reading and attempted the difficult task in the breeze of turning to the next but Dorothea stopped him.

'Never mind,' she said. 'We know the rest. All that matters.'

Her excitement was intense.

'It's fantastic, isn't it?'

'Incredible!' Paul said.

'You said there had to be something else behind it.'

'Yes. But never in my wildest dreams...' He broke off. 'Your father...'

'Didn't have a clue.'

'That's not what I was thinking about. What I meant was that New St James was bad enough but this...'

'Oh, Daddy's had it.'

Her brutality shocked him.

'I'm surprised he hasn't telephoned,' he said.

'Lawks, man,' she said. 'Daddy'll have too much on his plate getting to grips with this one to think of me.' She crossed for her cigarettes. He saw her hands were trembling with excitement.

'Do you think he'll fight it?'

'Oh, yes.' She was looking in her bag, fumbling for the packet. 'But he won't get anywhere.' She didn't even raise her head. When she did, it was to say. 'I haven't any matches.'

'Give it to me.' He took the packet and moved into the shelter of the changing-room beside the pool to light two cigarettes. When he came out she was still standing where he had left her, in the blazing mid-morning sun, droplets of water sparkling on her skin. Her lower lip was held between her teeth in thought.

'What is it, Dee?' he said.

She raised her head to him and for a moment he had the impression her eyes were unfocused, that she didn't see him. But then they were sharp-black eyes that flashed.

'I was wondering how it affected us. Thank you.' She took a cigarette.

'I don't see it really does.'

She drew on the cigarette, thinking. 'No,' she said. 'I suppose not. Not directly.' And after a moment. 'No wonder Kornblath was willing to offer you two million. Norfolk will be worth an absolute fortune if this comes off. And it will.'

She was standing one hand on hip, the other round the cigarette in her mouth, talking round it, drawing on it over quickly. The bikini was minute, in small pink gingham check and her hand pressing hard upon its bow threatened to remove it. Around one slender ankle she wore a thin gold chain but otherwise no jewellery. Her hair hung down her back, still too heavy with water for the breeze to move it. The smoke from her cigarette was whisked away as made.

'Paul,' she said. 'I wonder what your uncle's going to make of this.'

'He'll put two and two together.'

She shook her head. She was thinking very fast. 'No. Not necessarily. Kornblath offered you a seat on the Board of the company that's going to do all this. That could have been why you went to see Daniel. To talk about that.'

'And Kornblath introduced me as the man he was going to pay two million pounds to for Norfolk...'

'Only at the table. And he didn't see anyone else. Just me. And then he went off with Martin Tod and that other man...Hamilton. For a meeting. And he'll be back in England by now.'

'All the same,' Paul said, 'it's not going

to hang together is it?'

'How d'you mean?'

'Well if we go to Uncle Harry and tell him I've been offered two million pounds for Norfolk he's bound to connect the two.'

'Well obviously we don't.' She realized of a sudden she was forgetting her role.

'What d'you think Uncle Harry's going to make of this tax haven business anyway?' she said quickly.

'He's not going to like it one little bit.' He smiled wryly. 'I've already had his views on Nassau and that lot more often than I care to remember.'

'But there's nothing he can do about it.' She spoke more to herself than to Paul.

'It's hard to take, you know,' he said, 'that a few men can make a decision...and turn everything upside down. Nothing's going to be the same.' And he looked about him, at the bauhinia trees with their orchid flowers and long seed pods the colour of Dorothea's skin, beyond them to a tall palm tree its fronds flaring in the breeze, at the white painted great house. 'Don't *you* find that hard to take?'

She nodded dutifully. But she had passed beyond Cordoba—overnight it had become a staging post.

'Yes, I do,' she said. 'But I know it's going to happen. It's all been far too carefully planned.' She threw her cigarette away, over the hedge of Chinese Hat. 'And you know,' she said, 'it's people like your uncle who're going to find it hardest. The ordinary Cordoban...' She shrugged prettily. 'Those in St James will like it. It'll mean more money in their pockets and more cinemas and things like that. And those in the country...'

'Won't begin to understand what it's all about.'

'No. I suppose not.' She laid her hand on him. 'Come on,' she said. 'It's starting to get too hot.'

They went first to her room where she took off her bikini and with a towel round her middle made a business of combing her hair.

'You know what?' she said to his reflection in the dressing-table mirror.

'What?'

'If we are going to get married...'

'Which we are.'

'Then the sooner the better.'

'Check!'

Smiling, she swivelled on the stool. He was sitting on the end of the bed, the mosquito net drawn up by a pulley system, and the room being small she was easily within reaching distance. She looked, he thought, quite delicious with the white towel around her middle, the comb held paused in her jet black hair, her breasts firmed by her attitude, her flesh still slightly moist from swimming.

'What I mean' she explained, 'is that the sooner we get married, the sooner we can go and live at Norfolk.'

He was surprised, 'Live at Norfolk?'

'Yes,' she said. 'I think that's what we have to do. And as soon as possible.'

# Eight

It was three weeks to the Saturday following the Cane Cutters Ball when Paul arrived to take up residence at Norfolk Hall.

It was a hot, still afternoon. He ran the M.G. under the shade of the enormous cotton tree—Tom Long's cotton tree and reputed haunted—and stood for a few moments in the benefit of its shade looking at the mansion.

For the first time it wore for him an intimidating air. He could imagine that it, at least, understood his motives for coming to live in it. And as if not only would every stone of it resist him but it was confident of its ability to beat him. Two centuries it had stood there, unchanged except for decay and the minor modifications Harry had carried out to make such a mausoleum manageable to live in; it could withstand a six-months siege with ease.

He pulled himself together. This was absurd. As was the house. It had had its time. Already more than a third of it, the area beneath the platform which ran the full length and depth of the house, had been shut up, unused, for more than twenty years. Whatever happened that part would never be used again, would remain a vast empty area of corruption, wet with damp, with windows jammed immovable and dead spiders brittle in their webs. And of the upper storeys, what was used? The entrance hall converted by Uncle Harry into sitting-room, the sitting-room converted into rooms for Sophie and her maid. Part of the kitchens. And upstairs? One small room out of all the possible bedrooms Uncle Harry had chosen for himself. One small room on a floor large enough to house two or three families. It was an anachronism, Norfolk Hall—once it had been in scale, now it was preposterous.

He threw his cigarette away and humped his suitcase to the house, surprised there was no Uncle Harry leaning over the platform's balustrade, no Alexander come out to take his luggage. He crossed the broad-leaved grass, crunched along the weedy gravel drive, making his way slowly with a sense of slight uneasiness at this forbidding lack of welcome, sweating in the sticky heat and climbed the nearer arm of the broad double staircase and crossed the platform into the house itself. He stood for a moment, listening. But the only sound was the faint distant clink of a cutlass blade and the dulled shout of some worker by the factory.

Hesitating to go upstairs he put down his suitcase and looked around him as if this hall turned sitting-room was one he had never seen before. And, in a sense, he had not seen it before for he had never really studied it. He found it now a simple, almost a feminine room, which spoke of Harry's wish to lighten the atmosphere for Sophie. It was really out of keeping for a planter. The grey-white marble tiles on the floor were old but the lightness of the walls and the furnishings were new and even the old steel prints ranged in double lines around the walls had a modern air, as if reframed. In a corner there was a grand piano, never played, and there were ample chairs and sofas, off-white in colour picked out with scarlet cushions. The main stairs led off forming a minstrel's gallery out of what once had been a landing, superb stairs, the finest in Cordoba. The stairs had a curiously tempting air about them, as if beckoning him to use them, to escape from this unfitting sitting-room and be lost back in the folds of time.

He went outside again, on to the platform, and stood with hands out-stretched, leaning on its mouldering, lichen-stained balustrade.

The fields below were patchwork now, velvety and silver-green where the cane was not yet cut, otherwise rich brown with here and there small tufts remaining, little clumps of silver-green against the brown, breaking the straight line regularity. In the nearer fields there were men at work, their bodies dark and their khaki-covered legs hardly distinguishing them from the crops they cut and only the women, working with them, and the snow-white herons and the scarlet body of a tractor making real points of colour. But beyond the silver-green of sugar, beyond the coconut palms margining the beach, the sea was brilliant, turquoise, blue and jade, while to his right the sugar factory, Cuevas, was like a huge silver ship riding at anchor in a grey-green ocean puffing white smoke from its funnel.

'Counting your acres, Paul!'

He wheeled.

Sophie in her chair was watching him, a mocking, knowing light in her eyes.

'Come to turn us out, haven't you?' she challenged him.

He realized he had not taken Sophie properly into his calculations and that this was a mistake. Norfolk Hall without her presence was unimaginable but even so up to now she had been little more than that, a presence, Uncle Harry's cross, a difficult, forbidding, eccentric woman who must be excused because of all her suffering and disappointment but played no more part in the affairs of the estate than, say, the bed-ridden wife of a financier in his banking business. But the tone of her last remark swept away such an over-simplified assumption. For there was satisfaction in it. It was not merely that she had so accurately, and so economically, pinpointed his motives but more that she seemed to welcome them. He could hardly dismiss the monstrous proposition that he and Dee might have an ally here.

'If that's what Uncle Harry thinks,' he answered, 'I wonder he's agreed to my coming here.'

'He's a fool.' In three words, twenty and more years of unflagging care and consideration were dismissed.

'So it's not what he thinks?'

'How should I know?'

'Well it isn't why I've come. I've come to learn how to manage Norfolk.'

'You've had all these years to learn how to manage Norfolk. And when do you decide you'll start? Two days after this Costa business is announced!'

'May I explain?'

'Inside.'

She spun the wheelchair, banged the rims and sped inside. He followed her. She was already facing him from her corner; she could move in her chair as fast as a man could walk.

'Well!' she said. 'Let's have it then!'

He had to summon all his sense of purpose to hold her gaze while delivering the explanation he had hammered out with Dorothea.

'Last time I was here,' he said, 'it was because I was on my way to see Daniel Fonseca and I assumed he'd asked me to go and see him because he wanted to make another offer for Norfolk.'

'And he didn't?'

'No.' At least that was truth. 'Daniel's tied up with this New St James business. He had a man named Kornblath with him who's heading this consortium and Kornblath happens to know me because he leases a cottage at Coral Gardens. Apparently he's a higher opinion of my abilities than you have because he wants me on the board of the local company. And that sort of offer doesn't come often in Cordoba. It means being able to travel to England at someone else's expense. And it's a change. I was getting fed up with Coral Gardens. Anyway I couldn't do both.'

'But you can manage Norfolk while doing this...' she moved a stiff jerky arm, the nearest to a dismissive wave she could manage. Everything outside Cordoba was to be dismissed. 'This other business?'

'No, Aunt Sophie, of course I can't. But

112

it's going to be at least six months before anything positive happens on the New St James business...'

'So why not stay till then at that stew house you call Coral Gardens?'

'You think Daniel with all those shares in it is going to agree, me being there right through the summer when it's reasonably quiet, then leave just before next season starts?'

'So it's six months we're going to have you?'

'That's right.'

'H'm.' He could tell she was puzzled. Her instincts were against believing him. But it was a good fiction with enough truth in it to give it backbone and enough of matters foreign to her to weaken an attack upon it. And it had been well rehearsed.

'I hear you've taken up with this Sasso girl?'

Paul relaxed; the first hurdle had been cleared. This was safer ground.

'That's right.' He was intentionally contentious.

'You'll be sorry. Ring for tea.'

He obeyed.

'Dorothea, isn't it.'

'Yes.' He had had hardly time to sit.

She sniffed. 'Dorothea! Trust a woman like Alice Williams to give a girl a name like that. I hear she's black.'

113

It was not a remark with much to do with colour prejudice. Sophie was as dark herself. It was snobbery.

'You hear wrong,' Paul said.

Sophie did not pursue it.

'And now you've come to live here,' she went on, 'I suppose we'll have to put up with her as well?'

'I daresay she'll come over now and then,' he answered casually.

'Now and then? That won't do for you. You'll want her living here.'

'Uncle Harry certainly wouldn't agree to that.'

'It's your house, isn't it? If you want to keep your mistresses in it, you've a case. There's plenty of precedents. Only of course...' She jerked her head, nodding towards the floor '...they used to keep them underneath.'

'You assume she is my mistress.'

'Well isn't she?'

The question was fired at him too quickly; he couldn't deny it convincingly.

When he didn't try, she went on gleefully, goading him:

'How else you going to manage the business now you've given up Coral Gardens? In the bushes with ants crawling all over you?'

'We're getting married,' he said bluntly and it gave him pleasure to have caught her for once off balance.

Tea was brought in and served by Hesther who had been what had been known in Sophie's youth as the *schoolgirl,* the young negress taken on by Sophie's mother to be her companion as a child, her maid as a young woman and her children's governess. Only there had been no children. At the beginning Hesther, or Hetty as she had been, had drawn life from Sophie and Sophie had been her life. When she had been Hetty they had splashed together in the river pools and made secret houses in the mango trees and she had been bright and gay because Sophie had been bright and gay. When Sophie had been thin with adolescence, Hetty had modelled herself on her. When Harry and Sophie had fallen in love, Hetty had been eager for them. When they had married she had yearned for children with a warmth which matched their own. And when there were none and the creeping agony had come upon the woman who was the be-all and the end-all of her life, she had felt the agony as her own and Hetty had died and Hesther had been born.

She dispensed the tea but otherwise she might as well not have been there; conversation went on in front of Hesther as if she did not exist. Which in effect she did not except as an aide to Sophie.

Nothing she heard would ever be repeated, except to Sophie. In the world there was to Hesther only Sophie. She was a second Mrs Danvers.

'I hear that that boogooyagga, Rose, was at that disgraceful auction at The Fort.' 'The Fort' was an occasionally used nickname for Coral Gardens.

'That's right.'

'He'd be at home in that stew house. Who'd he take with him? Not that wife he's got, I wager.'

'He was a guest of Kornblath's.'

'Guest? In his pay more likely. Who else was there?'

She meant who else from Cordoba; the Queen herself would have interested her less than someone who gave her gossip ammunition.

'The Jagans...'

'The Jagans!' She was delighted. 'If ever,' she went on spitefully, 'I saw a hypocrite it was Julius Jagan. To hear him talk you'd think he'd never set foot inside the place.'

'He is a politician.'

'Politician? He's as two-faced as a star apple leaf!'

'Aren't all of them?'

'Who you put him with? The Fonsecas?'

'No. The Zaidies.'

'The Zaidies! Neville Zaidie!' Her contempt was blistering. 'What sort of man is that? All talke, talke, talke. Why one fools around with such a fellow?' She spent a little time destroying Neville Zaidie and his family, then came back to questions.

Paul obliged her with the answers. While she sipped her tea, holding the cup between her wrists, slopping it down her front, being mopped up by Hesther silently, he told her, table by table, which Cordobans had been allowed at the Cane Cutters Ball. And all the time while Sophie was docketing it away for future reference, Paul was hoping Harry would come in. When tea was over, when Hesther had been dismissed, they would come back to Dee and Norfolk. But Harry did not come in and when Paul managed to slip in a query as to his whereabouts it was summarily dismissed with a curt: 'How should I know? He's in the factory.' And then they were back to the Cane Cutters Ball and the questions neatly leading towards Hesther's dismissal.

'Of course *he* wasn't there?'

'He?'

'Don't be so innocent. It doesn't suit you. You know who I mean. Sasso. Get rid of it!' This last remark to Hesther, who rose obediently to stack cups and saucers on the trolley.

'No,' Paul said. 'Bertie Sasso wasn't

there. If he'd been asked he wouldn't have come. So he wasn't asked. No point in...'

'Must have hurt Alice Williams that,' Sophie cut in with satisfaction. 'Not to go. Not to see Bertie with the plums.' She laughed. 'Lawd Jesus, I can see him,' she declared. 'Him real fine gen'lman at last. Him *Mass* Sasso now. Him sit at teble wi' Counts and Lords. Him yam yam caviare and walla walla wine. An' all dem men an' 'oomen learnin' how to ketch him coat tails.'

Paul could not avoid it. He burst out laughing. But it did not please her she had managed to amuse him. He had interrupted her in mid flow.

'An' Alice nex' to him,' she added rather lamely. 'As wishy-washy as a Redleg.' And irritably. 'Take it away! Take it away!'

Hesther wheeled the trolley out, shutting the huge doors behind her.

'And you're going to marry her daughter are you?' Sophie said—and, she would, Paul realized, have rubbed her hands had it been possible for her to do so. Defeated by his interrupting mirth, she was ready to turn her claws elsewhere.

'Yes,' said Paul.

'When?'

'In two weeks time. That's the earliest we can arrange a licence.'

'Why so quick? She can't be in the way for you. Not yet.'

'People don't get in the way these days. They take pills.'

'Don't forget who you're talking to.'

'Aunt Sophie.'

'Why so quick then?'

'Isn't that my business? Our business?'

'Or her business?'

'What's that supposed to mean?'

'You're Paul Blades, aren't you?'

'You think she's marrying me for the money I haven't got?'

Sophie shrugged. 'Cap no fit you, you no tek it up,' she observed. She seemed satisfied. 'Well as I said, it will be interesting.'

'You don't mind her coming here...as my wife?' The irony was irresistible.

Again she shrugged.

'It's your house, not mine. We're only lifetime tenants.' She stirred—the audience was obviously at an end. 'Open my door,' she said. 'I'm going in to rest.'

But, at the door she paused for a final taunt:

'Much more better you keep her just as a mistress, Paul,' she said. And, lapsing into village talk: 'Marriage hab teet' an' bite hot, you know!'

She cackled—and slammed the door.

119

# Nine

'Well, where do we begin? Congratulations? Or introductions? What do you think, Paul?' And before Paul could have answered. 'What a lucky chap you are.' And Harry turned back to Dorothea. 'Come inside, my dear, it's far too hot out here for you. And in any case my wife is waiting to meet you.'

He was dressed in fresh and spotless khaki shirt and shorts with long neat socks and shining shoes. He managed to look compact rather than military. There was that eagerness about him which is seen in people who have looked forward to an event for a long time and find they are not disappointed and at the same time an over-enthusiasm Paul had never seen before and which he put down to Harry being faced with a situation he did not quite know how to handle.

Sophie was absurdly over-dressed and looked like a Victorian grand dame. Her manner was not much out of keeping.

'You may kiss me, child,' she said.

Paul found it all excruciatingly embarrassing. Dorothea seemingly did not and

120

played her part superbly. She bent and kissed Sophie on the cheek then straightened in front of her for inspection, crossing her hands, holding her big hat in front of her.

'Yes,' Sophie said. 'You're as pretty as they say.'

'Thank you, Mrs Blades.'

'Do you want to go up to your room?'

'Or,' said Harry, 'have a drink first.'

'Let's have a drink,' Paul said.

Harry was by the trolley on which was a jug of planter's punch and pony tumblers.

'It's a custom when we have guests for breakfast...' He paused, his blue eyes were twinkling, his soft white hair shifting in the breeze through the open doorway. 'We still call it breakfast, not lunch, you know, my dear...it is a custom to give them a glass of punch or two beforehand. The idea is to get them off to sleep so that we can go and get some work done.'

Paul found his chuckle not quite convincing and thought he understood: that Harry was embarrassed too, not because of Sophie—he was never ill-at-ease in front of others however outrageously she behaved, he had far too much sympathy for her, and far too great a sense of obligation—but because of Norfolk. If Norfolk had belonged to him outright,

121

Paul reasoned, Harry would have been less effusive. And less apologetic. His final words: 'I fear we're rather stuffed with old traditions here. I hope you won't find them too repressive,' were not necessary and were out of character; Uncle Harry was proud of Norfolk's traditions.

But Dorothea, even though meeting Harry Blades for the first time, understood better. She realized that his mind must inevitably be filled with memories of the day he had brought his own young bride to Norfolk. Whatever his father might have thought of the marriage, Uncle Harry—she had already begun to think of him that way—Uncle Harry would have been exhilarated, proud of his lovely young wife and facing the future with utter assurance he could handle it successfully. Almost certainly there would have been punches served just as they had been served now. And Sophie?... By all accounts she had been one of the most beautiful women in Cordoba. The world would have been hers that day. She would have taken in Norfolk Hall and its vast acreage and known that when Matthew Blades died she would be its mistress until death (and death at that age was an unimaginable proposition)...until death came to Harry and then it would be her son's. With no hint of the horror soon to strike her down or that her father-in-law the moment he realized there would be *no* sons, would will the property away to be Paul's eventually, would make Harry and herself mere lifetime tenants...with no inkling of such possibilities, she would have been starry-eyed with joy hardly daring to believe it could all be true. And Uncle Harry would be remembering all that as he spoke to her and not forgetting Sophie would be remembering too.

Dorothea did not reply. There was, nothing sensible to answer and, anyway, she knew he didn't want an answer from her. Besides Sophie was sitting in judgement and silence was more difficult to judge than speech. So she smiled, and said nothing, and stood holding her big hat in front of her. And, doing so, won the initial skirmish.

'Sit down, then,' said Sophie irritably. 'Somewhere where I can see you.' She jerked her head towards a chair. 'Sit down there.'

'Yes, Mrs Blades,' Dorothea said.

She had dressed very thoughtfully for this first meeting and not only for the meeting but for Paul as well. She wore a crisp cream shirt waister dress with her tiny waist nipped in by a simple belt. Apart from a small gold cross on a fragile chain and her engagement and wedding rings she wore no jewellery. She wore little make-up and, she had had her hair a little restyled to the nape of her neck and to a casual fringe. She looked cool and fresh and neat and younger, and less sophisticated, than the girl Paul had met in Daniel Fonseca's office.

The punch was delicious, very concentrated, sweet yet sour, made entirely from ingredients out of Norfolk. And it made for a few moments of easy conversation before Harry, standing, said:

'Well, I hope you'll be very happy here, my dear.'

She realized he was about to leave them.

'It's good of you...' she began.

'No,' he said, stopping her. 'You aren't a guest here, Dorothea, and you must never see yourself as one. This is Paul's house, not mine. And now I'm very sorry because there's so much I want to talk to you about but I've got to go down to the factory.'

'Now?' said Paul, surprised.

'Yes, Paul. I had Franklin up here, just before you two arrived.'

'There's something wrong?'

'Probably just a bearing gone.'

'Just a bearing...' He realized Harry didn't want discussion on it here. 'Do you want me to come down with you?'

'On the first morning you bring your wife to Norfolk. Certainly not.'

'But surely...' Paul insisted '...you'd have checked all the bearings before harvesting started... What did Franklin think?'

'All right, all right,' Harry said rather wearily. 'Yes, it could be Ryle.'

When the bedroom door had closed on Alexander, and on Thelma the maid detailed to Dorothea, she said:

'Who's Ryle?'

'You know I'm not sure I can go on with this,' Paul said.

She turned quickly and began to inspect the bedroom, looking out of windows, opening doors.

'We've got two bathrooms,' she discovered.

'Yes.'

'It's quite a fantastic bedroom.' Her tone did not convey she was impressed; rather that she had not been disappointed.

'I don't think I can go on with it,' Paul said again.

Dorothea picked up an ornament. 'I suppose this is *yours?*'

'I suppose it is.'

'And this one too?'

'I daresay.'

'These?' She patted one of the beds.

'Yes.'

125

'In fact probably everything in here? Almost everything in the house.'

He stood with a troubled face but the anxiety no longer worried her. She came across to him with a swirl of cream, cotton skirt and a flicker of pretty brown legs, kissed him full on the lips leaning forwards and upwards on tiptoe to do so, hands clasped behind her back, throwing her youth at him.

For a moment he resisted but her nearness overwhelmed him. The kiss became a passionate one. When it was ended she was breathless and her eyes were sparkling.

'Go and lock the door,' she said.

'Sophie's waiting.'

She chuckled. Already her hand was on the belt, undoing it.

'Just a quick one,' she said. 'While she's sharpening her claws.'

'So you were working for Daniel Fonseca,' Sophie resumed.

'Yes, Mrs Blades. For about six months.'

'Learnt all his secrets.'

'Not all of them.'

'This New St James business. He's mixed up with that.'

'Yes.'

'It's true then, what the paper says?'

'Yes.'

'But how much they leave out?'

'All they don't know.'

'Which you do.'

'No, Mrs Blades. It's been kept very confidential.'

'But you know more than's in the paper?'

'No, Mrs Blades, I don't think I do know any more than's in the paper?'

'Do you?' This was flung at Paul.

'Not really.'

'But aren't they making you a director?'

'When it starts to happen. I shall know more then.'

'And Norfolk doesn't come into it?'

'No.'

'H'm.' She sounded unconvinced. She turned back to Dorothea. 'What was the hurry?'

'What hurry, Mrs Blades?' Paul held his breath. Dorothea's reply had not been insolent; but there had been challenge in it.

'You marrying Paul so dyam quick?' Dorothea did not answer. 'You not in 'way for him, are you?'

'No, Mrs Blades, I'm not in the way for him.'

'You get married so dyam quick,' Sophie said. 'Lawd God, dem niggers all goin' say him advantaged you.'

Paul wondered why Sophie did this—this

lapsing into market vernacular. Dorothea understood. She was being tested. And it was against Cordoba Sophie judged.

'I don't mind, Mrs Blades,' she said, 'what they say.'

'Why not make you wait? You *wanting* all them niggers goin' roun' saying him advantaged you?'

'Pot,' said Dorothea, smiling, 'shouldn't cuss kettle that is black.'

Silent on the sidelines, Paul was aware that what was happening was important. They were testing each other but, more than that, each was voluntarily giving ground. Sophie's concessions were not in her words but in her manner; she was showing her claws but not really using them. Dorothea had brought a new dimension into her life for which she was more than prepared to tolerate her. Meanwhile she was going on:

'And now you're married you'll want to live here until Paul gets Norfolk and then be off.'

'I shall live here,' Dorothea answered quietly, 'for as long as *Paul* wants to, Mrs Blades. I shall live wherever he wants to live.' And she looked at him with a happy smile in which adoration was unmasked.

'Which isn't here,' said Sophie with a touch of anger which made Paul think the brief alliance was already broken—only for her to go on in a reasonable tone:

'There's Harry at the gate.'

'Really?' said Dorothea who had heard nothing.

'My hearing,' sniffed Sophie, 'is remarkable.'

'It must be, Mrs Blades. I didn't hear him.'

'What nature takes away in one direction, she usually atones for in another.' Sophie came back to her attack but not in an attacking way. 'You'll want to get out of Cordoba just as soon as you can.' She spoke as if this were agreed between them and the perfectly proper attitude for Dorothea to have.

'I've already told you, Mrs Blades,' Dorothea responded quietly. 'I just want to be wherever my husband wants to be.'

'Stuff and nonsense,' said Sophie, quite cheerfully for her. 'You want to go. That's why you married him.'

Paul was furious. 'Aunt Sophie...'

She rounded on him with withering contempt. 'Don't interrupt! You think she needs any help from you? You think she cares what you want? You're as big a fool as Harry is allowing her to come here.'

'Mrs Blades,' said Dorothea, 'I married Paul for one reason and for one reason only. Because I love him. It doesn't matter to me where I live—in Cordoba or out of

Cordoba. So long as I'm with Paul. So long as we are doing what he wants.'

She might as well have saved her breath. 'I shouldn't think,' said Sophie, obviously well satisfied, 'Paul's likes and dislikes matter to you any more than yesterday's cold porridge. You married him, I'd say, to help turn out Harry and then go off on the proceeds. Your mother taught you something. He can't walk out on you now; can he? Well it's going to be very interesting.'

She had timed it excellently; a moment later Harry had joined them.

It was a memorable first breakfast eaten in the dining-room—a vast room of dark floors and panelling with massive furniture including a dining-table at which two dozen could have been seated comfortably and was graced by glass and silver fit for royalty. Harry sat at the head with Sophie to his right and Dorothea to his left, and Paul faced Hesther who helped Sophie with her meal.

He could not escape, shut off from the world by a room specifically designed to achieve this feeling, the sense that here, at least, time stood still; that nothing would ever change. They made, counting in Alexander who served them, a microcosm of Cordoba: two blacks, two coloured women, and two men white but for a trace picked up along the way somewhere. They were representative of social stratas, of differing ways of life, of differing attitudes. Taking the dining-room as Cordoba, they made its population. And the meal was in keeping. A soup of pig's tail, salt beef and coconut milk—a soup exactly as that they would find below bubbling over the fires by the cane cutters' huts; a roast of lamb but with okra, yampie, gungo peas and rice, plantain and breadfruit spears; and a sweet of imported strawberries!

It was a meal of which Harry was very proud, a traditional planter's breakfast and he said as much to Dorothea but Paul now saw it as failure—as a coming to terms with what couldn't be defeated. The first few generations of Blades, he told himself, would have fought against this kind of mixture, would have struggled to lead a way of life entirely European—the beginning of Uncle Harry's tradition was no more than the end of a struggle lost. He had never thought this way before but then, as he told himself, his eyes had not been opened. He had thought himself a part of Norfolk; now he knew that he was not. To live his life out here, as Uncle Harry had lived out his, was unimaginable. But to live his life in Europe, or maybe in America, rich, with Dorothea to share it...he felt a sudden, burning impatience at the thought. Dee was right, there was no argument against her. Norfolk was an anachronism, a burnt-out case; it was as finished as Sophie Blades herself.

He looked at her, stumbling disgustingly through her meal, her dress stained with something slopped, the table top in front of her smeary with droppings, somehow conveying food to her mouth by wrists out of which grew hideous, useless, jewel-decorated claws, constantly upbraiding the patient dead-faced Hesther, ears pricked, eyes sharp, all attention on the conversation.

Harry was talking about the cotton tree under which Paul usually parked his car and which was known as Tom Long's cotton tree.

'...it's all rather confused, of course, as these things always are.'

'It's not at all confused,' said Sophie. 'Africans always believed in cotton tree spirits and always will.'

'Quite true,' said Harry. 'Only our particular example has got embellishments. For one thing they used to hang misbehaving slaves from it. So it's not just tree spirits who probably haunt it, it's the spirits of all those poor wretches too.'

'And Tom Long? How does it get its name... Tom Long?'

'Oh,' Harry explained. 'He was my grandfather's busher...like Franklin. And Joseph—that was my grandfather—was something of a recluse. When he was young enough he used to climb up that tree with a shotgun and blaze away at any strangers he saw heading for the house. Supposed to have killed quite a few.'

'And nobody stopped him?'

'Well you know, my dear, things were a little different in those days, and we were a very powerful family... Anyway. Tom Long. When my grandfather got too old to climb the tree himself, he had Tom Long take over. He was a rum one too.' He chuckled. 'You've married into a very rum family I'm afraid, my dear...' And he tried to bring Paul into the conversation. 'You finish it off, Paul.'

Paul was in a curious mood caused by Sophie's dismissal, the effects of which he had still to shake off and he was conscious of that irritation which men are inclined to feel when in moments of uncertainty the woman they love is showing herself able to fit easily into a situation which it is proving difficult for them to handle.

'It's probably all untrue anyway,' he said somewhat curtly.

'What isn't true!' Sophie rapped.

133

'About Tom Long.'

'Of course it's true. It's fully documented.'

'Yes,' said Paul. 'Fully documented. But that doesn't make it true...' He felt Dee's warm warning hand upon his thigh and strangely, instead of silencing him, this drove him on to recklessness.

'Every family that thinks as much of itself as the Blades have done, has to have its legends,' he declared. 'Most of them have haunted corridors—we go one better. We have a haunted tree. No one dares walk under it at night. It's fairly crawling with duppies...' He felt Dee's hand press harder. 'Tom Long was found dead under it one morning with a broken neck,' he said abruptly. 'He was supposed to have a look of terror on his face and there's a belief he was dead before he even hit the ground—although how anyone's supposed to have been able to substantiate that in the days before post-mortems, I do not know.'

'You think he just lost his footing?'

'Well of course he just lost his footing, Dee.' Her hand was back, resting lightly on the table. 'You try trying to climb a cotton tree at night with a shotgun in your hand.'

'He was dead before he hit the ground,' said Sophie.

'How do you know?'

'He was heard to scream with fear as he fell.'

'Why shouldn't he? I'd scream if I knew I was going to break my neck.'

'You don't understand,' said Sophie. 'You know nothing of Norfolk. I tell you Tom Long was dead before he hit the ground. He was killed because he mocked the spirits. And now his shadow...'

'Oh for goodness sake...'

'Be silent!' Her voice was suddenly shrill—and shocking. 'You'll find out.' She was leaning across the table, head thrust out, her stiff arms forward, her fingers rigid yet, seemingly, alive with accusation. 'We are threefold!' she cried, her voice taking on an odd religious tone. 'Body, soul and shadow. On the third day after we die our shadow rises from our body and sets on someone still alive. Look!' She managed to shake her hands. 'How do you think that I got these. They're Tom Long's hands. When they examined him, every finger of his hands was broken. Every one! And this is how he mended them!'

The vibrant triumph in her voice caused a *frisson* of shock to pass through Paul's body. There was no way of answering. And suddenly the thought of the months ahead filled him with trepidation. They had, he and Dee, done something unimaginable—they had entered into an unholy compact with a woman who was mad.

# Ten

Dorothea gave much thought to choosing the moment when vague generalities about dispossessing Harry should be translated into decision on what they should practically do. She knew she must not wait too long, that she must speak before her sexual hold over Paul began to slip.

In thinking of it in this way she was being true to the fundamental instinct of a people obliged to adjust to circumstances. To Dorothea sex was a vital thing but she was not tyrannized by it and she held the very practical attitude towards it of most West Indian women that, more than being a delightful game, it was a useful one which gave those who deployed it power over their men, and particularly so in an island such as Cordoba where the social structure of the past had not been based on family units, (which slave owners had done all they could to break up), and where the society had been a largely matriarchal one in which the men were inclined to *expect* their women to be authoritarian.

On the whole she had held the young men of St James in casual contempt and

137

managed them with little difficulty. But Paul had been, at first, a puzzle to her. She had assumed, and hoped for, the mastery from him she had not looked for in the young men of St James. She had imagined that a man of Paul's background would be far more difficult to rule. It was only as the weeks passed by that she gradually came to understand. With all the problems of a small island way of life, sexual relationships were difficult to manage in Cordoba and basically ended up as hasty, untidy and often purely oral affairs in cars...she, herself, had had to meet Paul to know for the first time the luxury of an uninterrupted night of lovemaking.

She assumed this would hardly have been a novelty to *him* but, getting to know him better, listening to all he said and reading between the lines, she had come to realize that even in Coral Gardens, Paul had been far less well placed than she had imagined. Whatever some of the matrons might have wished he had been the Coral Gardens manager and not its stallion and if he was to keep a job difficult to better, he had to be very circumspect. There would obviously have been women who enticed him, or he enticed, to cottage bedroom—but it would usually have been a jerky, hurried business, carried through under stress and often regretted afterwards. There might have been the occasional exception but even these would merely have thrown into clearer focus the untidy and frustrating overall management of the sexual life of a very sensuous man.

But in her he had found an answer—a girl beautiful of body, enthusiastic in sex and available full time. No more the disappointments, the frustrations, the fear of discovery, the next morning nervousness, the wondering what could have made him do it. No more the doubts of what was acceptable, and what was not. No more the haste, complaints on his performance, recriminations. It was hardly surprising he had been bewitched by her. But how long would this last? When would the time come when his enthusiasm would start to ebb and the other, the unsexual Paul Blades, would re-emerge? She had no way of knowing. But come one day it must and before it did she had to see that he would have been fully committed, had done things which made carrying through their project seem inescapable.

Her opportunity came a few days after her arrival at Norfolk. Their life had begun to fall into a pattern. It was the busy season with cane being reaped and crushed, when the factory poured its white smoke day and night, when the air was filled with the sickly smell of refining sugar, when the yard was choked with lines of carts laden with cut crop, when the marl tracks were littered with crushed pieces, when everything else was put aside to be done at a less busy time. Paul worked as hard as any of them, Harry saw to that—he had made it clear at the outset Norfolk could afford no passengers. Paul did not object. He had never been happier nor more occupied and his body responded to the work and regular way of life. He was off within an hour of dawn and not back 'till breakfast—riding the tracks, doing his stint in the factory, keeping an eye on the other aspects—the cropping of bananas, the picking of orange, lime and grapefruit, the spraying against pestilence, the marketing of copra.

Then, unexpectedly, Uncle Harry decreed a holiday:

'Too much work makes Jack a dull boy, Paul. Take her to the Falls. Do some mullet fishing. Swim. Fall asleep. Make sure it's in the shade. I don't want to see either of you back till nightfall.'

The property had a river, the Culebra, which was really a wide track of massive rounded boulders through which, except in times of spate, flowed shallow mountain water. A river which threatened to dry up,

140

yet never quite did this; a river from which you should run for your life if you noticed colour in its water. A river of stickles and small pools and only occasionally stiller stretches where the water was deep and slow.

At such a place was 'The Falls' as it was simply known, as beautiful a place as any in Cordoba. Here a pool floored by emerald rock was fed by white-frothed water sifting down the black face of a wall of rock in shadow at its base, sheltered by gigantic cotton-trees that were hosts to hanging vines. On one side the trees were close, old trees of many roots and buttresses, festooned with orchids and wild pines, forcing their way through pale pink mossy rock; on the other the trees drew back a little, cavern-like, showing below a sky of blue the starfishes of bananas, wild ginger with great sheaves of pink-white foxglove flowers, and branches weighed down with hordes of parasites and draped with liana as thickly as a Christmas tree with tinsel. It was cool here with the damp and gentle cool that only growing trees can bring and dim but for the clear colour of Dorothea's dress discarded on a rock, the sugar-white water sifting down and the scattered sunbeams fractured by a thousand branches.

She lay, nude, on the tiny beach of

rippled sand beside the blue green water just as she had lain by the pool at the Windsor Hotel when he had come out with the paper, her arms flat and her head between them, smiling at him. The line of her body was like a wave, from shoulders down to waist, then up to buttocks, then down and up to thighs, then down and up to calves, and then her tiny feet, pink-soled, toes dug into sand. He looked at her entranced. He was naked too. There would be no one here but them. This was Norfolk's land and all the Norfolk men and women were at work because this was harvest time.

They had made love and that wonderful sense of holiday lassitude had overtaken him. A young man who had largely led the life of an older man, who had largely mingled with older men and women, there was a special magic being here in this paradise with the girl he loved. He felt the urge to be absurd, to do childish things, to romp; but on the other hand just to lie and listen to the water and the birds, to feel the burning sun upon his flesh, to enjoy the freedom of a naked, unrestricted body, to lie beside her hour on hour, desire spent, to contemplate her loveliness which, incredibly, would be his for ever, was equally compelling. It was his happiest day.

Had Dorothea been able to make, as he could, comparisons, how different their lives might have been. For she was happy too. It was scarcely possible that a girl so confident of her beauty, so adored, so believing in her future, relaxing in so marvellous a place after the joy of successful lovemaking could have been anything but happy. The regret that she hadn't found in Paul what fundamentally her inner being cried for, a man who with the power to dominate her combined with the imagination to give free rein to her enthusiasm would lead her into the full life she sensed existed, this regret was numbed by the special magic of this place and her transient contentment. She felt at that moment a tenderness towards Paul she hadn't known before; with vision free, briefly, of ambition, she saw him for what he was: a romantic made intense by upbringing, placed in limbo by a will, struggling to justify himself, searching for a purpose. A man living, basically, without contemporaries, who had clutched at Coral Gardens simply because there was nothing else to clutch at. A man caught by the bewildering swiftness of modern change with both background and future geared to changelessness. An undemanding man—a man, as now, easily satisfied. Dorothea did not see it in this detail but the sum of all of this came across and she knew him for a decent man with a need for peace which she had met. And that was nice, even, for the time, sufficient. For the morning Norfolk was forgotten. They did childish things: up-ended boulders seeking crayfish, tried, absurdly, to catch mullet with bare hands, chased butterflies, played hide and seek, naked, amongst the river boulders, swam in the emerald pool amongst pink floating blossom which patterned their skin on leaving it like a beautiful disease, raced boats made of scooped out avocado pears with twigs for masts and Long John leaves as sails, toasted each other in frozen *daiqueries* from the ice box and ate enormously on previously prepared stuffed crabs and matrimony washed down with the fresh cold water of the river. And then they moved into the shade and slept.

In the tropics no afternoon has the magic of a morning—the promise has gone from the day, it is a time of waiting for the bliss of evening. And the heaviness of siesta dulls the sensibilities. When Dorothea awoke their morning was a memory. This did not depress her. There would be other mornings. In just such a casual manner did her subconscious dismiss her final link with innocence.

She looked at Paul beside her, thought

for a moment or two then, leaving him, quietly slipped into the pool to wash the sweat of sleep in heat away. The pool was deep enough for swimming and shallow enough to sit in with her head just out of water. It was pleasant to feel the steady press of the current on her flesh. From where she sat she could watch him all the time.

It occurred to her that after lunch he had wanted to sleep without making love to her and she realized with a faint start of surprise that this was the first time making love had not immediately preceded sleep between them. And now when she thought about the morning the recollection disturbed her. He had been too content. So she saw it now not as a memory to be treasured, but as an error; she could not conceive there would be a time when she would look back on it as a watershed. She did not have, as Paul had, the years behind her for comparison. There would be other mornings.

It was of a sudden absurd to be sitting in the pool, it was even cold. She left it, dried herself and put on her yellow dress. She washed the few lunch dishes in the river noisily, waking him. He sat up, heavy, comatose.

'What's the rush?' His voice was lethargic, coming through a yawn.

'No rush. Just thought I'd do them.' Her own was crisp and practical.

'Oh. Want any help?'

'No, thank you, darling. There's hardly anything to do.'

'Hot isn't it? Don't you want a swim?'

'Had one.'

He was silent, adjusting his mood to hers. She helped him on his way.

'Why don't you have a swim. Wake you up.'

'But I don't want to wake up. I want to go on eating lotuses. For ever and for ever and for ever.'

He could hardly have helped her more.

'They'd probably end up giving you indigestion.'

'I say,' he said. And then: 'Something up?'

She smiled at him winningly. 'No?' There was a query in her voice.

'Well I mean...well you're suddenly so horribly practical.'

'One of us has to be.' Her smile was just slightly reproving.

'Soon alter that.' He got to his feet with obvious intent.

'No.' She swayed away. 'You'll mark my dress.'

'Don't know why on earth you put it on.'

'You put on trunks.'

146

'Quite another matter. That part of a man isn't the most attractive.'

'It is to me.'

'Well...'

'No. Go and have a swim. I want a cigarette.'

She sat on a rock, smoking, watching him. When he got out he said: 'Do I get dressed or what?'

'We've got to talk,' she said. 'There are times for lotus eating.'

'Like now?'

'Not like now.'

'So I get dressed?'

She shook her head. 'No, of course not. Put a towel round you or something.'

He did so. And sat beside her.

'At your disposal, then,' he said. 'You can have ten minutes. Then we have sex. Or shall we have the sex first and then you can have as long as you like.'

'Ten minutes will do.' She flicked off ash. 'You never did tell me about this man Ryle,' she said.

'Not much to tell. His family's worked for Norfolk for generations. But he's a bad one. But we don't want to talk about Ryle on a day like this.'

'I do. What exactly did he do?'

'Started cane fires. And did his best to bugger up some of the machinery in the factory. We presume.'

'Are cane fires serious things on a sugar estate?'

'More of a nuisance than anything.'

'Not serious.'

'Well it depends... Dee...'

'No. I'm interested.'

'Well...no, they're not really serious. Not usually.'

'But doesn't it destroy the crop?'

He shook his head. 'No. But burnt cane has to be cut and ground quickly. And its filthy stuff to handle. And having to cut a field out of order upsets the system.'

'So if there was a big fire?'

'It's not all that difficult to put out a cane fire. Looks much more of a calamity than it really is.'

'But supposing there were several fires at once?' she persisted.

'Well, yes,' he admitted, grudgingly. 'If they were big ones, it could be serious then. But Ryle...'

She stopped him, a little impatiently. 'I wasn't thinking about Ryle. Well not exactly.' She threw her cigarette butt into the river and watched it whisk away. 'Uncle Harry lives on the income from the estate, doesn't he?' she said. 'Is it substantial?'

'Yes. Varies with the crop of course.'

'Doesn't the will say anything about the income?'

'A proportion has to go on maintenance of the house and property.'

'That has to come out first? Before Uncle Harry gets any income?'

'Yes.'

'What happens if there isn't any profit? It would be difficult for him to live here wouldn't it? Or does he have money of his own?'

'Only what he may have saved. Matthew Blades didn't leave anything worth talking about. Blued it all on gambling.'

'Well then?'

He had realized by now exactly where this was leading. He had a vague sort of notion that if he managed to prevent her bringing it to a head, it would all pass over.

'His wants are pretty simple, Dee,' he said.

'Don't be pyaa pyaa, man!' she said sharply. 'You know exactly what I'm driving at.' And she went on quickly before he could protest. 'If the estate lost money d'you think he'd put back into it anything he'd saved?'

'He might. Of course he's got Sophie to consider...'

'And an estate the size of Norfolk could swallow up savings pretty fast, couldn't it? Once things on it went really wrong. And of course you're right...he wouldn't

149

dare run down his personal savings with a woman as badly crippled as she is and who might, for all any of us know, go off her head completely. Anyway he wouldn't; he's not that sort of man. So what else beside cane fires would make the estate lose money?'

He shrugged. 'Bad weather,' he said dismally.

'Well,' she smiled faintly, 'we can't do much about that. But there must be other things we can.' She thought for a moment. 'Supposing,' she said, 'there was trouble amongst the men...you know, strikes...that sort of thing.'

'He'd hate it.'

'Yes. He would, wouldn't he.' She stared hard at the river, but now not seeing it.

'Malcolm!' she said suddenly.

'Malcolm?'

'Would he help?'

'I shouldn't think so.' He tried to make a stand. 'Look, Dee,' he said. 'We don't have to start thinking of draconian measures. We haven't even spoken to Uncle Harry, explained what's at stake...'

She demolished him with ease.

'You'll never persuade him, man. You know that's just damn foolish talk. And trying to will only give the game away in any case. Make it that much more difficult.' She had said what mattered.

Now she must be very careful. She must let him lead the conversation. 'Paul,' she said, laying a hand on his knee and looking at him with faint reproof. 'We have been through all of this before. That first morning at the Windsor and I don't know how many times since then.'

'We haven't been through committing arson! Or starting revolutions!'

'Is that a good idea?' she joked.

'It isn't funny, Dee.'

'No, man.'

'Please don't talk to me like that.' He paused—and then apologized. 'You remind me too much of Sophie.'

'Sophie.' She weighed the name. 'Paul?'

'Well?'

'It's not...' She hesitated.

'What?'

She raised her head, striking the attitude of a woman who had decided to face the truth.

'She accused me,' she said, deliberately, 'of marrying you for what I could get. And you didn't take her up on it, did you? Not really?'

'But I did!'

'No. Not really, Paul.'

He protested vehemently. 'It wasn't like that...you know it wasn't like that!'

She looked away.

'Dee!' he burst out. 'You can't think...

you can't believe...'

'No,' she said, quietly, as if she had been only testing him. And then, with a small smile: 'No. I shouldn't have said that. Forgive me.'

He was unconvinced. He grasped her arm.

'You couldn't have believed that I took that seriously. For God's *sake*, Dee!'

She did not answer.

'Dee!' he said. 'We've got to have this out. Once and for all.'

'You're hurting me, Paul,' she said.

He let go of her.

'You're quite right,' she said. 'We've got to have this out. Once and for all. I married you for one reason and for one reason only. Because there wasn't, once I'd met you, anyone else I could have married. I knew that the moment you spoke to me in Daniel's office. Do you remember? It seems a long, long time ago. And how many weeks is it? Just six.'

'The six weeks in my life that mattered.'

'And in mine.' Her quietness was very convincing. 'The only weeks, really. But you know, Paul, Sophie isn't all that far out. When you asked me to have a drink with you, that wasn't John Smith asking—that was Paul Blades. If it had been John Smith...' She smiled wanly. 'Well, I suppose it would have depended on what the particular John Smith was like... But, you weren't John Smith. You were Paul Blades. And being Paul Blades lifted you head and shoulders over the heads of all those damn idiots in St James. So I said yes. Because of who you were. Not what you were. And that's why I inveigled you into inviting me to Coral Gardens. Because of who you were. Because you could take me to Coral Gardens. And there wasn't anyone else in the whole damned island who could have. But somewhere along the line in just that one day it stopped being like that. Because *you* took over. I stopped thinking about you being the great whatever of Norfolk Hall and started to think of you in other ways. Like going to bed with you.' And she remembered that this was true and there was no way he could have disbelieved her—because it was exactly how she had felt. 'I started to think...' she spoke very simply. 'Of this.' And she put out her hand and rummaged beneath the towel until she found his penis. 'I started to wonder what it would be like inside me. That was nothing to do with Norfolk. Nothing to do with Coral Gardens. Nothing to do with being rich.' She closed her hand around his penis, feeling it swell. 'It's a funny business, sex, Paul, isn't it? It doesn't matter all that much to some people, I suppose. But it does to us. We only have to touch each other...' She let go of him.

'I don't know,' she said, 'where sex ends and love begins and I don't really care. Perhaps when you don't move me sexually, I won't love you any more. I'll grow tired of you. But as of now...I think of you all day. Think of you coming back from the fields and what we're going to do. I even...masturbate sometimes, thinking of you.' She looked away from him. 'I want Norfolk, Paul. And I want it so that we can sell it. And there's nothing I won't do to get it. I'll start cane fires; I'll incite Uncle Harry's workmen to be against him though all the time I realize what a kind and decent man he is.' She smiled again, faintly. 'I'd even start a revolution if that was possible and useful. You see'...her hand was back on his knee...'you see, Paul, I don't believe that it could last between us. Not at Norfolk. For a day, a year, maybe two. Days like today? Wonderful. Unforgettable. But they'd pall. They're holidays, darling, not part of life. If only they could be. But they can't. It's not how we are made...'

She had defeated him.

'I'll speak to Ryle,' he said.

# Eleven

A few days later there was the first heavy rainfall of the year; the clouds which day by day had gathered, broke suddenly and torrents fell unceasingly from dawn until well into the afternoon; then the rain stopped but the skies refused to clear so that with the ending of the cooling rain leaving the hot humid air trapped between the steaming ground and sullen clouds, the atmosphere was stifling. Dorothea, finding Norfolk Hall unbearable, drove down to the factory and sent a message in to Paul. When he came out it was to find her standing by his M.G. unperturbed by the curious looks of the depressed workmen and apparently oblivious of the mess of sodden lengths of crushed sugar cane which littered the yard about her feet. She was dressed in yellow slacks and a strident shirt; she might have been waiting for him on the patio of some smart South of France hotel.

'Can you get away?' she asked.

'Yes,' he said. 'There's not all that to do.'

'I can't stand it in the house. And I

wanted to get out of it before I get stuck with that damn tea performance.'

'What would you like to do?'

'Just drive around.'

'There's not many places to drive around to, particularly on a day like this.'

'Never mind. There's one or two things I'd like to pick up in Pilotte.'

'All right. I'll just let Uncle Harry know.'

When he came out, Dorothea had already turned the M.G. and was sitting in the driving seat.

She drove out through the factory gates on the marl road which for once was not a cloud of dust. Here there was sugar growing on either side, still waiting to be cut and every blade of it dripping steamy wet. A cart, its splaying out sides stacked with cane, blocked their path.

'Come on! Come on!' cried Dorothea impatiently.

'You'll have to back,' said Paul. 'He can't.'

'Damn!' she said.

It was torture waiting in the thick wet heat. 'I'm a puddle already,' Dorothea said.

The cart came slowly, steam rising from the hides of its three yoked oxen plodding through the pools of a road as white and slimy as china clay and the driver too low in spirit even to touch his sodden cap. Norfolk looked at its utter worst. Paul was drenched in sweat; impossibly it felt hotter here even than in the factory. He glanced at Dorothea and saw her face was gleaming too.

The cart passed at last and Dorothea let in the gears, crashing them in her haste, slithering the wheels before they took a grip. She drove without speaking. The only thing on her mind was to get some speed, to cool themselves with slipstream. When she met the main road, the road from French Bay to Pilotte, she spun the wheel hard, barely slowing, and at once accelerated. Beside them lay a sea as surly as the clouds with long spindrifted waves rolling in with dull monotony to expend themselves on the beach that was only vital because it was white. Today it could have appealed to no one, today it was as depressing as Pilotte itself, a draggletown of dripping tin-roofed shanties and crude painted concrete buildings.

'I thought there were things you wanted,' Paul protested as she drove through without stopping.

'They can wait. Ugh what a hole it is on a day like this!'

Where can we go, thought Paul. Where is there to go? There was that sense of constriction inescapable on a bad day on a tropical island with a single circumnavigating road and no town of consequence within forty miles.

'We could drive to French Bay and have tea at the Windsor?' he suggested.

'Sit in that damn echoing place,' said Dorothea. 'No, thank you, man. There must be *some*where else! Where does this road go?' She had slowed at the sight of an opening on their right.

'Copra Valley. Malcolm's place...'

'Why don't we go there?'

He wondered if she'd planned it, then thrust the first disloyal thought aside.

It was too late to protest without making a meal of it; she had already turned, skidding a little, into the road.

For perhaps a hundred yards, already climbing, the road was metalled but round the first bend it collapsed to a rutted lane with occasional shabby huts with palm-frond roofs and walls inside decorated with old newspaper pictures and advertisements. Slimy-looking paths wandering from huts to smallholdings leaked muddy rivulets, women peered disconsolately from crooked doorways. Then came a sagging, peeling gateway which was never closed because the gatepost had rotted off—the entrance to Malcolm's property.

'In here,' Paul said glumly.

What had been a lane became a track, narrow, two ruts with high wet grass between which made a rushing sound as it brushed the belly of the car. There were coconut palms on either hand with the ground beneath them soiled by decaying fronds. Occasionally there were piles of nuts, green and unhusked, waiting to be collected. They passed the copra factory, a bungalow-sized building, thatched and smoke-blackened, like Norfolk's, except that here the pile of reddish, brittle shells was high enough to dwarf it.

The house came suddenly: another gateway with another sagging, peeling gate; a track so narrow they could have touched the growth on either hand; a sudden, steeper turn. And there, perched on its inevitable mound it stood—Copra Valley.

Paul saw that Dorothea was alert, studying it. If she had not seen this house before, she had seen all of its component parts: the double flight of curving steps masking the archways of its lower stuccoed floor; the continuous balcony fretworked in a diamond pattern of painted, peeling woodwork; the pairs of narrow louvred windows either side of the double louvred entrance door; the roof of corrugated iron. It had a strange ramshackle charm as it stood there rising from a cluttered

159

mess which just remained a garden so that it was seen through a haze of dripping purple bougainvillaea interwoven with yellow allamanda and the hanging stars of white thunbergia—Copra Valley, one of a score of such houses in Cordoba, of a thousand in the Caribbean, crumbling houses of small, defeated planters whose lives had become aimless and habitual.

Malcolm must have heard them coming from a long way of for he was on the balcony. But he only bothered to see who his visitors were when he heard the car door slam. He came to the balcony edge and stood looking down. Dorothea saw a man wearing jeans and a torn blue string vest over a matted chest. He was unshaven and his thick, black, lustrous hair uncombed.

'Hallo, Malcolm!' Paul called up to him.

'Come up,' he said, looking only at Dorothea. And when they had reached the balcony. 'So you're the one who married him.'

'Yes, Mr Blades.'

'Malcolm.'

'Yes, Malcolm. I'm the one who's married him.'

'And what do you want with me?'

'Your help?'

He laughed. 'You must be pushed.'

He had been guarding the entrance to the balcony making Dorothea stand on the topmost step tilting her head to look at him. She noticed in him a blend of virility and femininity. He was an attractive man.

'Well,' she said. 'Can we come in?'

He stood aside. 'All right.' And nodding to Paul. 'You too.'

The balcony was unfurnished but for a rickety, rattan table and some wooden chairs. On the table was a bottle of rum, a jug of water, a half filled glass and an open book; beside it, hanging from a rafter, was a long length of smouldering rope for lighting cigarettes. The low walls at the ends were disfigured by cracks and broken termite runs, the floor a sorry mess of fractured paving.

'Sit down then,' said Malcolm looking at Dorothea insolently and making a gesture of mock courtesy towards an unsafe looking chair.

'Thank you,' she said easily, sitting in it. 'May I have a cigarette?' Paul must be livid, she was thinking.

Malcolm picked up a limp packet of cigarettes and spilt one to her. 'Why should someone who looks like you marry someone like him?' he mocked.

'Because I preferred him to anyone else I know.'

It made him laugh. 'You're out of your

class,' he said to Paul.

'Would it be possible,' Dorothea asked, 'to have some tea. I want to take an aspirin. I've got a headache.'

Malcolm bellowed 'Aggie!' and when there was no immediate response, bellowed it again and there was the sound of grumbling and then the sound of heavy feet and then the woman, a surly black with skin like earth and enormous breasts sagging unfettered in a shapeless scarlet dress, appeared. On her head was a plaid madras and great brass gypsy ear-rings swung indignantly. Her feet were bare and dusty and her legs badly scarred with yaws.

'Tea!' said Malcolm. 'For two.'

'For one,' Paul said. 'I'll have Scotch.'

'Go and get it then.'

Paul followed Aggie in, hearing her muttering to herself. He scarcely knew the house, although it belonged to him. It was no more than a sitting-room with kitchen behind and an inner staircase leading to bedrooms below he'd never seen. The sitting-room had a white matchboarded ceiling sloping to meet walls lined with planks of split coconut palm. Termite runs drew gritty looking, dun-coloured lines across it. The room was shabby, slovenly and poorly furnished. There were many books.

He poured himself a whisky far larger

than he needed, then went outside again to find Dorothea leaning back in her chair with her arms held wide as if to show herself and Malcolm eyeing her with real, if mocking, interest. He was shocked, there was something so utterly shameless about her posture, something so insolent about Malcolm's gaze.

'What was the rush,' Paul heard him saying. 'You can imagine the talk.'

'She's had that already,' he snapped. 'From Sophie.'

'She would.'

Paul struggled to show nonchalance. The man is a worthless drunk, he told himself—by mixing it with him, I only demean myself. As for the idea of him helping over this Norfolk business, forget it.

He leaned on the balcony rail, casually but carefully—the rail looked flimsy. As soon as Dee's had her tea, we're off. And not coming back again. So he told himself. Meanwhile... He sought inspiration and, looking down, a long way down, he noticed, beyond the overlapping spiders of coconut palms the bow of a banana boat moored at Pilotte Wharf.

'What ship's that?' he demanded briefly.

'How should I know. I deal in coconuts, not bananas.'

The rail tested and found secure enough,

163

Paul turned, leaning back against it.

'How's business?' he said offhandedly.

'Bloody.'

'What's the trouble?' And when Malcolm didn't answer. 'I said what's the trouble?'

'And I didn't answer because I don't answer damn fool questions.'

You're making a mess of this, Paul, thought Dorothea—you can't carry it off, so you shouldn't try.

She rescued: 'What is the trouble?'

'I can't get pickers.'

'Why not?'

'Because they're all working for Uncle Harry. Because I can't afford to pay what Uncle Harry can. Because when cane is being cropped they always work for Uncle Harry.'

'Couldn't you grow sugar too?'

'I could.'

'Why don't you then?'

'Because it needs attention and would interrupt my drinking.'

A weak man this, she thought. But he attracted her. There was something so *physical* about him. That he was more than fifty mean't nothing to her. She knew at once that he wouldn't be weak in sex; that no woman would ever manage him in sex the way she managed Paul.

'You're proud of your drinking, Malcolm, aren't you?' she said.

164

He laughed again. 'I told you. You're too bloody good for him.'

'They adjoin, don't they,' Dorothea went on as if he hadn't spoken. 'Norfolk and Copra Valley, I mean. If your father had left the property differently, if he'd left you part of Norfolk, d'you think you'd have grown sugar too?'

I must speak, Paul told himself. I must stop her. In a minute it'll be too late.

But he didn't speak.

There would have been time. Malcolm didn't answer at once. It was as if he sensed what Dorothea was leading up to.

Yes, I can risk it, Dorothea thought. I think he understands. 'Would you?' she repeated. And now there was an edge which had not been there before.

'Would I *what?*'

'Grow sugar if you had more land?'

'That's a different question isn't it?'

I shall speak, Paul told himself. I've got to stop this. And as if he *had* spoken, Dorothea turned her head to him. And nodded. He heard his own voice. He could not believe what he was saying.

'We've come to offer you a piece of Norfolk.'

He saw Dee's smile, noted the satisfaction with which she ground out her cigarette. And he was suddenly afraid.

'Bog Pen,' he said desperately. 'It's good land.'

'And not yours to give.'

'It will be.'

'I'll be dead by then.'

'Not necessarily.'

'Oh?'

It was easy now. The past was over. Done and finished with. Like climbing a long slow mountain. It might be only emptiness ahead, but the climb was over.

'I've had an offer for Norfolk...'

'You're always having offers.'

'Not like this.' Am I saying too much? Is this relevant? He looked at Dee for guidance. But she was watching Malcolm. 'Not like this,' he said again, making his voice very firm, as if he were already owner, as if he were already wealthy. A man of affairs. 'But first I've got to persuade Uncle Harry to let me sell it. That's where maybe you can help. And if you can I'm willing to make the Bog Pen sector over to you. It's not bad land and there's over a hundred acres...' No, I'm talking too much. 'Take it or leave it, Malcolm.' What an absurd way to end.

'Take or leave what? Uncle Harry won't go. You know that, man.'

He felt the flush rising to his face. He had to beat it.

'He might. With a little persuasion.'

166

There. It was said. He was weak with relief.

'Persuasion?'

'Persuasion.' The firmness was genuine now. 'Are you interested?'

Malcolm was nodding slowly. 'I might be.'

But just then Aggie came stomping through. 'Where I put it?' Her voice was surly.

'Where do you want it?' Malcolm asked Dorothea.

'Can I have it inside?'

'Any time you like.'

'I meant the tea.'

'On the table, Aggie.'

They followed her in, followed a waft of stale sweat.

'Observe,' said Malcolm to Dorothea, 'the difference in a date of birth. Oil lamps instead of chandeliers. Bare boards instead of marble tiles. Calendars instead of Corots.'

Dorothea surveyed the long narrow room with its flaking ceiling and its coconut panelled walls.

'I could, of course,' Malcolm went on, grinning, 'have a neat and tidy home, however humble.'

'Could you?' She picked up a book lying on the top of a cheap bamboo bookcase filled with books, and opened it. It was

167

eaten through by worms. She put it down again.

'It isn't just conceit, living like this, you know,' Malcolm said. 'It's making the best of things. The trouble with being a poor white isn't being poor, it's being white. Now if I were black and smartened up the place a bit that would be commendable...'

'But,' interrupted Dorothea, speaking quickly as if to get it out of the way, 'as a rum-soaked white it would be pitiful.'

For the moment it looked as if this had annoyed him; then he grinned again and patting her bottom left his hand against it. 'You win,' he said.

'Take your hand off her,' Paul said.

Malcolm turned his head, contempt on his face: 'If you think your hand's the only one that's felt her bum or the last that's going to...' But he took his hand away. 'Let's sit down,' he said, 'and plan the way to dispossess poor old Uncle Harry.'

Aggie had come in, making the whole room shake, carrying a tin tray, banging it on the table, tossing her head. She went out again, slamming the door behind her. She might not have been in the room for all the notice Malcolm took.

'What would make you go?' said Dorothea, pouring tea.

'Me?' said Malcolm. 'I shan't go.'

'What makes you stay?'

'Being here.'

'That's all?'

'That's all. If I were somewhere else, I'd stay there too.'

'But if your troubles with pickers went on and on, wouldn't you go then?'

'Where to?'

'Couldn't your brother say the same?'

'He could. And probably would.'

She saw he was enjoying this. She wondered why he wore a cross. He could be religious. Even a Catholic. She wondered why she wondered if he was Catholic. How did you get to the bottom of a man like this? How did a man live so dissolutely and stay so strong? How could a man who was so weak convey such power?

'Suppose...' she tried. 'Suppose your coconuts were ruined by disease, would you go then?'

'I doubt it.'

Paul was impatient. This slow approach demoted him. It was his land after all.

'How far are you prepared to help us for Bog Pen?' he snapped. But Malcolm merely looked at him as if he had no business to be there and he had forgotten that he was.

'Well?'

'Well, go on,' Malcolm said.

'I've tried persuading him and it's no use. He's got to be made to go.'

169

'How?'

'He's got to be forced to go.'

'How?'

This was the wrong way. The words should have been put into Malcolm's mouth; the suggestions come from him.

'I thought,' Paul said, 'that if we stirred up labour troubles. If there was a whole series of cane fires...'

He broke off. A sudden squall made doors bang and louvres rattle. A blessed coolness rushed into the house. Malcolm cursed and got up from the table to shut the balcony door and close the louvres, shouting: 'Go on!' Paul watched him at work, seeing behind him the palm trees bent, their fronds streaming out like women's hair. 'Go on! I can hear you!' Malcolm shouted again. His buttocks looked powerful in tight blue jeans, his matted back threatened to split the string vest further. 'Bugger!' Paul heard him say as he opened the doors again to go out for his bottle. Through the open door the rain was seen thick as a bead curtain blotting trees from sight. It was very dark. Malcolm came in again, dripping bottle in hand. His massive arms glittered with rain the hairs held from his skin. He fetched a glass. 'Go on, then!' he said, half filling it with rum. 'Or have you changed your mind already?'

170

'No,' said Paul.

'That the lot then?' He went through to the kitchen to fill his glass with water and came back with a jug.

He sat down. 'Well?'

'Yes,' said Paul. 'Strikes, cane fires...'

'Why should cane fires bother him?'

'If they're big enough and happen often enough...'

'And are accompanied by trouble with the men,' said Dorothea.

'Oh ho, ho, ho!' shouted Malcolm. 'You're in this as well my pretty, are you?'

'Why shouldn't I be. I'm Paul's wife.'

'If you keep telling me often enough, I may come round to believing it!' He drank about a quarter of his rum and water. 'Cane fires,' he said. 'Cane fires mean bugger all these days. A lot of smoke and flame and damn all else. And Uncle Harry's as used to them as Paul to bunkers. They'll not bother him... Unless...'

She could not restrain herself. 'Yes?'

He laughed aloud. Even above the amazing drumming of the rain which threatened to stove the tin roof in, his laugh rang out.

'Unless, my eager Jezebel,' he cried triumphantly, 'the bulldozer doesn't work and the Land Rover's got a puncture! Unless there's a norther blowing and

171

they've got to put it out with beaters! Unless it's not just five acres like Cuevas absorbs two or three times a year but a hundred and started from several points at once! Then even Uncle Harry might be bothered!'

She felt a thrill of pleasure. He's going to help, she told herself He's sat here all these years in this sordid little house and every morning when he's got up and every evening when he's sat out there filling himself with rum, he's had Norfolk Hall to look at. Oil lamps instead of chandeliers. Bare boards instead of marble tiles. Calendars instead of Corots.

'So you'll help,' she said.

'Maybe. How much has Paul been offered?'

'That's my business,' Paul interrupted.

'Two hundred thousand dollars above the market price,' lied Dorothea.

'Is it tied up with this New St James business?'

'Indirectly.'

'Uhm.' He sat tapping his tumbler on the table, thinking about it. Dorothea close to him, watched him with eager expectation. Paul across the table could watch them both and he realized he had been genuinely quite forgotten. Of a sudden he was aware that the business had passed from his control. He was like the first front man of a revolution who is swept aside when he has served his purpose. And like that man he began to see, for the first time, the real character of his lieutenant. For Dorothea's guard was down. Caught up in the excitement of the moment instead of keeping the end in view she had given all of her attention to the project, and her new ally in the project. This was not the girl Harry had seen cool and pretty, demure in a fresh cream cotton dress, holding her big hat in front of her, conscious of inspection—this was a passionate young woman in a strident shirt unbuttoned enough to show the line of breasts, skin glossy with sweat, tense in body, eyes glittering and pulses racing—a girl who had forgotten herself in the intoxication of the venture. In one bewildering, horrifying instant Paul saw another Dorothea. Sick in his stomach he stared wildly at the two of them, his wife, his uncle; brown glossy flesh, matted hair; silk shirt, string vest; youth, age. And he, forgotten. Trapped.

'For Bog Pen, for twenty-five per cent of your two hundred thousand and for the pleasure of kicking out Uncle Harry, I'll help you.'

Paul realized that he was being spoken to. But he could find no words. Too many emotions fought for precedence. He remembered his whisky but not where he had put it down. Was it outside—or had he brought it in with him?

'Paul!' There was rebuke, impatience in the word.

'What?'

'Do you agree?'

'You can agree for him.'

But the moment had passed—the guard was up again.

'It's not my property, man.'

'True.'

The word sealed a compact. Paul saw that with awful clarity. Between them, he told himself, I am dismissed. But I have my function. And of course they have to pander to it. They've given themselves away. I must be more cunning.

'Agreed.' He injected all the crispness he could manage. And he smiled inwardly at the faint curl of Malcolm's lip. 'Right then,' he said briskly. 'Let's get down to details.'

'What's the hurry?' Malcolm was leaning back, glass in hand. The pose stretched the torn blue vest across his barrel chest. Errol Flynn? thought Dorothea. Well, in a way. She was aware of an added excitement going beyond the project. The rain was still thundering down. It gave their conspiracy a curious intimacy. It shut off the outside world, sealed in their secret meeting. She wondered what might have happened if she

174

had come up alone. It occurred to her that life was a ratchet and pawl affair; once you had passed out of one attitude you never went back to that attitude again.

'What's the point of wasting time?' she countered.

'You've left it a bit late this year, Jezebel. Half Uncle Harry's crop's in already.'

'There's still the other half.'

'You'll have to do more than burning cane.' He changed tack. 'Does Uncle Harry know about this offer Paul's had?'

'No.'

'Why are you supposed to be there then?'

'I'm taking up a directorship in the New St James business in six months time,' Paul said. 'I've packed in Coral Gardens and I'm using this as a filler in.'

Malcolm stood, crossed the room, switched on the light. There was no response. 'Aggie!' he shouted. 'Bring a lamp!'

'Will it have gone everywhere?' said Dorothea.

'Shouldn't think so. Anyway you don't have to worry. You've got a stand-by generator.'

'I'm surprised you haven't.'

'You know how many crates of rum you can buy for a stand-by generator.' He emptied his glass as if to make the point, refilled it and sat down again.

'Now, listen,' he said. 'It's pretty late to do anything this year but maybe there's just time. But don't start doing anything yourself. That goes for you too, Paul.' Aggie came stomping in with an oil lamp; he waited until she had plonked it amongst them on the table and stomped out again, slamming the door. The drumming drowned her muttering.

'I'll deal with the cane fires,' Malcolm resumed. 'Otherwise I won't touch it with a barge-pole.'

Paul felt the frustration boiling up.

'We don't need...'

'Yes, you do! You'd only make a botch of it. You don't know Cordobans in the field. You get ten years for starting cane fires.'

'So what do we do?'

'You, Jezebel? You concern yourself with politics. With your father who he is you ought to be able to find out who the agitators are. Who doesn't like Uncle Harry. When all this happens it's got to look like something other than it is. There's no better camouflage than politics and with that old witch Sophie you're going to need all the camouflage you can get.'

'And Paul?'

'Paul?' He spoke as if he had to dig deep to find something for Paul to do. He paused. It was not night yet but it was

176

so gloomy that the lamp threw light and shadows on his face. It was quite cold now. The cold had mingled with their sweat and lay on them clammily. Yet they were still sweating, adding to the clamminess all the time. 'Yes,' he said, discovering something so it seemed. 'The best way you can occupy yourself, Paul, is by learning the precautions that are taken, where all the machinery is, where it's dodgy, who looks after it, what his habits are. That sort of thing.'

Paul let it pass...he had decided what he was going to do.

It was another hour before the rain eased sufficiently for them to leave and by then it was quite dark, a night without moon, damp from the sodden growth and lowering clouds. Such tropic nights depress the spirits.

But Paul was not depressed. He had decided what he was going to do.

'Drop me off at the wharf, Dee, will you?' he instructed her.

'What for?'

'We're loading bananas. There's things I've got to do.'

'But you didn't even know what the boat was called?'

'I was just making conversation. It's the *Annotto*.'

'I'd like to come and watch. I've never seen banana loading.'

'I'd rather you didn't.'

'But why not, man?'

'I'd just rather you didn't.'

'That's not an answer.'

'It's all you're going to get.'

'What is this? Paul!' He felt her hand of a sudden on his knee.'

'You'll have us in the ditch...'

'Paul!' She brought the M.G. to a slithering halt. It was too dark to see anything except the cave of growth ahead. But there was a sense of thick wet bush all around them. 'What is this Paul?' she demanded. 'What's the matter?'

He constructed anger. It was not a difficult thing to do.

'I suppose you didn't notice how he looked at you?'

'Well of course I noticed. Most men look at me that way. What of it?'

'And you didn't lead him on?'

'Well maybe I did. We want him on our side. Paul...' Suddenly she laughed. 'Man, you're jealous!'

'Too bloody true, I am. You're my wife. You sit there with your shirt wide open and so bloody close it's an invitation for him to start feeling up your leg... You'd have let him. Wouldn't you?'

'I think,' she said, restarting the engine.

'I'd better drop you off.'

'You can't answer, can you?'

'Of course I can answer. But I'm not going to.'

'Yes, you are. We're going to have this out.'

'No we're not.'

Back in control now, thought Paul. Back in control, aren't we?

'What are you going to tell him when he asks you to go to bed with him?' he shouted.

She didn't answer. She let in the gears and set off again. The headlights picked up the usual swarm of glittering insects against a moving background of shining undergrowth.

They didn't speak until they reached the main Pilotte road when she said quietly:

'Paul, I don't want us to have our first fight...'

'We've already had it.'

'It takes two to fight. And I'm not fighting.'

'It's easy...'

'Please. Let me say what I have to and then I'll drop you by the wharf. I did make up to Malcolm. Perhaps I went too far. If I did, I'm sorry. It won't happen again. But we need him. And now we've got him on our side. But you don't have to be jealous. You need never be jealous of anybody. I

179

got a bit carried away...but not by him. What is he?' She thought of the grin, the tossed black hair, the sensuous lips, the mocking eyes. 'A failure pickled in rum!'—It was a catch phrase stolen from her mother. 'You think a man like that could interest me?'

He felt a weakening of resolve. It was tempting to let reassurance in. He had cast off from a blissful land in which for weeks now he had lived contented—it was so easy to turn around and paddle back again. But if I do, he told himself, that will be the end. I shall never know self-respect again. And he had decided what to do. It was only a few minutes to the wharf.

'He interested you today,' he said dispiritedly. 'I had the feeling that if I hadn't happened to be there you would have.'

'Would have what? Say it, man. Don't say Mr Dog when you mean dog.'

He took her at her word.

'Let him fuck you,' he said. And he knew it would never be the same between them.

The bananas from Norfolk and Palmira were delivered to the loading station prepacked in plastic but those from the village smallholdings were carried in as cropped, long hands, still green, borne on

180

their owner's heads for miles to be put into their plastic bags in the shed itself. This was a huge wooden and corrugated iron building its length parallel to the quay but, long and high as it was, dwarfed by the enormity of the silent ship which lay alongside.

The fruit when ready was stacked on sugar sacks in great blocks, higher than a man, with passages between; it seemed incredible that any one ship could take such a vast quantity of bananas yet all the time trucks and carts were still arriving.

It was an event, the banana loading, and half Pilotte was there to work or watch and between the wharf entrance and the shed there was a small line of huts, temporary rum shops, a grocery and so on. You could buy sticky cakes or ladles of grey goat stew and there were girls from Mildred's Alligator Club hoping to catch the seamen. The huts were illuminated by flaring naphtha lamps, and the shed was brilliantly cold from electric light while the ship, massive and aloof, borrowed such light as escaped except for the loading bays, which were floodlit, and the warmer, yellower lights escaping from portholes which indicated some other way of living which was private and nothing at all to do with the two or three hundred milling men and women in and around the shed.

The stench of sweating bodies was pervasive and the clamour indescribable. Lorries hooted and screeched and raced their engines, men shouted and cursed and laughed, young girls giggled and old women cackled, megaphones blared and all the time with the regularity of a ticking clock the tallyman's bell tinkled. The tallyman had an antiquated machine from which hung a knotted string; the women (for the loaders were mostly women) had cottas on their heads onto which a hand of bananas in its plastic sack was lifted and were at once off, at a fast, graceful walk which took them to the tallyman and his machine. The woman or the girl (for many were little more than that) put out a hand and pulled the string which rang the bell and with the same hand took the small metal tally from the tallyman and transferred it to the pocket of her apron. There were, it is a true, a few men who put the tally in their pocket, but the great majority were not men and the line of loaders was a long sinuous shift of brilliant colour. Once past the tallyman the carriers broke into a half run out of the loading station, across the quay between them and the ship rearing bright and clean, impersonal, into the floodlight, to the bottom of one of a pair of gangplanks where the hand was lifted off their heads by the first of a line of pairs of men who passed it over their heads to the next and so on up the length of the steeply sloping gangplank where it was handled in to disappear from sight. And already the woman who had carried it was running back to the beginning of the conga line to start again.

Paul could find Ryle nowhere. He walked along the alleyways between the stacks of fruit, amongst the carts and trucks and investigated the knots around the rum shops. There were many men, mostly blacks, some working, some sleeping, some in groups—but Ryle was not amongst them. They eyed him curiously for most of them knew who he was, some touched their caps, a few greeted him. Paul nodded, or occasionally answered briefly. Franklin, Harry's busher, stopped him, surprised to find him there, and Paul was obliged to pass the time with him. Even then his eyes were alert, seeking Ryle. He did not question what he was going to do—the decision had been made. His mind was shuttered.

In the end he found Ryle—at the very end of the quay, where the bow of the *Annotto* curved sharply away to show the water inky-black and oily looking in the starless night. Ryle was leaning against the wall of the loading shed—a small, angry-looking black with very thick lips, a very spread nose and a neat moustache. When Paul went up to him he quickly threw away the stub of his cigarette which fizzed out in the puddle near his feet. But the smell of ganja clung.

'Ryle!' Paul called.

Ryle pushed himself upright by his shoulders.

'Hear tell you've lost your job,' Paul said.

Ryle stared at him suspiciously, his round eyes very white. 'Yes, Mr Blades,' he said.

'Not found another?'

'No.' His manner was clipped and surly.

'Maybe I can find you one. Come to the Alligator Club in half an hour.'

The Alligator Club was the best place of its kind in Pilotte. There was a street bar underneath the bedrooms and at the back a dance floor lit by naked red and green bulbs. The roof of this rear part was hung with Christmas decorations and its walls were split bamboo except for a low wall dividing it from the lower area of bar portion which was concrete blocks painted crudely with an alligator.

When Paul went in, it was still quite empty. There was a quartet of men off the banana boat sitting at the matting bar,

184

looking unsure, a few of the girls, half a dozen blacks and Mildred, who owned the place, a great fat negress whose painted lips made an unpleasing pattern of patchwork brown and carmine.

'Why Mass Blades,' she said, coming out from behind the bar to him at once. 'I don' expect see you heer with season on.'

'I'm not at Coral Gardens now,' he reminded her. 'I'm at Norfolk.'

'Tchut!' she said, slapping her huge thigh with a great ham of a hand. 'You don' marry Bertie Sasso's gal. I clean forgot.' But she was only making conversation. 'What you come here for then, man. Is it for rest?' And she exploded into a huge burst of laughter.

The blacks and the seamen and the girl behind the bar watched with casual interest. In here Paul Blades was not the Paul Blades of Norfolk Hall. He was just another man, not black, not white, not of one class or another—at least not to Mildred. In a brothel a man sheds everything except that he is a man with male lusts.

'You too damn facey, Mildred man,' Paul answered briefly—and loudly enough to be heard above the ska.

Mildred was a shrewd woman—she knew when to stop. She wiped the grin away at once.

185

'Come you this way, Mr Blades,' she said.

She led the way to a table covered with very old and very cracked American cloth, calling to the barwoman. 'Partina!'

The woman came over.

'What you want, Mass Blades?' Mildred asked. 'Whisky?'

'Beer,' Paul said.

'Give Mass Blades a beer, Partina,' Mildred said. 'An' don' you charge him.'

She went off and Paul settled himself to wait for Ryle. This is the acme of entertainment possible in Pilotte, he told himself; the best available to Malcolm. With the days of house-to-house entertainment the planters once knew over and done with, if work and books and sleep are not enough for a man, this is his alternative. And he wondered, uneasily, if Malcolm might come in before he'd done his business with Ryle.

But a man and woman came from a table at the back catching his attention. The woman, a madras on her head, wearing a brownish flowered dress, was impossibly thin with a firm belly and buttocks and small breasts which she covered with her hands caressingly; the man was lithe and thin in tight blue jeans. They began to dance, well, rhythmically, swaying forward from the hips, thrusting at each other, their hands moving more than their feet. They were like a floor show. The seamen were relieved at having something to watch not having drunk enough as yet to be sufficient in themselves. Meanwhile the place was beginning, slowly, to fill up. Paul saw Hezzy Matt come in, a Pilotte character, a deaf mute. He joined the couple dancing, dancing by himself, standing by the juke box, sensing the music somehow. If the other two were thin, he was wafer thin, with drugs, mongoloid and negroid all in one, using his hands like a Siamese and his feet like a West Indian. On his face was total insanity. Then a girl came down, from the upper floor. A girl of about sixteen, thought Paul, maybe even less. She was minute, perfectly formed, dressed in scarlet pedal pushers tight as skin and a white, waisted, sleeveless shirt unbuttoned to her navel. She looked around, hesitated, then not knowing who he was, came over. She stood beside him waiting for a sign and when he gave none, suddenly hopped on to his knee and stared at him like a precocious child. She wore no bra and she wriggled on his knee to show her nipples. He was conscious of a sense of dispensation, like a man given an evening off by his wife to do exactly as he pleases. He put his hand inside the girl's shirt on to her breast. Her breasts were very firm, like moulded rubber. He felt no lust at all and what he was doing was not even an expression of defiance. The girl was there with naked breasts so he put his hand on one of them. He knew the quartet were watching covertly and this amused him. He felt the head of the girl come forward, against his shoulder and smelt her sweat. He wondered if she had just come down from earning her keep. He gave her breast a final, good-natured squeeze, then took his hand out of her shirt, shoved her off his knees and gave her buttocks a hearty slap. The girl pouted, then grimaced, then went off to the seamen. Another girl came in, a negress like a Zulu, fat, with a yellow band around her head pushing her hair up like a shaving brush, an ugly creature with skin of creosote lined with wrinkles like an old man's face. She knew who Paul was and perhaps Mildred had already spoken to her for she passed by, her dress a shapeless splash of purple, her nose coarse and flattened, her lips wet and pouting, her eyes shot with bits of blood. She joined the seamen, one of whom was already pawing the girl in pedal pushers. Before they were done most probably two of them would take each girl upstairs. It seemed extraordinary that two would actually pay to fuck the Zulu.

'Good evening, Mr Blades,' said Ryle.

He's got a hang-dog pride, thought Paul—he won't call me 'Mass'.

'Partina!' he called. She came across. 'Give Mr Ryle a rum,' Paul said. 'And put it on that table.'

He indicated the table next to his own. Ryle, taking the point, sat at it, looking at the seamen at the bar.

'You were a bloody fool, Ryle, starting that fire... Don't look at me!... And don't waste my time denying it.' He took a prepared packet of cigarettes from his pocket and threw it on Ryle's table. There were notes inside it. 'Have a cigarette,' he said. 'And keep what's in the packet.'

He sat for a moment or two longer, finishing his second beer, taking no notice of Ryle. Then, getting up to go, he said:

'I'll be at Eight Mile Bridge at half past ten tomorrow morning.'

# Twelve

He could hear the car coming from a long way off—all the way from Granpaw's gate. He heard the screech of brakes. But still Dorothea didn't wake. He waited for the sound of running feet. But there was just the sound of a car door slammed and then a silence which could only have meant the driver had parked on the grass. But you didn't park on the grass when you came to rouse the house because the cane was burning—you stopped by the steps and ran up them. So it was puzzling—this silence. And now these footsteps, quick, firm, triumphant even. But not hasty. Well it would be explained. He reached under the mosquito netting's edge and switched on his bedside light. Dorothea stirred. He sat up and flicked the sheet covering them away and Dorothea awoke. 'What is it?'—'Be quiet,' he whispered her to silence. 'Pretend to be asleep. Uncle Harry'll be coming in, in a minute.' 'But...' 'Do as I say,' he said. 'Pretend to be asleep.' And, after a moment: 'Turn the other way so that you're facing the door when he throws it open... Shh!'

He listened, hearing the sound of a man striding along the passage, the rap on a door, voices. Now he was more than puzzled, for one of the voices was Malcolm's.

'That's Malcolm, isn't it?' he whispered.

Dorothea listened. 'Yes,' she said. 'That's Malcolm.' The voice was loud and cheerful, but some way off and the doors were three-inch doors. Nothing spoken could be understood. Only the tone which was without alarm.

'What is it?' Dorothea probed. 'What's happening?'

'We'll soon find out,' he said. And he heard hurrying steps towards their room. 'Now shut your eyes,' he ordered. 'And pretend to be asleep.'

There was a formal bang and then the door flew open. 'Paul...' he heard Harry start—but then he must have seen Dorothea lying naked. There was just time to catch sight of his face before he turned away—and he looked old with the cruelty of sudden wakefulness on all but the truly young.

'What is it, Uncle Harry?' Paul called out, over the shoulder of Dorothea who, playing her part superbly, had first sat up, then grabbed at the sheet to cover her nakedness.

'There's a cane fire.' Harry's head was

191

averted and for once he was unsure.

'Where?'

'At Hill Flat.'

'Is it bad?'

'No.'

And he was gone, closing the door behind him, gently. As if he'd happened to have been passing with a minor piece of news.

Dorothea was not asking questions any more. She was thinking what Paul had believed she would. That Malcolm had arranged it. And she was puzzled. And trying to put reasons to it. And she wondered if Paul had met him at the banana loading and they'd arranged to do this and not tell her. But the thinking didn't slow her. She was already out of bed, sliding deftly underneath the mosquito net and crossing the room quickly to pull at drawers. He watched her covertly. Saw her pick out a bra, hesitate, then swiftly drop it back and start putting on a shirt. She was the more quickly dressed, in the shirt, and slacks tucked into riding boots and a scarf tied round her hair.

Malcolm was downstairs, in his hand a glass. He can't want that, Paul thought, it's just that he has to look the part.

'What are you doing here!' he asked contemptuously.

But Malcolm just grinned: 'My brotherly duty.'

Paul brushed past with a good show of impatience. From the platform he could see the flames, not directly, but reflected in the sky. He was aware of Malcolm beside him.

'Is it bad?' he asked.

'Much as expected I should say.'

Dorothea was there as well, still playing her part.

'Expected...but it's accidental surely?'

'It's all right, Jezebel, Uncle Harry's far too busy.'

She rounded on him. Her eyes said eloquently what she wasn't given time to say: 'Don't look at me,' said Malcolm. 'I didn't start it. Look at Paul!'

Prompted by his comfortable scorn, Dorothea instantly read the situation—and as quickly responded to it. She wheeled on Paul. 'What have you done, man?'

'Nothing,' said Paul. It had been, he realized, a mistake not to have explained. He tried to shift the emphasis. 'Did you report it to Franklin, Malcolm?'

'No. He might have put it out before you'd had a chance to see it.'

'But what's Uncle Harry going to say? He's going to be damned suspicious you've come all this way when Franklin's only half the distance.'

'I'd say you've got a problem.'

'Me?'

'Isn't this your handiwork?'

'Of course it isn't.' But even to his own ears it sounded unconvincing.

Uncle Harry came out just then, dressed in khaki drill, carrying his hat.

'I was just telling Paul,' Malcolm said to him. 'I clean forgot to tell Jim Franklin.'

Harry looked hard at his brother.

'What a strange chap you are,' he said.

'What are you going to do, Uncle Harry?' said Dorothea. 'Shouldn't we hurry?'

'There's no hurry, my dear. Franklin will have it in hand.'

'But how will he know?'

'One of the rangers...the watchers, will have told him.'

'And what will he be doing?'

'Waking the tractor driver and getting the equipment out.'

'But how do you put out a cane fire with a tractor?'

'You don't...'

It was going all wrong. The whole purpose of the exercise being wasted. 'Uncle Harry!'

'It's all right, Paul. No call to be impatient. There isn't any panic.' He turned back to Dorothea. Paul could see her shirt was open, unbuttoned too low, showing a naked breast. He remembered how she had deliberately dropped her bra in the drawer. For Uncle Harry, she would tell him—to make him ill at ease. But he didn't look ill at ease. He even looked less tired. 'You can't put a cane fire out, my dear,' he said.

'What d'you do?'

'You treat it,' said Harry, 'exactly as you do a termite's nest.'

'A termite's nest!'

'Yes,' said Harry, now clearly enjoying the situation. 'Do your shirt up my dear, would you?'

'Oh!'

Harry went on through the flustering of fingers exquisitely well done. 'This is what you do. To destroy a termite's nest. You make a hole in it with a bit of stick or something and then you take a pinch of the little beggars out and squeeze them with a little calomel...or if you can get it, Paris Green is even better. Then you put 'em back. They're scrupulously clean insects, you see, and to get rid of the dead bodies they eat them up. And poison themselves in the process. And so it goes on until there's none of them left. Did you know that, my dear?'

'No, Uncle Harry.'

'Well you do the same sort of thing with a cane fire, let it destroy itself. You put a Caterpillar on a loader and then you pull

195

the loader with a tractor up to it and the Caterpillar cuts a path to leeward.' He chuckled. 'But Franklin's going to have one hell of a problem with this one.'

'Why, Uncle Harry?'

'Because, Mrs Blades, there isn't any wind.'

They had all been concentrating their attention on Harry. No one had seen Hastings coming. Dorothea started, Paul spun round. Malcolm was amused. Harry might have been expecting him.

'It's a strange night, Mrs Blades,' Hastings added, 'to start a cane fire.'

'Dorothea, my dear,' said Harry. 'This is Inspector Hastings.'

It was a strange time and place for her to meet him—on the platform of Norfolk Hall in the middle of the night with the sky sullen with reflected fire.

'How do you do?' said Dorothea. She did not find it difficult to be calm. She was daughter of the Chief Minister designate and future mistress of Norfolk Hall. This was a policeman. In such a situation there was a way she should behave. 'I believe you know my father.' She saw the faint wrinkling of his brow and wondered if she had been too cool.

'Yes,' said Hastings. She read him at once for what he was, a proud man. He wouldn't talk any more to her, not now she'd spoken of her father. He was incorruptible. She must be careful, very careful. What a damn fool, Paul had been.

'I came up to be sure you knew,' Hastings was saying to Harry.

'Very good of you.'

'I passed Franklin on the way. The bulldozer's on the road.'

'Good.'

'If you're going down I can give you a drop and bring you back.'

'My brother says it isn't bad.'

'No. Not bad.'

Oh, God, thought Paul, he's not even going to bother to look at it. He saw Malcolm grinning knowingly—and Dorothea shooting him a warning glance.

'Can I come too,' she said, excitedly. 'I've never seen a cane fire close to!'

And then she remembered something. 'Did you say *start* a cane fire, Inspector Hastings?'

'Yes, Mrs Blades.'

'You don't think this is accidental?'

He showed no humour. 'Cane fires don't start themselves. And never in the middle of the night.'

'How would it have been started then?'

Malcolm broke his silence his voice mocking, airy: 'A match and a bottle of paraffin, I'd say...wouldn't you, Paul?'

197

How does a man trying to mask his crime yet bitterly jealous manage in front of an experienced policeman to answer that? thought Dorothea. What a damn fool situation in which to place himself.

'Probably.' (Not too bad, she thought. But how long can he go on and not give himself away. Doesn't he realize you get ten years for arson? Or did he forget that in his damn fool jealousy?)

'And what do you think's behind it, Paul?' (Stop it, Malcolm...stop it or you won't be getting your fifty thousand dollars, your hundred acres of Bog Pen. It'll never be ours to give.)

'Politics?'

(Don't take him on, Paul! He's a man with nothing to lose. They're the strong ones, the ones with nothing to lose. You've got to get rid of him. Have your fun tomorrow. But have it in *private*. And anyway, that way, when he humiliates you there won't be spectators.) And aloud, she said:

'Politics? You think it's politics, do you, Paul? How about that, Inspector? Would you think its politics?'

'I shouldn't think so.' His voice was dry. And Harry's puzzled, and a trifle irritated.

'Why on earth should you think that, Paul? You've seen enough cane fires. You

198

know why they're started.'

'I don't,' said Dorothea.

'Well,' said Harry in such a different tone that it was clear whatever suspicions he might be harbouring they did not extend to Dorothea, 'it could be spite, a man laid off or something. But most probably it's no more than that they want to get on with cutting a particular section. Once cane's burnt, it's got to be cut quickly...'

'You mean they'd set a field on fire just to cut it?'

Harry nodded his head of soft white hair.

'One of the commonest reasons for cane fires, my dear,' he said. 'Is trash that cuts the hand. Burn the cane and you burn the trash.'

But Hastings added: 'And that's what's so suspicious about this one. It isn't that kind of cane.'

'Nor,' said Malcolm, 'that kind of night.'

And Harry was thoughtful again, staring at the painted sky. Dorothea plucked his arm.

'Will you take me to see it, Uncle Harry?'

He turned his head and slipped his arm around her waist.

'My dear,' he said. 'I couldn't deny you anything.'

The Land Rover's blazing headlights darkened the outer darkness as they set off, swaying and lurching over the uneven ground; but the air whirled with glinting insects.

'It's thrilling, darling, isn't it' Dorothea was chattering gaily. 'If Uncle Harry doesn't mind we must have cane fires more often!'

He couldn't think how he would have answered that if it had been as her manner made it out to be. He felt her physical presence—her side against his own in the confines of the cab, her warm hand on his knee. But otherwise she seemed far away. Unreachable. Because he lacked the power to reach her. I have gone into my shell, he told himself, this is what they mean when they say that. And from in my shell there is no one I can touch. Not Dee. Not Uncle Harry. And there is no one else to touch. I'm locked in here until I find some method of escape.

The gate was open... Gran'paw picked up like a mote and gone, frozen to a gesture. The huts fisked past, murky shapes and glows; the copra factory sprawled, asleep. The road flicked straight, the fields flat as a lake on either hand. The frogs whistled and croaked and the cicadas shrieked.

Harry was silent, his straw hat on his head, Dorothea next to him tense, excited. Paul wondered if Malcolm and Inspector Hastings would be following. They ran on to the Pilotte road, their headlights raking the secret sea behind its grille of palms, watching it break on an empty beach, calmer than it had been, yet still impressive with the breakers the storm had brought. Then the sea was gone and there were only trees, a million flying insects, a sudden village, huts on stones, a mangy barking cur, a Coca Cola sign. A shadow ran—and then a second. A machete glinted. They paused for a halt that was not a halt and then went racketting on again.

'Big Sam gone on?' Harry, not turning, asked of the fellow still clambering over the tailboard.

'Yess, Mass Harry.' The voice was breathless. 'Him gone on wid Mister Jim.'

'How long him gone?'

'Ten minutes, maybe.'

'Where was the 'dozer?'

'Water Valley, Mass Harry.'

'Damn!' Harry said.

Paul glanced round, over his shoulder and was shocked to find there were four of them, not two. Four. Two on either side. Like troops being taken off to war. The sudden stench of sweat was appalling.

'Hill Flat!' pronounced Harry suddenly.

But there was no sign of the fire, only a palisade of uncut cane which the fire would have reached by now had there been a wind. Then that was passed and Harry was shouting, with a kind of exultation.

'There she is!'

It was not the fire which, curiously, from here was not even a glowing in the sky, but the low loader caught in the lights with the yellow bulldozer on its back. It was lost in a lurch and then picked up again, bigger now, the loader army-green, the beetle of its tractor, red; the bulldozer brilliant mustard. The sea seemed to push it to its right and the raking headlights probing beyond the breakers found slithering lines of waves and then, as they rounded the curve as well, the huge bulk of the loader came smacking up towards them and Dorothea was hard against Paul, then gone away while the huge conglomeration of machinery scraped past going backwards and near enough to touch. Paul turned his head to look at it. The black who had spoken to Uncle Harry was eyeing Dorothea but the other three were looking away, at Big Sam high up on the creeping tractor.

And then the next curve took it all away except for faulty headlights winking briefly.

'There it is,' said Harry like a man finding something of only average interest.

But Dorothea was alert and because she was, Paul felt life creeping back into his veins. It was a thrilling, aweing sight. First a sudden reddened sky as they emerged from a tree tunnel, a sky like that of a city seen from a distance, and then as they breasted a rise the fire itself. It all seemed to come together: the smoke, the flames, the sparking of spitting cane, the smell of burning sugar, sweet and thick and tarry.

Paul heard Dorothea gasp with pleasure. 'But it's beautiful!'

They could feel the fire's heat and see the trash floating like burnt paper in and above the flames. They swept along a smooth marl track whose white dust rose and came in through the back. On one side the cane was burning, on the other not. The heat was choking, burning the air away before it reached the lungs: dry, electric heat. The flames danced in the coiling smoke. The dead wisps of trash were like an uncertain snowfall. The red sparks shot and sputtered. The fire was self-sufficient, talking to itself with an indifferent roaring and a crackling and the pistol shots of cane exploding. And Harry's hair was pink and there were shadows in the valleys of his wrinkles.

Beyond the fire he stopped, backed and turned the Land Rover.

'There you are, my dear,' he said to Dorothea, almost with pride, an uncle with a Christmas present.

'I've never been so close to one before!'

'Impressive, isn't it?'

He got down from the cab, nimbly—a man of seventy. The blacks came round from the back. He spoke to them, shouting, waving his arm. Dorothea stood beside him. The sweat had soaked through her shirt which clung, moulding her breasts. Her face was shining as it had shone at Copra Valley. Her body was as taut, her eyes as brilliant. Paul knew this wasn't acting. He had been so near succeeding.

He heard her shout to Harry: 'Isn't there anything we can do until the Caterpillar comes?'

'Only scuff it out if it jumps across the interval.' Picked out by his own headlights Harry began to walk towards the fire. The first of the blacks was chopping at a stalk of cane, the second stamping out the beginnings of a small fire. Ahead the other two were misty in the swirling smoke. Harry went up to the nearest of them.

'Go cut me a coupla stalks of cane, Wilson,' he said. And when Paul caught up with him, his hand was out feeling the trash with his fingertips. 'You see, Paul.

It's not the kind they usually fire.'

Paul felt the cane obediently: the trash was soft. And Ryle was cunning.

The man named Wilson came up with the stalks of cane and Harry took them from him and gave one to Paul and one to Dorothea.

'If it jumps across, beat it out with this.' But he glanced up to the smoke which was shaped like a poplar tree. 'Not that it's likely to,' he added. 'Not on a night like this. What a damn fool time to start a cane fire.'

The loader came, lumbering like a close-eyed monster in a fog, driving them back while the headlights of the Land Rover cast strange shadows on the swirling smoke, shadows which came and vanished, pieces of the creeping loader, even once Uncle Harry in his hat.

Big Sam, high up on the tractor, silhouetted against smoke and flame looked like the Devil's Drayman. He stopped and they brushed past him, between the loader and the pliant cane, to watch the bulldozer clanking off, grinding the marl, mixing white dust with smoke. There was shouting and the fire's sounds. Paul stepped deeper into the cane, carelessly, and felt a sharp edge slice his hand. Dorothea was glazed with sweat, her shirt clung and her upper body was as good as naked. But the excitement was having an effect on her, stimulating her in a sexual sort of way. She came up to him, gripping his hand, not knowing it was cut, making him cry out. She looked up. And laughed.

Now the bulldozer was at work dipping at the cane, drawing back, dipping and driving again, rooting up earth and cane, dipping and driving like an angry bull head down pawing at the ground. It slewed and dug, dipped and dug, turned, drove and dug, pushing the earth and cane in front of it, pushing it towards the fire, building a wall against it. Each time it dug a little deeper, each time it started straight then slewed towards the fire, moving along the interval all the time. Around it the Cordobans with their switches jabbered. Their bodies glistened patchwork through their ragged clothes, their leathery feet were powdered white with marl. Uncle Harry stood apart, Norfolk's unquestioned master. And again the shadow of his hat was thrown high in the air, and huge, like a symbol against the swirling sparking smoke as he followed slowly along the interval. Now the heart of the fire and the barrier neared each other and the heat was fierce again and sweat liquefied smuts to ink that ran smarting into eyes. But dawn was coming and the fire was fading. The smoke became determinate, sullen, very black, flowing off towards Norfolk in the freshening morning breeze which had come too late for Paul. Unexplained sounds showed themselves as animals escaping and the fields turned grey, then green. The sky coloured yellowish with coppery clouds above pale blue to the east, pearl with grey and pink towards Norfolk in the west. And suddenly it was done. A brown gash of earth littered with crushed sugar cane ran beside a barrier of cane and earth and stones and marl which damned the fire and starved it out.

'That's all,' said Uncle Harry. 'We might as well go home.'

Franklin came down, clambering from his cab.

'Jim,' said Harry. 'Have you met my nephew's wife?'

He was a tall, thin man about as dark as Dorothea. She didn't interest him. 'Shall I go through?' he asked of Harry, nodding his pith helmet at the *cul-de-sac* cut into the cane.

'Don't bother with it,' Harry said. 'What a damn fool cane fire that was.'

Harry drove back at a leisurely pace. It was quite light now. On the sea a bark canoe rose and fell amid the swell; on the road a man with a hand of green bananas on his head came slowly along towards them, walking to Pilotte; on the estate the burnt-out margin stood desolate. But only the trash had burned: the cane still stood, stained and blackened. The field was like a shell-shattered wood showing curious unburnt islands. The smell of burnt molasses cloyed the air.

It was too late for bed. In the bedroom Dorothea stripped naked and stood for a moment and Paul knew it was an invitation. The fire had done for her exactly what he had forecast, exactly what conspiring with Malcolm had done at Copra Valley. But he was as burnt out as the fire.

There was a note from Malcolm, delivered with first breakfast. They were sitting in the silence of a man and woman who have come to the end of their road but have for the time being no other one to take. They were fresh and showered and Dorothea was wearing a white towelling wrap and a matching turban. They sat at a small round table and between them was a great dish of fruit: pau pau, grapefruit, star apples, uglies, the first mangoes of the season. Beside them another table with a jug of soursop, silver *entrée* dishes, a pot of coffee. On each of their new unfolded serviettes was a single red hibiscus. Thus had first breakfast always been served at Norfolk Hall. And nothing had yet changed.

Paul read the note and handed it without a word to Dorothea, who did the same.

'Well?' she said.

He put it into his dressing-gown pocket, shrugging: 'It's about what I expected.'

'Will you go and see him?'

'Yes.'

'I'd better be there as well,' she said.

# Thirteen

They met Malcolm in a squalid bar beside the Pilotte waterfront; he wore soiled white ducks, white shirt and plimsolls. They sat on two bar counter stools and he stood next to Dorothea, his back against the counter. He turned his head to tell the young black with little blisters underneath the skin: 'Beer! And Coca Cola for the lady!'

The barman moved the fat cigarette resting centrally in his enormous lips and rolled it to one corner of his mouth and, watching Dorothea attentively yet with marked lack of interest, reached for the bottles from the small refrigerator beside him.

There were two others in the bar sitting at a plastic-covered table: one was in a red shirt with a notebook poking from his pocket, the other was bearded and had plaited hair on which a beret balanced. On their table lay a milky-looking roll and two pint-sized glasses of sherry-coloured liquid.

'Learn all you needed, Jezebel?' said Malcolm, grinning. 'Feel you're properly blooded?'

'Yes, man,' said Dorothea shortly.

The bar had stable doors hiding the waterfront so that only the rusting corrugated roofs of minor warehouses could be seen but the man with the plaited hair going to them and opening a flap to put his fingers to his nose and blow snot onto the cobbles disclosed momentarily a line of long black barges which before the harbour had been deepened had been used for ferrying out bananas to the roads. That, had been years ago. Now they had been impressed for fishing although very clumsy. They had been thickly tarred but the tar had flaked off in patches.

When the man came back from blowing his snot, Malcolm said to him: 'That was a damn fool cane fire at Hill Flat, Walter?'

The fellow touched his hair respectfully. 'Heer'd so,' he said.

'Who you think fool roun' like that?'

'Well,' said the bearded one with dignity. 'From the way I look 'pon it heer, I do think I know who done it.'

'Is who done it then?'

'Mass Malcolm...' His voice was reproving. 'Now you know I can know who done it, but I can not talk who done it.'

Malcolm showed sudden fury.

'Since when,' he shouted, 'you become so dyam stoshus!' And he banged his drink down on the counter and came round to

211

the fellow, towering above him.

'I done say it wrong,' pleaded the man, clearly terrified. 'I didn't see who done it. I heer'd who done it.'

'Hearso make no pickneys!' Malcolm bawled, seemingly in the most fearful rage. 'You make me so dyam mad, I good mind go get me cutlass, lick you down an' chop you! Who you heer say done it?'

'George Ryle,' whispered the hapless black.

'Nex' time you tell me fust time I ask! Now get the rass from heer dyam quick!'

'Yes, *sir!* Yess, Mass Malcolm,' the man said, grabbing at his roll and sidling an escape along the wall and never for a moment taking his eyes off Malcolm as if fearful he might at any moment whip out a machete from somewhere and make good his threat.

'You too!' roared Malcolm to the other. 'Get you out!'

The second man, the one in the red shirt, followed, knocking his chair over in his haste. Malcolm crowded him to the doorway, then shouted: 'Walter!'

Walter stopped twenty yards away as if a knife had been stuck into his back. He turned, slowly and fearfully.

'Ketch!' shouted Malcolm. And putting his hand to his pocket he took out a handful of loose change and threw it.

He came back grinning.

'Now,' he said, 'we can talk about the fire. Quacko!' He picked up the chair with one hand as if it were feather-weight and pointed to the table with the other. 'Come make you clean it up!'

The barman, who had remained un-moved through this performance and had not even put his fingers to the stub now rolled back to the centre of his mouth, put out a slow hand for a dirty dishcloth and came rolling round the bar to swab the table.

'That'll do,' said Malcolm, pulling out a chair for Dorothea and when she had sat in it putting a hand on her shoulder. 'Sit down, Paul. Sit down and tell us about the fire you paid Ryle to start.'

Paul looked at the two of them. It was as if they were posed: Dorothea, slender and straight, tense, her black eyes bright as ackee seeds; behind her, a huge dirt-ingrained hand with broken nails firmly round her shoulder, Malcolm, sensuous of lips, black tossed of hair, pouched of eyes but for once shaved. His other uncle. He felt dismally alone and totally inept. He had tried to assert himself and his miserable failure had made him contemptible; he all but lacked the strength of purpose to try again. He was being challenged and not just by Malcolm. Dorothea's acceptance of that insultingly possessive hand said as much as any speech. And the reason was in the tautness of her body and the brilliance in her eyes. She was hot for his own uncle. It was a form of incest. A form of incest made public in a squalid bar of his local town.

With a flash of understanding he realized what his mind when he had decided on that fire had been groping for. The way to Dorothea Sasso—how odd his mind should think of her as Dorothea Sasso—was the way of power. Power of money, power of purpose, power of fire, power of insolence. There were a hundred forms of power and any of them turned on Dorothea Sasso sexually. On that platform of rock when he had shown her Norfolk the power of his possessions had released her spring of sex. There, and on the beach of Coral Gardens, he had been in command. He should have exerted that authority, against her resistance, and by not so doing he had damned himself. She was of the stuff of which mistresses of Greek shipowners, kings and presidents were made and he was damned for evermore a commoner. Only she had this weakness—which probably the mistresses of the Greeks and kings and presidents could control—the weakness of the flesh.

He became very calm. 'D'you think it's

214

sensible making that kind of accusation in front of witnesses?' he said.

Malcolm laughed. 'Quacko? He's dumb. Had his tongue cut out because he talked too much. Right, Quacko?'

Quacko nodded. The tongue business was a joke of course. The dumbness was correct.

'And he can't read or write. Don't be so fidgety, man. If you're going to go around committing arson, you mustn't get *agitato* in public. ''tone wall hab yeye', you know. That right, Quacko? ''tone wall hab yeye?'

Quacko nodded. In a moment the stub would burn his lips.

They think I'm frightened, Paul told himself. They don't realize that dead men can't be frightened. They don't understand and I must see they go on misunderstanding.

He constructed a look of perturbation and, copying the accident of the man in the red shirt, stood, knocking his chair to the floor in apparent alarm and made for the door.

Malcolm was very quick, shooting out a powerful hairy arm and grasping him by the wrist. His grip was like a vice—but his voice was gentle.

'I shouldn't go if I were you.'

'I'm not staying here while you create

a witness,' Paul said, trying to wrench his wrist free.

'But I've created one.' Malcolm let go—for moments the pain remained.

'Do sit down, darling,' Dorothea said lightly. 'Let's hear what your wise old uncle's got to say.'

She could hardly have chosen words to anger him more; he could without the least compunction, have strangled her there and then.

'Well?' said Malcolm, mockingly.

'All right. It was my fire. I did use Ryle.'

'How much you pay him?'

'Five hundred dollars.'

'Five hundred!... You're mad!'

'He's only had two hundred so far...he gets the rest...'

'I don't give a bugger when he gets the rest! Five hundred dollars was far too much. And Ryle's far too bloody cunning.'

'But surely he was a good choice, Malcolm?' Dorothea said.

There was momentary suspicion in Malcolm's bright blue eyes. 'He wasn't your idea?'

'Don't be so damn foolish, man.'

'You didn't know about the fire?'

'Not until Paul woke me. But why wasn't he a good choice of Paul's?'

Always this establishing of guilt and innocence, thought Paul. Maybe he's dumb. Maybe he can't read or write. But he can nod or shake his head.

He listened to Malcolm. 'He was not a good choice. He was just about the most goddam awful choice anyone could have thought of. If there's anyone knows you don't start cane fires on still nights, it's Ryle. That's why he chose one. To exonerate himself. And in so doing he's exonerated all the other likely suspects. Of all the unintelligent...'

Paul broke in. 'If you call this intelligent! Discussing our affairs in front of...'

'Quacko?' Malcolm laughed. 'I know enough about Quacko to get *him* ten years. He won't talk. Anyway he can't.'

'He can nod his head.'

'He'll lose it nex' day if he does. Besides who's going to ask him questions he can nod his head to? We're the only ones who know you hired Ryle. You and me and Jezebel who's just made sure that Quacko knows that the first she heard about the fire was when you woke her up. Now she's really got you properly parcelled up and labelled.'

'No,' said Dorothea.

He waved a hand. 'Don't bother, Jezebel. There's no purpose in it. Now...brother Harry. If he suspects...'

'He doesn't.'

'How do *you* know?'

'Paul was rather clever.'

'Oh?'

'Had me show myself naked when he burst in.'

'Really!' A thrust out lower lip and tilted head was a mockery of respect. 'She's done you good, Paul. If only you'd met her years ago... Now. Listen to me.' He became...efficient. 'The next fire...if there is one...' But he changed his mind; Quacko, after all, could nod. He stood and, coming behind Dorothea, laid both hands on her shoulders.

'I think,' he said, 'we've achieved all we set out to, haven't we?'

'Take your hands off her!'

'Oh my God, Paul, don't be so bloody predictable.'

But he took his hands away and moved towards the door where he paused:

'By the way,' he said, 'there's just one other thing. I shall want Hill Flat as well. It'll be appropriate.'

'You'll have what you are given.'

Malcolm shook his head.

'No, man,' he said. 'Not what I'm given. What I decide to take. Whenever I want to take it.'

The waterfront was a curving line of wood

218

and corrugated iron huts part of which faced a small harbour which was like a dry dock which had had its gates taken away; across the harbour were more huts and behind them was the huge banana loading shed. Between the huts on this side and the water was a broad strand of cobbles. Where the cobbles petered out a beach of sorts began. Its sand was black, dusty above the ridge the all but tideless ocean left, glinting and with a metallic smell below. The sea was blue, stained muddy where it broke. It was all quite different from Norfolk's beach a few miles to the west and was a hard, harsh place appropriate for what had to be said except that there were too many curious Cordobans watching them. So they trudged on through the soft black sand Paul, and Dorothea in a shift of vivid orange which went well with her smooth dark skin, with sandals on her feet and around her head a black and orange scarf, walking, for all the yielding sand, with grace and certainty.

They walked for a long time in silence, side by side, passing a rusting jetty and the last of several bark canoes until they came to another bay where, through some vagary of tide and wind, the sea was wilder and the sand, still black, picked out with enormous baulks of driftwood sunk deep, immovable, like skeletons of beasts long bleached in a forgotten desert—an eerie place, endless, stretching on and on with the sea pounding in in great grey rollers, with no buildings and no people, only the dead trees and the roots of upturned palms, washed out of life, like yard-long shrimps, bloodless and disgusting.

They stopped at last in a part where a few meagre palms grew listlessly and Dorothea sat on a log—a fallen trunk salt and wind had petrified. She looked up at Paul, her scarf peak continually collapsing and recovering in the breeze and her eyes said: 'Well, get on with it.'

'What a pity,' Paul said, 'Norfolk didn't have a beach like this one.' And he looked along the desolate shore with its sullen, grey rollers pounding in, and its sand, like ash, littered with rotted coconuts and odd things thrown up by the sea, looking in the direction of Norfolk's beach as if he would turn white sand, black.

'That's ridiculous,' Dorothea said with small impatience.

He shook his head. 'You know,' he said. 'We could have been very happy.'

'If Norfolk had had black sand?'

'Yes. Isn't it extraordinary that the colour of a beach could alter so many lives?'

'You're in a funny mood,' she said.

'I'm in a funny situation.'

'You're in a difficult one. Man, why did you do it?'

'But you know why I did it. You know exactly why I did it.'

She looked perplexed. 'You understand nothing, do you? Even after what's happened in the last half hour, you still don't understand. Sit down.' She tapped the log. 'You were a damn fool having Ryle start that fire but it isn't the end of the world.'

He sat beside her.

'Tell me,' he said, 'which offer are you going to accept? Kornblath's? Or Malcolm's?'

'Offer!' She laughed. 'Malcolm hasn't made an offer. He's issued an ultimatum.'

'Which we accept?'

'It's not you that has to choose.'

How clever, she is, thought Paul. Before she's done, she'd have me thinking it a sacrifice.

'I don't have to give him anything,' he responded, with seeming naïvety. 'Not Bog Walk. Not fifty thousand dollars. Certainly not Hill Flat.'

She shook her head wonderingly. 'You don't understand, Paul, do you? You think he's rowing in with us for land? And money? What's the good of them to him? What would he do with more money if he had it? Buy a few more crates of rum?

221

Sleep with a few more prostitutes? Can't you see...' Her hand was on his knee, as if appealing to him to think. 'It's far more fundamental.'

'He hates Uncle Harry.'

'Yes, of course he does. But that's not the reason. He hates *himself*. His life isn't worth a fig to himself or anyone and he knows it. Oh, yes, he hates Uncle Harry. He's sat up there all those years in that mouldering slum while down below, there for him to look at every time he sits on that messy balcony, there's Norfolk Hall. He can't not see it. So of course he hates Uncle Harry. So would you if you'd been in his position. So would anyone. But it's gone beyond that, Paul, don't you see? It's eaten into him. He's been left enough to live some sort of life on. The best thing he could have done was to get out of Cordoba. But he didn't. And now he can't. He's locked in. He can't even sell what he's got, not that it would fetch much if he could, because it belongs to you eventually. So what's left? Drink and women?'

Yes, thought Paul. And lording it in rum shops. And of a sudden he felt a respect for Malcolm he hadn't felt before. If he couldn't be someone in his own right, at least he'd be a character. 'What's he like? Malcolm?' Dee had said. At the beginning.

'The local Errol Flynn,' he'd told her. 'A lot of women like him.' And a lot of women had liked him. He might use the local girls...while there were only local girls available...but there'd been others who hadn't been local girls. Others like Dorothea only too eager to share his bed. And Malcolm *had* set out to be the local Errol Flynn—to create a personal identity. To be something, if only a little, more than a whoring alcoholic. There was something quite noble to it. A refusal to be totally swamped by circumstances. The more he thought about it, the higher Malcolm rose in his estimation and the less he thought of himself. It was, after all, he told himself, very much in my hands. I could have given Malcolm Copra Valley, given him the right to sell it. It would have been quite valuable ten, twelve, fifteen years ago. And Malcolm what? Thirty odd? Young enough to start again somewhere. And it never crossed my mind. It must have crossed Malcolm's mind. At least he could have *asked*. But he hadn't. Weak he might be, but Malcolm had pride. And courage. And a kind of grit which had prevented him from entirely succumbing. How frustrating then. Dorothea put herself in Malcolm's shoes on Malcolm's balcony looking down with envy on Norfolk Hall. But there was more to it than that. There was frustration—at what he might have made of it had it been his. And at the years passing by unused. And then...we come along. We offer him the chance of *doing* something. And of course he doesn't want me to do it. He wants to do it himself. To turn out Uncle Harry personally. So many things at once. Revenge. Self-vindication. Something to do—a project. So now what happens. What do *I* do?

He glanced at Dorothea. Tired of waiting for him to speak she had scrabbled her hand amongst the sand and found some pebbles which one by one she was throwing back-handed towards the sea, not reaching it. Probably, he thought, she'll go to Kornblath if he'll take her. Kornblath she would respect—in his soft fat hands lay tremendous power. She will go to Kornblath and her being his mistress will be a spring board. In a few years the glossies will be full of her. But will he take her? If he can't get Norfolk? And he realized that Norfolk remained important, was the nub of it. Not the two million pounds itself but his being able to dispose of Norfolk as he wished. If it was his he could give of it generously to Malcolm and hand to Dorothea the prize of being able to take it along to Kornblath and out of the proceeds he could take care of Sophie and Uncle Harry.

'The solution, of course,' he said aloud, yet hardly to Dorothea, 'is to persuade Uncle Harry to make Norfolk over to me.'

'How?' Her head had turned sharply. One hand with a stone ready for throwing stayed where it was, aloft.

'Explain everything,' he answered simply.

'Oh, don't be so damn foolish!' She threw the stone but without concentration and it fell into the soft sand this side of the ridge. It made no sound that he could hear at all.

He didn't bother to persuade her. It hardly seemed worth the effort.

'You think,' he observed, 'that Malcolm would tell Hastings?'

'What do you think this morning was all about?'

He remembered Malcolm's words.

'You helped him,' he said.

'He made out I did. I didn't know what he was going to talk about.'

'It was pretty well signalled once he'd started.'

'I didn't think he'd go that far. Do you think I'd have agreed to go there if I had. Not tried to stop you going? What sort of girl d'you think you've married, man?'

And that was pretty well signalled too, he thought, wearily yet without rancour—the change of tone, the insinuation of lightness

225

with just that touch of affection. Not too much not to be withdrawn from—so slight, in fact, that it might have been something misunderstood.

But something to build on if effective.

What a clever girl she was.

'What are you thinking about most of all?' he said. 'Me getting ten years for arson. Or that clause in the will.'

'Clause?'

'Oh for God's sake!'

He was genuinely annoyed. The thought of a Cordoban gaol didn't disturb him because it was, as yet, too unreal to be imagined. But the clause was very real.

'You know all about that clause!' he snapped. 'I gave you a copy of the will to read. Don't tell me that you didn't read it. Or that you didn't notice that clause about my forfeiting my rights if I hurried things up by dispossessing Uncle Harry.' But his annoyance was already passing. 'Of course,' he said, quite conversationally, 'what Matthew Blades would have had in mind was my doing him in. I don't suppose it crossed his mind for a moment I'd try to grab Norfolk by lighting cane fires! He wouldn't have been so petty. If he'd been in my shoes, he wouldn't have hired Ryle to start a fire but to cut Uncle Harry's throat. What a dull world we live in nowadays.'

'What a curious mood you're in,' she said, clearly puzzled. But she went on quickly: 'That wasn't what I was thinking of at all. I was thinking of you.'

'I wonder,' he said thoughtfully, and not unkindly, 'if you know what you're thinking of at all.' He faced her. 'You were never in love with me, were you?'

'I don't know,' she said. 'The first day? Yes, Paul I think I was in love with you.'

'Until you went to the bar with Solly Kornblath.'

'I didn't really come back from him a different person. It was that...' She broke off.

'That I didn't measure up to new requirements?'

She nodded slowly: 'Maybe.'

'But that wasn't the whole of it?'

'No.'

He smiled, wryly. 'You see,' he said. 'How right I was?'

'What d'you mean?'

'If Norfolk's sand had been like this...'— he kicked it with his foot and it was dusty stuff, depressing—'I would have made love to you up there and you'd have spent the evening with me in Coral Gardens and then the night in my cottage...'

'What are you going to *do?*' she interrupted.

'Leave it to Malcolm. What else can I do?'

'Why did you have to light that stupid fire? Nothing's going to hurry him now.'

'That doesn't worry me,' Paul said.

'We had six months. We've used up six weeks already...'

'That doesn't worry me either. I'm not all that impressed by Kornblath's threats. If he doesn't want Norfolk, someone else will. As far as I can see there's absolutely nothing that's going to stop Costa pushing his New St James Bill through. In what, six weeks, it'll be law. Then we shall have people falling over themselves making bids for Norfolk. No, it's something else that worries me. Us. Yesterday I was in love with you. Half an hour ago I could have killed you. Isn't that an extraordinary thing, Dee, that a man can love a girl one day and hate her the next? But I tell you something else even more extraordinary. I've stopped hating you. You just don't mean anything at all. Except perhaps that I'm a little sorry for you. For both of us, really. Because I think we could have had a very good thing going.'

And he had a mental vision of how it had been that morning when he had come stunned out of Daniel Fonseca's office and there had been Dorothea, standing by the gate in the Fonseca uniform, waiting to let him out. He had needed someone to talk to, someone to help him make sense of things, someone to hold his hand, someone to steady him until he came down to earth again.

'It wasn't your fault,' he said. 'It was mine. I was far too selfish. I didn't think of your point of view at all. What a thing like this, like two million pounds, just thrown at you, could do. And then it all moved so fast didn't it? In the morning we hadn't met and Norfolk was just a family estate that one day I was going to inherit; by the evening I was in love with you and desperately jealous of a man I'd hardly given a moment's thought to up to the day before and thinking in terms of being able to live the kind of life he lived. Fantastic when you come to think of it.'

'Are you sure we can't go back?' said Dorothea.

He shook his head. 'We're different people, Dee. That man who came out of Daniel's office. That girl who was waiting for him. They lived centuries ago. They're dead. And in their place are two new people who happen to be married to each other and have got themselves all snarled up in a situation they can't get out of on their own.'

'Why,' said Dorothea quietly, 'weren't you like this before?'

'Because these things hadn't happened to me.'

'Light me a cigarette.'

He did so. She smoked for a little while in silence, staring at the rollers which endlessly, and seemingly pointlessly, crashed to destruction on the black sand strand.

'I'm not sure,' she said, not looking at him, 'that we still couldn't have a good thing going.'

'So long as I stay like I am now.'

'Yes.'

'But you forget.'

'What?'

'Malcolm's going to expect you to sleep with him.'

'Yes.'

'Will you?'

'You wouldn't mind, would you?'

'As between us, no.'

'As between you and Malcolm?'

He thought about it—'No,' he said.

'You minded before.'

'Because I hated him.'

'And you don't any longer?'

He shook his head, slowly.

'It's a curious emotion, hatred,' he said. 'It has an annihilating effect. On everything except oneself, I mean. You can't stand apart from the thing that's causing you to hate and so when its got you by the throat you can't see anything in perspective. You don't really hate another person—what you hate is what that person is doing to you. But if suddenly you see it doesn't matter, what that person is doing to you, then you stop hating. Dead men don't hate.'

'You're not dead, man.'

'In a way, I am,' he said. He half laughed. 'Oh I don't mean permanently. Men don't die permanently until they really die...or at any rate not those who have something to look forward to. When there's nothing to look forward to—then they die. But I've got something to look forward to. After all, there's Norfolk. So no doubt I'll recover all right. But at the moment? Yes, at the moment I feel pretty dead. After all...all Malcolm's got to do is have a chat with Hastings and I'm booked for ten years in a common gaol less whatever I get off for good behaviour. That ought to worry me. Normally the thought of it would send shivers up my spine. At the moment...it doesn't. It's just that simple.'

'Malcolm will always be able to talk to Hastings.'

'Yes,' said Paul. 'But I don't think he will providing he gets his way. Besides if he leaves it long enough, he'll be an accessory, won't he?'

He slipped from the log.

'We'd better be getting back... Or I had anyway. Uncle Harry'll be wondering what we're up to.'

'And Sophie,' Dorothea said.

'Oh she knows already,' Paul replied. 'That's the worst part of the whole sickening business. That Sophie knows and doesn't say anything about it. Just sits there like a spider watching flies struggling in a web it didn't even have to spin.'

# Fourteen

After his discussion with Dorothea on the black sand beach, Paul became a different person. For the first time, and Harry saw this, he stopped living consciously only for himself.

For the first time there were signs in answer to many years of Harry's prayers that the nephew he had wanted to look on as his son, might become as his son. Harry did not fool himself that all was changed—but if there was ever to be a change there had to be a beginning and maybe, thought Harry, this was it. And he would do nothing to arrest that change. If Paul gave thought to his uncle in these days, which he did, it was as nothing to the thought his uncle gave to him. Under the crushing influence of New St James, Norfolk might fall. If Harry could stop it falling, he would; but if he could not, at least there was a breathing space which he must use.

Paul did not think this deeply because it was so great a relief simply to accept things as they were. His subconscious fought against involving himself in deliberations which might destroy the sense of peace which this new way of life had brought. Day followed day with different things to do yet basically unchanging. His body responded to hard work and routine. He was conscious that Franklin's initial contempt was changing to grudging respect. He found pleasure in pausing to gossip with the men and women on the estate something which (with the exception of Gran'paw at the gate where it was unavoidable) he had hardly done before. His mind was occupied with both problems he had to solve and new discoveries. Torrid heat, which at Coral Gardens was something one managed more or less artificially, was now something to be endured and, for the time at least, the drama-loving side of his nature found satisfaction in it. There was Harry's friendliness, the bringing back to life of childhood memories, the beauty of Norfolk and the knowledge of ownership. These and many other influences cast a protective shield over him so that Norfolk became his life and he resisted other thoughts. By half-past nine he was as ready for bed as was Uncle Harry and even the sadness of Dorothea, maintaining far more than he did the subterfuge (which he was quite sure no one by now believed) that they were still in love, even Dorothea slipping naked beneath the single sheet under the mosquito net to the double bed in tandem with his own, couldn't keep sleep from him. Even the strange, almost weird closeness which seemed to be developing between her and Sophie and the knowledge that she was seeing Malcolm, did not really disturb the cocoon being woven round him. There was Norfolk. And there was the rest. And of the rest he refused to think.

And then came Hamilton's telegram: 'Please telephone me urgently at Coral Gardens. Gordon Hamilton.'

It was like the smoke of a ship seen by the castaway content with his desert island. He could answer that telegram or ignore it. He could go down to Pilotte and make the call and that would be exactly the same as the castaway gathering brushwood to light a signal fire vastly increasing the possibility of being rescued into the advantages and disadvantages of the real world. In the end he made the call because in the end he saw he must. He was not alone on his desert island—there were others laying the preparation for the escape in which he must in due course join. But the method of escape, if it was escape, was a perilous one. He could not ignore other possibilities. If he must escape then perhaps he could find a better way. And so, although angry and uneasy, he went to the Post Office in Pilotte and telephoned

Gordon Hamilton.

'Mr Kornblath asked me to contact you to see how you are getting on. I'm in the island for a couple of days.'

Paul was conscious of a mixture of annoyance and relief. Was this all it was? A stock enquiry. Had his haven been broken into, his new-found peace of mind been disturbed, just for this? He quite overlooked that Hamilton would be assuming alarm that a lack of reported progress might presage a withdrawal of Kornblath's interest; that Hamilton would be imagining that his life was being shaped by the fear of losing two million pounds.

'I'm sorry but I've nothing worthwhile telling you,' he answered shortly.

Hamilton took this as defensive.

'You appreciate, Mr Blades that Mr Kornblath put a time limit...'

'And there's only four months left.'

'Exactly.'

'I can't imagine if he's really interested there's any magic in a six months' date.'

Hamilton had thought of that as well. And that if Kornblath withdrew there would be other suitors. It didn't affect him directly whether Norfolk Beach happened or didn't happen—but it would be a feather in his cap to go back and report progress he could claim he'd brought about. He adopted a less hectoring manner.

'Well, Mr Blades,' he said. 'I wouldn't count on that. Mr Kornblath is inclined to allocate only a certain time to a project and if that time's exceeded write it off. Still we needn't assume the worst, need we? And anyway I've a suggestion to make which might help things on their way. You're still there, Mr Blades?'

'Yes.'

'I thought it might be a good thing if Mr Tod—the architect, you remember—if Mr Tod flew over with me. And he has. And I was wondering if it might be a good idea for him to come over with me and meet your uncle tomorrow...'

'I'm afraid that won't be any good, Mr Hamilton. He's going into St James and I'm going with him.'

Like many unsure men Hamilton disliked having to fit in his arrangements to suit others he considered lower in the hierarchy; however there was no help for it.

He made a virtue of necessity:

'Actually that would suit me rather better.' He coughed. 'One moment.' He consulted a non-existent diary. 'Yes. If I can get through the meeting I'm having with Mr Rose this evening...and I believe I can... Yes. I've one or two appointments in St James and I'm catching the evening flight up to New York...yes...perhaps Mr

237

Tod and I could meet you sometime in the morning. Will you go in early?'

'I really can't see the point,' Paul answered. 'In fact I'm not even sure it's a very good idea.' But even as he spoke he asked himself if there was *any* opportunity he should discard out of hand.

Hamilton picked up the hesitation. 'Well surely nothing can be lost?'

'But how do you think...'

'Mr Tod can be very persuasive, you know.' Hamilton disliked having to say this but he'd noted results Tod had achieved in what had seemed to him much more unlikely situations.

'I don't know,' said Paul. It needed much more thought. 'I haven't mentioned Mr Kornblath's offer...'

'Ah!' said Hamilton. 'Well, I suppose... Does he know you've met any of us?'

'I shouldn't think so. I haven't told him.'

'Well suppose we hadn't met and I'd contacted you because I was acting for someone who wanted to put a proposition...'

'No,' said Paul. 'I don't like it one little bit. I don't think it'll achieve anything anyway.'

'Let me finish. I could simply have told you I was on the island and wanted the opportunity of meeting your uncle...'

238

'I believe,' interrupted Paul who was beginning to find this nauseating, 'that would be the worst possible thing to do. Anyway, for all I know, my uncle might have heard I'd met you and not mentioned it to me. There's not much that stays secret in Cordoba, Mr Hamilton.'

'Well perhaps at least *you'll* do the courtesy of meeting me, Mr Blades,' Hamilton said waspishly and only because he was determined not to be defeated utterly.

Paul felt a weariness come over him. It all seemed so unreal: Hamilton, Kornblath, two million pounds. Norfolk was the only reality these days.

'All right,' he said. 'If it fits in. Where do you suggest?'

'Shall we say the Darien Hotel. It's where Mr Tod is staying. At half-past twelve. We could lunch together...'

'No good.' Uncle Harry wouldn't miss his liar dice at the James Club and he'd expect Paul to be there with him. 'I could manage eleven o'clock. But if that doesn't fit in with your other appointments...'

But somehow it was fitted in, and so arranged. Then, no sooner had he put down the telephone receiver, than Paul regretted it and before he had got back to Norfolk decided he would cry off from St James on some excuse.

# Fifteen

Although many different influences have to exert their pressures and many coincidences take place before any event involving man occurs, there is usually one happening which because of its inherent dramatic flavour, or perhaps because it is easy to grasp comes to be taken for the root cause of the event.

In the case of Cordoba it was to go down historically, and incorrectly, that everything was to be quite different from how otherwise it might have been for one reason only—that a thief should have decided to break into the cottage at Coral Gardens which Errol Rose happened to be occupying. In fact one could have selected at least a dozen, and probably a hundred distinct and different reasons all the way through from the decision that some cottages should be built for letting to the ability of Solly Kornblath to use the weaknesses of others to further his own ends, as being equally responsible.

But the exploits of the thief was what was chosen because the connection was direct, the happening easy to headline and the content dramatic.

Why look further?

The thief's name was Raleigh and he had a hut in which he lived high up in the wild unbushed hillside above French Bay. He was a tall man, very black, of Koramantee descent, immensely strong and he would have been handsome but for a hideous scar which gashed his face. His woolly hair was short and curly and he wore a small fringe of beard. He was about thirty, in his prime, cunning, agile, ruthless, fearless and with an absolute hatred of authority.

He made his way down through the tree covered hillside until he struck the spur off the Smithstown Road which ran westwards towards Coral Garden's entrance. He kept to the side of this, through light scrub and, entering the peninsula, easily avoided being seen or heard by the policemen in the guard hut; thence he made his way through the wooded areas between the fairways, watching, silent, swift, a dark shadow flitting from covert to covert. Then having prospected for and found a suitable spot near enough to 'Spathodea' which, on the advice of his informants, he had decided to rob, he took the satchel from around his neck and, laying down his machete, stripped naked. From the satchel he took a bottle of coconut oil and anointed himself from head to foot. Next he cut a switch from a clump of nearby bamboo, took from his satchel a pad of cotton wool and tied it to the thinner end with fishing twine. Finally, from the satchel he took a small bottle, then folded and packed away sweater and trousers and put it down in a place easily relocated.

From now on he moved with exquisite caution towards 'Spathodea' looking, with the bamboo switch in one hand with its white tip gently swaying, rather like a fisherman, yet still a menacing figure with his black oiled body gleaming in the moonlight and the machete in his other hand held ready. There was small cover now—only occasional clumps of bamboo left for scenic effect, and a few tall trees or palms so that when he reached the boundary of the property Raleigh at once headed for the cover of its surrounding hibiscus hedge and edged along in its shadow. Nearing the entrance he peered through the driveway gap. All was still, the only movement that of the night flying insects swarming round the lights which, fixed to every corner of main house and guest annexe, threw unbroken illumination in opposition to the brilliant moonlight on the lawn. Seeing there was no point in concealment now, he moved quickly,

242

avoiding the stony driveway, immensely tall, glistening, dangerous, machete raised, casting a fearful shadow.

He had decided on the bedroom annexe to 'Spathodea' because he had heard there would be two guests in it occupying separate suites and the chances of money left lying on bedside table doubled. His plan was simple. If there were louvres open he would pour chloroform from the bottle on to pad of cotton wool and, thrusting the bamboo tip through, wave it over the noses of the sleepers, then break in boldly; if the louvres were closed he would seek some other form of access and chloroform them from inside and if need be kill them. For Raleigh had already killed. He had been put into the St James gaol for a small offence—an alley brawl—and those three months had been anguish to his proud nature; he had left the gaol knowing he would kill to avoid as much as another day of it and he had killed and was now that most dangerous of men, the man with nothing to lose but liberty.

The plan went awry. Raleigh moved silently but not so silently that the cicadas did not hear him move. Not many Americans or Englishmen on their first night of a holiday in the tropics would have noted the sudden pausing of the cicadas' stridulation but Errol Rose was a

Cordoban and he noticed it as instinctively as others would have noticed the sudden ceasing of a traffic undertone.

It was silent in that bedroom which Rose and Charlotte were using. The talking had been done, the instructions given, the equipment used and during the time while Raleigh had been moving swiftly across the lawn Rose had been busy with the final preparations. Now he was ready, or perhaps it is better said that Charlotte was ready, for she was tied by wrist and ankles spread-eagled to the four corners of the bed. She was not naked but was dressed in a schoolgirl's uniform, in fact in a set of Errol Rose's own daughter's Hendriks' uniform. She wore gymslip, blouse, and stockings, even shoes—all that she lacked were bloomers. Rose had had little trouble persuading her, the prostitute soon becomes accustomed to the perversities of her customers and as there was apparently to be no flagellation, there was no danger. As to why Errol Rose, unlike the huge majority of his fellow countrymen who are rarely inclined to what Cordobans call 'dirty' sex, should have for years nursed a desire to act the pederast to a white girl dressed in schoolgirl's uniform who can say? Perhaps the idea was picked up from another prostitute in London or from a *Playboy* magazine; or perhaps it

244

was that to an imaginative mind this was the greatest degradation he could conceive inflicting. At all events the ambition was at last about to be achieved and Rose trembling with lust having tied the final knot around Charlotte's left ankle, stood back to view his victim unhurriedly and dwell on the sensual feast ahead, at the very moment when Raleigh, the thickness of a wall away from him, began to creep cautiously round the corner of the annexe and the cicadas quietened.

Rose heard that sudden utter silence and his blood ran cold. Lust died and a sense of horror moved into its place. If he was right, and he was sure he was, that there was a sneak thief prowling the house, he had little time, perhaps no time, perhaps already through some clink in the louvres he had been watched. Perhaps the fellow was even now moving away to spread the news. There was no time for thought, only for decision; if this came out his career and future would be in rags. He listened, in an agony of mind, and heard the faintest sound which his concentration translated as a footstep. There was no time to hesitate, no time to untie Charlotte. The man must be stopped. And Errol Rose knew how he was going to stop him. There would be nothing but praise for a minister who killed a burglar. There were far too many burglars in St James. One less on Cordoba would cause few tears.

He went quickly to the chest of drawers and opening it took out the gun which like many in Cordoba he always took with him against just such a situation. Charlotte turned her head. Rose put a finger to his lips and pointed to the wall behind her. He had just time to see the dawn of alarm in her small eyes before he quietly opened the door and left her. Like Raleigh, Rose moved quietly but he hadn't Raleigh's training and, still fully dressed, wore shoes. Careful as he was, Raleigh heard him. He looked about him quickly. There was a pergola on the bedroom window side thickly planted with shrubs for shade—allamanda, thunbergia, bignonia. Laying the bamboo switch on the ground, within two quick steps Raleigh was into the pergola, hidden by its luxuriance yet able through the barest gap to watch.

He stood silent, naked, his oiled body sheening even in this dark walkway, listening. He heard every sound. The opening door on the far side of the bedroom, a whispered call from Charlotte inside, the pat of careful footsteps on the grass. And he waited.

He did not think while he waited that it was odd that the woman's voice came from the same room as the opening door because Raleigh did not think of the people of Coral Gardens in that way. They were strangers and nothing to do with him in any way—he did not relate them to Cordoba. Indeed he hardly related them to human beings. He did not envy or hate them or object to their being where they were and having a guard room and their own policemen. Except insofar as they represented a mine of wealth they were beyond his range of thought.

And so he was surprised when around the corner of the annexe, fully floodlit by the burglar light, he saw a tall, gaunt black man with hooded, yet protuberant eyes, fully dressed and somehow familiar, cautiously advance. But what caught his attention more, and was more important, was that the man held a gun. It was a terrible mistake of Errol Rose to have brought that gun to Coral Gardens. Raleigh was cunning but he was a simple man. He had never owned a gun and there had always been in his mind a wish to do so. He saw a gun as a talisman which would give total and final protection from authority—by owning a gun his liberty would for ever be assured. There was nothing, he had reasoned, he could lack if ever he owned a gun. His prestige, high as it was, would soar. A cutlass was all right but it had its limitations—also it could impede. It did not occur to him how far more terrifying he would appear standing tall and black and powerful with that hideous scar adding a macabre touch and a machete in his hand, than holding a mere revolver—a machete was to him an instrument, it held no symbolism. And so now, as he watched Rose drawing nearer alongside the cottage annexe, his mind was filled with a single compulsion, to have that gun.

So he waited and now because of the angle he could not see Rose but he heard the sound of his progress suddenly stop and a half stifled cry of surprise and he knew exactly what that was, that the bamboo lying on the ground had been seen. With lightning speed and instinctive cunning he acted. He lobbed the bottle of chloroform ahead of him a yard or so to the right of the bamboo switch and at once leapt out from the pergola, machete raised.

Errol Rose momentarily distracted had no time. Turning sharply he saw a naked man with an awful scar towering half a head above him and as he raised his gun a machete coming down and in a single stroke severing the wrist which held it. He heard the gun go clattering on the path which circumscribed the cottage and the extraordinary plop of his severed hand joining it a moment later, and then the machete was raised again and there were two eyes glaring at him and a hideous scar...

And Errol Rose, Minister of Finance for Cordoba, was dead. And with his death died New St James.

It was the falling gun which woke Hamilton. It had been an uneasy sleep. All through the evening he had known the bitter jealousy of one man with another man and a beautiful woman who, when they leave him, will do so for sex. As he lay tossing and turning his angry mind flickered from one resentment to another. His mind was crowded with the catalogue of his defeats—defeat by Kornblath, defeat by Tod, defeat by Blades and now, if of a different kind, defeat by Rose. There had been nothing but defeats in Cordoba and not one victory. And now, in his lonely bed, he knew what seemed at the moment the worst defeat of all—the defeat of manhood. In such a state of mind he fell asleep.

He attached no significance to the sound of the falling gun but lay awake brooding, knowing he wouldn't sleep again. He would have taken a pill but he had none with him; if he had been in a city he would have dressed and sought bar or night club; if he had had work to do he would have done it. Instead there was nothing to occupy his mind but the sound of the June bugs absurdly colliding with the walls, the sight of the fireflies flickering endlessly and his own gloomy thoughts. And then he thought of Charlotte Amalie in the annexe, her bedroom scarcely a hundred feet from his; his thoughts at first wistful became lascivious, making him more restless still and at length he got up and, barefooted and in pyjamas, opened the bedroom door and stepped out on to its private patio. The moon was past its zenith now, riding in a mackerel sky so thin as barely to dim its light. A coconut palm above his head was a sheaf of swords and the sea was beautiful. There was a scent of perfume filling the air, rich, sweet and cloying. It was warm and magical.

He felt cheated in his loneliness. With no particular plan in mind he began to walk towards the annexe. He passed the end of the main house and it was when he came to the path which led past both of the bedroom suites he noticed the faint, thin bars of light which escaped through the louvres of the further bedroom. He listened, carefully, cocking his head up to the moonlit sky for any sounds. And presently he heard a low-pitched testing call and at length deciphering this realized, to his astonishment, that his name was being called. 'Mr Hamilton! Mr Hamilton! Mr Hamilton!'

It suddenly blazed across his mind that it was Charlotte calling to him. How she could have realized he was there he didn't understand, but there was no doubt of it. She was calling to him, softly, so as not to wake Rose. Calling to him. And there could only be one reason. Triumph, mingled with excitement, came flooding in and he turned to go around to the other side of the annexe—but as he did so his eyes fell on the dark shadow of Errol Rose lying just off the path athwart the grass.

He did not at first realize this was a man because of a thicker skein of cloud momentarily obscuring the moon but almost at once this cleared and there was no doubt of it. His immediate reaction was one of fear but his feet were too rooted to the path to let him move. And then again he heard his name being called softly, testingly, from inside the farther bedroom. He looked with horror at the body and the horror was of a sudden made even worse as he noticed that also on the paving was a crab clearly heading for the body and the crab was the confirmation of his suspicion that the man was dead. In instinctive anger and disgust he kicked at the crab with his bare foot but instead of the hardness he expected his toes met relative softness and he bent his head to see what it was that he had kicked and saw it was a hand.

Charlotte did not know that Rose was dead. The clatter of the gun falling on the paving had been unmistakable for what it was, but the sound of the machete slashing him and of his hand dropping on the concrete had been puzzling, while the sound of his body falling had been softened by the grass. She had thought too that she had heard the footsteps of someone running away but even of this she could not be sure. Rose himself had made no intelligible noises, no speech or cry, merely a kind of gasp for the second cut had been clear across his throat and wielded with tremendous force. Few men had died more quickly than Cordoba's Minister of Finance.

Charlotte had realized the possibility of something similar to what had actually occurred but also imagined other explanations. At first she had lain still, petrified at the thought of a marauder having dealt with Rose coming in to deal with her but, later, with the night quiet apart from the normal tropic sounds, she had tried desperately to free herself. But Rose in the careful attention to detail which had given him slow pleasure had done his job well—the cord knots were tied too cleverly and Charlotte succeeded only in chafing her skin. She was left with the two alternatives of attracting attention or waiting to be found. She was very hesitant about the former—there could be some explanation which had eluded her and Rose might yet return; on the other hand if there had been a sneak thief, or even an assassin, he might be lurking near at hand and a cry could bring down on her what otherwise she might escape.

But if she did not attract Hamilton's attention how could she be sure that it would be he who would be the first to find her—or if she tried to attract him by shouting, might she not lose the one chance out of this mess, that he might be the first to come knocking on Rose's door? Might not someone else hear her instead?

Charlotte had, for less money than Kornblath paid, endured worse indignities at the hands of men than merely being dressed in schoolgirl clothes and tied to the four corners of a bed, but always these indignities had been either private as between herself and client or if in front of others, those others had been active participants. But, like most prostitutes, she had her standards. She no more wanted to be found in such an embarrassing situation than would the wife of a man who had similar tastes to Errol Rose. Indeed in some ways she was even more anxious than such a wife might have been. Cordoba was not her country, there might be laws against this sort of thing, she might find herself imprisoned or at the least deported. The publicity could be damaging—some kinds of publicity had value, this kind did not. Again she had not as yet been paid nor wanted to lose such a valuable contact as Kornblath had proved himself to be. And so she kept quiet, now and then making another attempt to free herself, sore of wrists and ankles, cramped of body and very angry and frustrated.

Hamilton stared at her in astonishment hardly able to take in this new phenomenon. She twisted her head and stared at him with animosity.

'Undo me, you fool!' she hissed.

'He's dead,' Hamilton said in a perplexed sort of way. 'Murdered.'

'Murdered!' She was shocked to silence. But only for the moment. 'For Chrissake hurry then!' she raged—although in muted tone.

'They cut his hand off. I kicked it.' He glanced at his foot and said 'Oh, God!' The bottom of one pyjama leg was scarlet with blood. He came in unsteadily and sat into a chair, feeling sick again. Doing this took him almost out of her range of vision however much she craned her neck. 'Didn't you hear anything?' she heard him ask.

'Will you undo me!'

'Oh.' For the first time through the fog of shock Hamilton began to understand Charlotte's predicament. As in a dream he stumbled to his feet and pulled vaguely at the nearest knot but in the midst of doing this he felt the retching in his stomach and knew he was about to vomit. He clapped his hand up to his mouth and instinctively ran towards the bathroom. He was far too late and he ended leaning against the doorjamb with the sick all over him. Charlotte stared at him in helpless frustration, a wretched figure of blood and mess, ashen face, hard dismal eyes, thin clammy hair sticking to his scalp. She watched him stagger away, into the bathroom; she heard the sound of his ablutions. She strained against the knot he'd fumbled with but he hadn't loosened it at all.

Hamilton was a long time cleaning up and the process gave him time to think, or at least to settle more towards a state where thinking coherently was a possibility. He was calmer when he came back in.

'You didn't hear it happen?' he said,

puzzled. He had taken his pyjama jacket off. His body was old and white and spare.

'I heard something. For Chrissake when are you going to undo me!'

'I can't.'

'Of course you can!'

'I can't. My hands are shaking.' He held up his hands. They were trembling like poplar leaves.

'You can't let anyone find me like this. Someone could come any time. Get on with it.'

'I can't anyway.'

She felt a chill run through her body. 'What's that supposed to mean!'

'He's been murdered. Rose. He's out there dead. On the path.'

'Okay. Then the sooner you untie me the sooner we can get the cops in on it.'

'No.' He was shaking his head.

'Get on with it, you jerk.'

'No.'

He stared at her and she saw his eyes were not on hers but on her body. She could feel from the discomfort under her stomach that in her efforts to free herself the gymslip had rucked up, from the comparative coldness of her buttocks that they were exposed. It was unimaginable he would not untie her.

'For God's sake,' she begged. 'Untie me.

What's in this for you? Look untie me and you can fuck me if you like. Do anything. But untie me first.'

But his eyes back on hers were hard, the eyes that many supplicants had seen across that desk in that office in Berkeley Square with the row of deckle-edged invitation cards on the mantelshelf behind their owner's head. Eyes that were not to be persuaded. Because there was nothing the supplicant could say or do sufficiently to Hamilton's advantage to persuade him to change his mind. And there was nothing Charlotte could do, nothing anyone could have done.

For Gordon Hamilton had seen suddenly thrust into his hands power such as he had never imagined, power at a stroke to revenge himself on Kornblath, on Tod, on Paul Blades, on Cordoba itself. It could be commercial suicide but, at that moment the future meant nothing.

'I'm not going to undo you,' he said. 'I'm going to have them all look at you. The more the merrier.'

'You bloody bastard...'

But she saw him heading for the alarm switch and hastily changed her tack: 'Just a minute...'

He paused, turning to look at her in her schoolgirl's uniform, her buttocks bared, her titian hair tumbling down her back, her wrists and ankles pulling legs and arms into a cross.

'Let them see what you are,' he said. 'It's not my business going round untying whores. Anyway—when there's a murder you're supposed to leave everything exactly as you found it. And that's what I'm going to do. No one can object to that, can they?'

And he flicked the switch and the alarm bell clanged out over Coral Gardens and Hamilton smiled and went to telephone the police.

## Sixteen

Just beyond the opening on to the French Bay to Pilotte road Harry pulled the old Ford into the side where, against the background of a yellow green croton hedge, her hand upraised, stood a portly black woman dressed all in her best with a great shining face and great gleaming eyes.

'Mornin', Liza Ann!' he called.

'Mornin', Mass Harry!' Her voice was a gurgle of cheerfulness. 'You is going into 'James?'

'Yes, Liza Ann.'

'I'm considerin' askin' you something, sir.'

'Yes, Liza Ann?'

'Seein' as you is goin' into 'James an' seein' as how I is goin' to see my sister up by Wagtown, would you be giving me a drop?'

'Only too pleased,' said Harry. 'Would you mind, Paul?'

The Ford was two doored. Paul got out and Harry pulled back his seat.

'Hop in!' he called to Liza Ann and when she did so, quite filling the door opening, he helped her as courteously as he might have a duchess and she with equal dignity for all the ridiculously small space at the back settled herself, spreading her starched dress stiffly, placing her fat hands folded in her lap.

'You know Mr Paul,' said Harry as they drove off.

'I know Mr Paul,' the woman said, for all the world as if there were only the two of them in the car. 'I know him when pickney.' And then, as if accepting Paul's presence. 'You done marry Mister Sasso's daughter.'

'Quite right,' said Paul.

'I saw her drivin' to Pilotte a few days back. She's a very lovely gal.'

'Yes.'

'Be much more better when Mr Sasso Chief Minister.'

'You think so?' Harry said.

'Know so,' said Liza Ann with absolute certainty. 'When you think we get rid of that reskil, Mass Harry?'

'What rascal?'

'That reskil, Costa.'

'Oh that'll be best part of two years, Liza Ann. But isn't everyone saying what a good thing he's doing? This New St James business?'

'Well I don't know,' said Liza Ann. 'From the way I look 'pon it things is not so bad as they is, an' if the good Lawd wanted 'James like they say we is goin' to have it, he would have made water deep.'

'Water deep?' Harry had missed the point.

'All this dredging they is goin' to do.'

'Oh.' Harry laughed. It was still cool, the sun still shafting through the palms bordering the ocean strand, but he wore only shirt and shorts. He was one of the few men left who still went about his business in St James in shirt and shorts. But he looked neat with well shined shoes and military socks.

He drove very slowly and carefully, chatting to the woman all the time, but not turning his head to look at her at all. Every now and then he threw out bridges to bring Paul into the conversation. But Paul scarcely crossed them. His mind was too occupied with whether he should or should not keep the meeting arranged with Hamilton and Tod—and in any case he lacked the freedom of communication Uncle Harry shared with Liza Ann.

Two months earlier this would not have troubled him but now he listened with envy and even a slight annoyance that the woman should by her obvious uninterest in him, dismiss him.

He would have liked to have asked a

question of Liza Ann. 'What will it mean to you when Uncle Harry dies and I am running Norfolk?' He would have liked to ask the question not because he could not have made a fair stab at the answer if given truthfully but because of the stirring towards Norfolk in his soul which had been growing over the past few weeks which was now insisting he should be punished. In a way this journey was a punishment, because of his exclusion—but that was only a punishment to fit the crime of disloyalty. But his crime had been far greater, and merited more than this casual disregarding. She had called Costa a rascal, and no doubt he was, but at least Costa's scheming was grand scale scheming. History forgave men their crimes if their crimes were big enough. But there was no forgiveness for petty criminals who lit stupid little fires, petulant little fires... This thinking brought him back to Dorothea. 'I saw her drivin' to Pilotte a few days back. She's a very lovely gal.' Yes, she was. And why was she driving to Pilotte? To shop? Or on the way to Copra Valley? Would she go there today? Quite possibly. For sex with Malcolm? Or to plot with Malcolm? But what could they plot? Removed from, as it were, the scene of action, from Norfolk, Paul asked himself quite seriously what they could do. And he could think of nothing sufficiently devastating which would make Uncle Harry quit Norfolk. Cane fires? Well it was too late now in any case. All but the last of that was in. Trouble with the men? What men? A few scruffy discontents like Ryle...would they, withdrawing their petty contributions, so much as make a dent in the deposit of goodwill Uncle Harry had built up through the years? Then what?

He could think of nothing. The whole idea was laughable. And yet it had seemed so real. So believable. Supposedly it had just been possible. Supposedly a properly planned campaign of arson, sabotage and the sowing of discontent might have made Uncle Harry throw his hand in. Supposedly. But supposedly as well it might only have hardened the resolve of a man who had seen through crop failures, banana blights, falling sugar prices and all the rest... Had he really believed?... Oh, yes—one evening three conspirators heads together in a shabby house while the rain beat down in torrents on the roof! How many conspirators in such an atmosphere had put their heads together and plotted, and believed in their plot, to pull down even emperors' roofs above their heads? And after they had failed, when their petty plots had fizzled out? Probably, he mused, if you stood away from most plots they looked comical. Why else the caricature of the assassin in his long black coat holding a smoking time bomb? He was real only if the bomb went off and killed somebody. And they would be real only if they succeeded.

And how could they succeed?

He did not pursue it—it no longer seemed to matter. Success, if it was to come, had to be a long time off in any case. Long beyond Kornblath's six months limit. Not that that mattered—there'd be other buyers.

Then what did matter?

Well it was in Malcolm's power to have him clapped in gaol—out of comicality at least that non-comical by-product had been created. And Dorothea? Was she affected? Had this made her become the girl she was? Or was that the real inner Dorothea anyway? Had the comicality brought to the surface what was latent—or had it dramatically changed a girl who in the normal progression of life would have married a respectable St James' youngster and settled down to the humdrum life of a Cordoban of her background? And Uncle Harry? This decent man driving so carefully and chuckling away at some remark of Liza Ann's. What was this going to do to him? Yes, he, at least, was bound to be affected. There was no possible course to be taken which wouldn't end in savage hurt to the one man, the one person in the world who had love for him. There was no way to avoid it now. No way.

They dropped Liza Ann at Wagtown, a sort of suburb on the outskirts of St James—a mere clutch of buildings, poor shabby huts knocked up from wooden boxes and scraps of tin where fat-bellied but healthy-looking children put fingers in their mouths to stare in wide-eyed wonder. They dropped her, a brilliant massive flower amongst a shabby dun-coloured mess which had sufficient pride to give itself a name. They watched her treading heavily up a slope towards her sister's hut and they saw her become half hidden behind the leathery shields of banana leaves. And she knew her dignity better than to look back at them.

'I'm supposed to be meeting some people at the Darien.'

'That's all right, Paul,' said Harry. 'I'll drop you. You can get yourself a taxi down.'

'No,' said Paul. 'I'm going to duck it.'

'Man, that's not reasonable.'

'They wanted to see you too.' And at Harry's frown. 'A man named Hamilton and Kornblath's architect.' He came out

265

with it. 'Kornblath wants to buy Norfolk too.'

'Ah,' said Harry. 'Was that why you had to see Daniel?'

There had been no hesitation. It was as if Harry had known all along.

'Yes. How did you know?'

'I didn't. It was just suddenly obvious.'

Paul waited for the expected question and when it didn't come said: 'It's not just the beach. He wants all Norfolk.'

'Lawks!' said Harry.

'And he's offered me two million pounds.'

There was a moment or two of silence. 'Pounds?' said Harry unbelievingly. 'Not dollars even?'

'Pounds.'

'Lawks,' said Harry, very quietly. 'What a lot of money.' And with hardly a pause. 'You should have told me before.' And from those few words Paul realized that Harry had understood all along.

'Uncle Harry,' he said. 'Why don't you come along and meet them?'

Harry nodded: 'Why don't I do that?' he said.

'How d'you do, Mr Tod?'

Watching them shaking hands, Paul realized that in a way they were very much alike. He was not thinking from a physical point of view (although in fact both compact and bright of eye they were not all that dissimilar) but of quiet assurance which made no difference of the fact that here was Harry on the *loggia* of the Darien Hotel a known and respected figure while Tod was a total stranger. Alert to each other they both might be, but they were not wary. They made him the odd man out.

'Is it too early for a drink?' suggested Tod.

'No,' said Harry and Tod ordered beers. It was pleasant enough sitting here on the *loggia* of the Darien Hotel which ran tangential to a sweeping semi-circular drive bordered with ornamental palms beyond which was a semi-circle of lawn planted with beds of yellow and scarlet cannas beyond which again was a view over the roofs of St James to the sea. Outside the James Club it was the regular meeting-place; even at this time of the morning there were quite a few pairs of men or women or small groups of three or four as well as individuals glancing through their notes whilst waiting for their appointment to arrive. The Darien was a last lingering reminder of a past age which had been slow to change, in which there had been no sense of any pressing need for change, and so long as it still stood, acknowledged and used, it would exert no bad an influence on those who came to meet and discuss their business there.

'I've no idea,' said Tod, 'why Hamilton should be so late.'

'You haven't telephoned him?'

'No.'

'I will if you like,' said Paul, half rising.

'I shouldn't bother. If he hasn't left by now he's not going to get here.' Tod paused to light a new cigarette from the old, flicked the stub over the wooden *loggia* railing and asked cheerfully: 'Any idea what we're supposed to talk about?'

'Yes,' said Paul. 'You're supposed to persuade my uncle to let me sell Norfolk to Kornblath.'

'Really,' said Tod and gave Harry his full attention. 'Well, Mr Blades, where do you think I should start?' His eyes were full of fun. He managed to convey the impression not that he and Harry were on opposing sides but that they were involved in some joint enterprise.

'You could start, Mr Tod,' said Harry, 'by telling me what you intend to do to it when Paul's sold it.'

Tod hauled up the brochure resting against the brief case beside his chair.

'We've just about got room,' he said and after the shifting of glasses laid it on their table. Harry studied it unhurriedly, his fine hair shifting in the breeze, his mouth making the small signs of a man impressed and meaning to show it. He came to the end then, closing the brochure, handed it back to Tod who stowed it beside him.

'Well?' Tod said, a broad grin on his face.

'I'm glad to see you've left the house,' said Harry dryly.

'Yes,' admitted Tod. 'It's a bit of a cheek, isn't it?'

'Impertinence might be a better word.'

'Or plain bloody impudence?'

'Without which...' Harry indicated the brochure with a movement of his head, 'that sort of thing would never get put together, I suppose. Tell me something, Mr Tod, how long did you spend at Norfolk altogether?'

'I walked halfway along the beach and back.'

'That's all?' Tod nodded. 'Did you talk to anybody?'

'Hamilton. And a man named McCallin. Both of whom were against touching it with a bargepole.'

'But you didn't talk to any of the men and women who live there?' Tod shook his head. 'You don't think it's a good thing to talk first to the people whose lives you're going to turn upside down before you do it, Mr Tod?'

'You think that's pretty arrogant?'

'Well, of course. But that's neither here nor there. I'm not too much worried, I'm afraid, Mr Tod, about your affections. What I'm much more worried about is your affect.' He picked up his beer as if considering drinking some of it, then put it down again.

'You know, Mr Tod,' he said. 'I don't think I could have been an architect. Or if I had been one, I think I'd have limited myself to doing very small things. I don't think I'd have had the courage to do a thing like that. I think I'd have been terrified when I started drawing lines at what I was doing. That's a pretty impressive thing you've put together. If it happens there won't be one single man or woman in Norfolk, in Pilotte for that matter, whose life isn't going to be turned upside down. Even the children yet to be born are going to find themselves in a different world from the one in which they were conceived. That's one hell of a responsibility, you know. But I suppose that isn't your business.'

'It should be.'

'Yes, it should, shouldn't it. In fact I would have thought it ought to be the point from which an architect ought to start. Of course I don't suppose we'd get much done that way. But maybe that wouldn't be so awful. Maybe a moratorium on anything new at all for the next ten years, say, wouldn't be a bad thing.'

'Stop progress in its tracks!'

'Progress?' said Harry. 'Well.' He waved to a new arrival up the steps who came over and passed a few minutes time of day.

When the man had gone, Harry said: 'What is the job of an architect, Mr Tod?'

'In a sentence?'

'If you can.'

'To interpret the times we live in?'

'Ah! Sweep away everything that doesn't fit! Replace it with something more appropriate to the times we live in!'

'When there's a need.'

'There's a need to get rid of Norfolk? To cover it with hotels, golf courses and marinas?'

Tod smiled.

'Funny thing, need,' said Harry thoughtfully. 'One starts with shoes to get about and ends up with motor cars. Then you hardly need the shoes you started out with. You used the word 'arrogant' just now. We're pretty damn arrogant, aren't we? Each generation telling the one before its ideas are old hat and taking not the least notice that that generation said the same thing of the one before and so on

271

backwards. We always think we've reached the end of the line as it were. That the next generation following us is going to say what splendid chaps we were and got it all tickety-boo. This thing of yours. What's it to be called?'

'Norfolk Beach.'

'Norfolk Beach. Yes, well if it's done it's going to be there for a long time, isn't it? And the effects of it. Norfolk as it is has stood the test of time and on the whole's not been too badly thought of.' He told him about Liza Ann. 'She thinks it's not too bad and I daresay if you took a straw poll locally that's about what they'd say. But your thing? Norfolk *Beach?* Well who knows? Next generation might think it ought to be all swept away as you'd sweep away Norfolk as it is to do it. And they won't be able to put Norfolk as it is back, will they?' And when Tod didn't speak. 'You see it's all very well, Mr Tod, pulling things down and replacing them with what happens to be the current fashion of the time but there's just two snags. The time may just happen to be a commonplace and senseless one. That's snag one. And pretty important. Snag two's the one that counts though. When you change the way people live their lives, you change the people too.'

'If there's many people in Cordoba think

like you,' Tod said, chuckling, 'my client's going to have one hell of a time getting New St James through!'

'Uhm,' said Harry and went on: 'You'll get...or rather your client will get New St James through because that happens to make good politics for a rat named Vernon Costa the people of Cordoba were so misguided as to put into office. Norfolk's something different. Nothing to do with politics. That's all to do with me and my nephew.' And for the first time he turned to Paul. 'Does Mr Tod know the situation?'

'My uncle has lifetime tenure of Norfolk,' Paul told Tod, 'and unless he's agreeable there's no way I can sell Norfolk. And he didn't know until five minutes before he met you that Kornblath wanted to buy it—let alone was willing to pay two million pounds.'

'If I may say so,' Tod observed to Harry. 'You seem to have absorbed the situation quite remarkably, Mr Blades.'

'I may have seemed to,' Harry answered briskly. 'But I haven't. In fact I've never been in such a devil of a situation in my life. On the one hand I've got all the people who work at Norfolk...'

'To say nothing of the tradition of a family owning it for generations...'

'Yes, well we'll have to put that aside for

the moment. I've got all those at Norfolk, and a lot in Pilotte too. On the other hand, I've got Paul who owns the place and hasn't any obligation to share my views... After all. Two million pounds. That's one hell of a lot of money. And what right have I to stop Paul getting it when what your man wants to buy belongs to him? Maybe if I say no and your Mr Kornblath goes somewhere else there won't be anyone following up behind...'

'There's bound to be,' said Paul.

'Well thank you for that,' said Harry. 'Because as you say there's bound to be when all that lot gets done.' He waved a hand vaguely towards the town. 'Still it mightn't be two million. Mr Kornblath may be overvaluing it.'

'No,' said Tod.

'You don't think so? Well I daresay you know. Two million pounds. Lawks! What a lot of money. Who'd have thought it.' He finished off his beer.

'So, Mr Tod,' he resumed. 'What do I do? Hang on to Norfolk like grim death for however many years I've got, which mayn't be too many? Or get my old arse off it and let a man who's waited patiently enough and God knows decently enough have his turn?'

'I don't think you really have a choice, Mr Blades, do you?' said Tod.

'No,' said Harry. 'I don't think I do. Let's have another look at that damn thing of yours.' He waved his glass at a passing waiter.

'Mornin', Mr Blades.'

'Mornin', Henry. Same thing.'

'Sure thing, Mr Blades. Nice to see you in again, Mr Blades.'

'Nice to see you too, Henry.'

Henry went off with the glasses. The brochure was back open on the table. Paul sat back with narrowed eyes, astounded.

'Well you'd better explain it,' Harry said.

Tod did so. Harry listened patiently. At the end Tod said:

'I'd be grateful for any comments.'

'You'll get them,' Harry said. 'By the wagonload. But not now. You'd better come and stay with us for a week or two. Come tomorrow.'

'There is nothing,' Tod said. 'I'd like better. But I happen to have another appointment tomorrow.'

'Lawks...' Harry began.

'In Hong Kong,' Tod said. 'But perhaps I could call in on my way back.' There was a huge grin on his face.

'Why not do that,' Harry said. He stood. The second beers had long since been drunk. 'By the way,' he said. 'What are you doing in Hong Kong?'

'Just one hotel,' said Martin Tod. 'And I'm afraid I neither write nor speak Chinese. But I'll remember what you had to say.'

When he had gone, Paul said, amazed. 'You mean you're going to agree. I don't believe it.'

'The trouble with you, Paul,' Harry said, 'or rather one of your troubles, is that you haven't yet made your mind up about what kind of man you want to be and until you do you'll be hopeless at judging other people. And until you can judge other people you can't make an intelligent guess at what under particular circumstances they're likely to do.'

'Maybe,' said Paul. 'But when I stayed at Norfolk the night before I saw Daniel, and that was before I had any idea Kornblath was interested, you made it perfectly clear...' He remembered. 'Not one acre of land, not one foot of beach,' he quoted.

'Quite right,' said Harry equally. 'That was under the circumstances as we were then discussing them. But the circumstances are quite different now. There's this New St James thing and there's two million pounds. One has to know when a thing's got too big for one. And two million pounds is too big for me.'

'You mean all I had to do...'

'Well I don't know...' Again Harry broke off to chat to someone passing by their table.

'What was I saying,' he said, when this person, in this case a lady, had continued on her way. 'Oh, yes. If you'd come straight back from your meeting... No, probably not at once. For one thing I wouldn't have had all these weeks getting used to the fact that Costa's going to turn Cordoba upside down anyway. For another...oh several things. You weren't married. I hadn't had you living and working with us at Norfolk...'

'I arranged that cane fire,' Paul blurted out.

'What a day for confessions this is...'

'You mean...you guessed!'

'Let's say I didn't put it beyond the bounds of possibilities.' He smiled, rather wearily now, at the thin anxious dark face of his nephew. 'Easy, man, easy,' he said. 'I'm not going to the nearest damn telephone to let Hastings know.'

Paul looked away, staring at the green and brown rusting roofs of nearby shabby buildings below their level.

'Makes me pretty futile, doesn't it,' he said with bitterness.

'Well,' Harry said phlegmatically. 'Does us all good to feel that way sometimes. It's when you're always above things you stop noticing them.'

He laid his hand on Paul's arm.

'Paul,' he said. 'Listen to me.' Paul looked at his uncle and saw how kind and understanding Harry's eyes were and he felt such shame as never in his life he had known before. 'You've done no lasting harm and that's what matters. You've put yourself in a false position but not one you can't withdraw from. At least I hope not.'

Paul knew he was thinking of Dorothea.

'What do you mean?' he said.

'I mean,' said his uncle, looking at him very directly, 'when you enter into relationships with people that are wrong relationships.'

'And if you have and it's as wrong to withdraw as go on?'

'Then,' said Harry, 'you have done lasting harm. Let's hope it doesn't apply.'

'I'm ashamed,' said Paul. 'I have never in my life been so ashamed.'

'That's no bad thing either,' said Harry comfortably. 'But let's not carry this sackcloth and ashes too far, shall we?' He chuckled. 'All right for priests. Part of their terms of reference. Not part of yours.'

'What are my terms of reference, then?' He spoke dully while realizing he would never meet another man as good to him as

278

Harry. That there were few men so good.

'Well,' said Harry. 'That man Tod. I rather took to him. He's an honest man,' and he went on: 'I'm not so enthused about the times we live in. In fact I think they're a bit commonplace and certainly without much sense. But he doesn't see it that way. If you asked him what he thought, he'd say he thought they were splendid, I daresay. He's a modern-day adventurer, you know. Nothing wrong in that. The world would be poorer without adventurers. We certainly would have been. Wouldn't have had Norfolk but for Drake and so on would we? Eh? The way he sees it is that a three-mile white sand beach must inevitably be covered with hotels, etcetera.' He held up a hand. 'Yes, I know, you said that too. But that wasn't in the context of New St James. Now when they've stuck a runway a couple of miles through Criolli and they've got the jumbos coming in...he's probably right. I can resist it for a year or two...' He broke off for a moment. 'You see I only have the right to hold you up if it's right to hold you up *and* there's the possibility that by holding you up I can prevent something happening...assuming of course I'm right it shouldn't happen. But if it's going to happen anyway... Well if it is, for God's sake let's have a man who's doing it for

279

the thing itself. Not just for the money.' He paused again. 'I believed in that man, Paul,' he said. 'From the moment I shook his hand. You can usually tell. So...back to your question. Your terms of reference are to get out of any false positions you've been such a purblind idiot as to get yourself into and after that to see that whatever we do end up with at Norfolk is as good as it can be for the people it's going to affect. And you make sure there's none of this guard-room nonsense.' He glanced at his watch. 'Well I'm not going to see Geoffrey Borland this side of lunch that's for sure, so let's go down to the club and throw a few dice, shall we?'

As they went down the wide steps towards Uncle Harry's old Ford parked in the drive a man rushed past them, paused as if to speak to them, then continued flying on his way. Unaccountably Paul felt a clutching at his stomach.

'Come on, Paul,' Harry a pace or two ahead called to him.

Paul looked at the man standing talking excitedly to some of those seated on the *loggia*.

'Come on, man!' said Harry.

Paul followed him slowly to the car. By the time he got into it there was quite a small furore going on up above them with others leaving their seats to join the excited group.

'Mundall seems to have some news,' he said.

'He always was an excitable chap,' said Harry, switching on the ignition.

'Shall I go and see...'

'Don't bother with it,' Uncle Harry said. 'If it's important we'll hear it at the club.'

They heard about it in the club, a bungalow of a building set in the middle of a large concrete car park railinged in from the town and planted with trees for shade. If there had been a stir at the Darien, here it was ferment. The bar was packed and the dining-room which by now would normally have had at any rate a sprinkling of the staid and serious who didn't drink at lunchtime, was quite deserted. The billiard table was unused. But the entrance *loggia* with its round tables and its comfortable chairs which would normally have had only one or two members picking at the London and New York papers and the business magazines, had become a busy overflow with men with drinks in hand, standing in groups, shouting and laughing and joking with each other and the neat lines of the papers and periodicals, usually so tidily overlapping, were in disarray.

281

'What's on earth's going on?' asked Harry of Paul but he did not have to wait long to hear. Joe Hernandez, the man who had sold his shares in Coral Gardens to Daniel Fonseca, Joe Hernandez huge, good-natured, eyes gleaming behind his pebble glass, spotted him.

'Uncle Harry!' he shouted and he pushed his way through the press and put a massive arm around Harry's shoulders. 'How are you, man!' It was as if the gathering was now complete.

'What's going on?' said Harry.

'You don't know? You haven't heard?'

Harry shook his head and meanwhile Roger Savage, one of the younger men, was joking at Paul: 'Which post you going to pick, Paul?' And Paul, instinctively aware that this was a moment of great significance to him, waited with a beating heart for the explanation.

'Errol Rose has had his throat cut.'

'You mean he's dead?'

'As mutton.'

'Good God!' said Harry. He stood quite still, holding his old hat, in khaki shirt and shorts, neat socks and shining shoes, looking up at Joe Hernandez towering above him and because he was so liked, and so respected, those near at hand fell silent long enough for Hernandez to explain:

'That's only the beginning, man,' he said. 'The old bugger had some girl dressed in his daughter's school uniform tied down to a bed all ready for his attention.'

'Lawks!' said Harry, awed.

'Where was this?' Paul demanded.

'Your place. Where else?' said Savage.

'You mean...at Coral Gardens?'

'Right.'

'In Kornblath's guest suite?' It was out before he could stop himself. 'Who did it?' he said hastily.

'That man Raleigh they reckon,' someone said.

'Cut his throat? What? With a machete?'

'Bloody near right through.'

'And his hand... Clean off. Pow!'

'According to this man Hamilton...'

'Hamilton. You said Hamilton...'

'After his gun...'

'What a bloody idiot...'

'What about Hamilton?'

'Found him. Lying outside. With his head damn near cut off and his hand lying a yard or two away...'

'Did you ever meet the girl, Paul? Real dolly bird named Charlotte Amalie?'

'You've got to be joking! Charlotte Amalie!'

'That's in the Virgins.'

'This one wasn't!'

283

'Ever meet her, Paul...'

'I could use a drink,' said Harry. 'And you look as if you could use one too, Paul...'

'Uncle Harry! How are you, man?'

'*Ai! Ai! Ai!* What's happening? Someone struck oil?'

'Yes. Bertie Sasso!'

'How about that, Paul...'

'Excuse me, Savage...'

'What'll it be, Paul...'

'Not a blast! This one's on me. Charley! Russian Bear and soda for Mr Blades! Paul?'

'Gin and tonic...'

'Will someone tell me...'

'Someone's taken a cutlass to poor old Errol...'

'But, man, his position's quite untenable...'

'They're going to call themselves the Cordoba Degenerates...'

'And have children's dress parades. C.D.P.'s.'

'...kicked his hand thinking it was a crab...'

'By the time the police got there...'

'Hallo! Hallo! Hallo! Who have we got here?'

'Bertie!'

'What for you come in so untidy man? What sort of place you think this is?'

'He thinks it's the House of Represen-
tatives!'

'Thanks, Joe.'

'Paul.'

'Thanks.'

'Looking at you.'

'Your father-in-law's just come in, Paul.'

'What's this damn thing?'

'Eh?'

'This!'

'Oh that's from Cecil Bryden.'

'Pretty damn quick off the mark isn't
he?'

'What's it for, Bertie? To wish you
luck.'

'Your son-in-law's in there. With Uncle
Harry.'

'What damn fools they think we are?'

'No man. What damn fools they are.
Only jackass him bet on mawgah hoss.'

'Mawgah!'

'What for you stand there like damn
black jigga nanny? You think all you got
to do get in Buckingham Palace is blow
out yo' belly?'

'You tell me.'

'You don' really think you goin' lick
out Costa? Man did you hear him at
Sussanna's Hill las' night? Man, he had
them spellbound!'

'Sweet words don't fill him belly... Paul.
Is Dorothea with you?'

'No... I came in with Uncle Harry. I didn't know about this business...'

'Uncle Harry!'

'Bertie!... Buy you a drink... Charley!... How's Alice?'

'Fine. Fine.'

'Must be having one hell of a time with her girls if all we hear is true...'

'It's true all right. What a damned arse. If he'd got to do it, why the devil didn't he do it off the island?'

'The thing's incredible. The man was always pontificating...'

'Perhaps he wanted to teach the girl a lesson!'

'Not very funny, Morgan...'

'Bertie looks pretty happy.'

'Paul Blades looks anything but...'

'What about Daniel, eh?'

'Patrick, me bhoy...'

'Same thing, Charley...'

'Uncle Harry! Good to see you...'

'What price New St James now.

'You should have waited Foxy...you're not going to unload that lot in a hurry.'

'What a lot of nonsense! He's going to dig a canal through it and let off moorings!'

'You heard what the Cordoba Degenerate said to the People's...'

'Hallo, Paul. Quite a thing, eh? You knew the girl didn't you. I saw that

photograph taken at the Ball. Wouldn't
have minded tying her down myself...'

'...a game of dice?'

'Don't be such an idiot. Who you thinks
going to play dice...'

'Man dey carry 'traw mustn't fool wid
fire...'

'Seriously how long d'you give Vernon,
Bertie...'

Paul was glad when it was over. His head
was splitting, not because he had had too
many gin and tonics, although he had, not
even because of the hubbub which after
an hour had hardly lessened, but from the
sheer strain of a mental state so complex
that he had found himself hardly able to
think coherently or talk intelligently. It was
utter relief to be back in the old Ford with
Uncle Harry and on their way back to
Norfolk. He barely noticed the cauldron
heat of early afternoon, he had forgotten
he hadn't eaten.

'What about your meeting?' he said
dully.

'Blast the meeting,' Uncle Harry said.

A little later Paul said: 'Are they right?
That's the end of Costa?'

'The end of Costa. And the end of New
St James. Bertie'll get in by a landslide.'

'Was McIndoe right? About Kornblath?'

'He should know, Paul. He's a lawyer.'

'D'you think they'll do anything about Charlotte Amalie?'

'Charlotte Amalie!... No, Paul, I shouldn't think so. Just ship her back to the States and be glad to be shut of her. You hungry?'

'No.'

'Well I am. We'll try Belle's. Not likely to be anyone round our necks there anyway.'

They were at Belle's twenty-five minutes later—a modest place well up the hillside which was popular to run out to in the evenings.

'For you, Uncle Harry,' Belle said. 'Yes. For anyone else, no. So what you want?'

'Cling cling beef?'

'With Worcester?'

'With everything.'

When Belle had gone off to her kitchen, Uncle Harry said. 'Well there it is, Paul. And it's going to look pretty much like that in ten years time, I daresay.'

St James was at their feet, the dining area a hard oblong projection with iron railings on three sides. Above their heads was a rattan canopy and at fifteen hundred feet the air was cooler. Paul stared at the patchwork of wide criss-crossing streets which lost their form quite soon, blurring to a muddle of shanty shacks. He could pick out almost everything: King Street running down to Victoria Square. Daniel's office where it had all began; the club where it had ended—the dream of wealth. He looked at the vultures circling gracefully, soaring on the up-currents, tipping their wings, searching for dead things. It was rare one looked down on vultures.

'Yes,' he said. 'I daresay it is.'

'It was to be a big thing, Paul.'

'Fantastic.'

'It's a bit frightening isn't it?'

'What?'

'That a couple of men can get together and play games with the lives of entire populations. What sort of man is he?'

'Kornblath?' He thought of Kornblath, soft and clean and gentle who always smelt as if he'd just got out of his bath. Who'd a continuing invitation not yet withdrawn for Dorothea to live in comfort in London in a flat he'd provide. He wondered if she'd heard from him; if they had regular contact.

'I suppose,' he answered, 'he's an adventurer as well. It couldn't have been for the money.'

'But surely he wasn't...'

'Oh, no. It was all tied up with a major insurance company and some lot from Las Vegas or somewhere. And there was a Canadian Bank. I don't know which one.

I daresay there was more to it than that.'

'Mafia most likely,' said Harry with a little gloom.

'Wouldn't be surprised.'

'Well,' said Harry, cheering up. 'There's going to be a lot of disappointed men before the day's out. Including a whole heap of Cordobans...'

'Who'll have to go on paying taxes.'

'Well, actually, I wasn't thinking of them. I was thinking about people like Foxwell. Joe tells me he's bought himself a coupla thousand acres of swamp in what was to be industry or something!' He chuckled. 'Poor old Foxy. Got it wrong this time anyway!' And, after a moment, chuckling: 'You know what you ought to suggest to your father-in-law as the first thing he does when he gets in office? Sets up a new Ministry. The Ministry of Anti-Tourism!'

Paul understood what lay behind the joke.

'You're not serious,' he said, half laughing.

'Well I don't know,' said Harry, becoming a little serious. 'I'm not at all sure it wouldn't be as bad an idea as that. I never knew many countries which really benefited out of tourism for all the talk.' And having made the bridge it was easy to go on, 'You're going to be a pretty important person, Paul. You're not going to get your two million quid. But there's a lot of compensations just waiting round to be picked up.'

'Yes, but that isn't true,' Paul answered quietly.

'She's very young, Paul.' Harry said, 'Don't judge too harshly. Be gentle with her and you may be surprised. You didn't know her faults when you married her; why should you assume you know her virtues now?'

# Seventeen

'You're back early,' Sophie said.

'I don't imagine I have to tell you why,' responded Harry. 'Tea, Paul?... Ring the bell will you, there's a good chap.'

When he came back, Sophie said: 'So your father-in-law's going to be Chief Minister.'

'That's the general opinion.'

'It's not a question of opinion. It's one of fact.'

There was unusual eagerness about her. Her eyes were avid for gossip. Not for years had such a plum as this been tossed in her lap. He wondered vaguely how she had heard, what she had heard. Probably Dorothea had told her.

'Where's Dorothea?' he asked.

'You're not supposed to be back for hours. You don't think she sits around all day here, do you?'

Harry stopped mopping his brow.

'How did you hear?' he asked.

'It's impossible not to hear. The island's buzzing with it.' She was back to Paul. 'That girl, the one he tied up—she was with him at The Fort when they had the

292

Ball, wasn't she?'

'Yes, Aunt Sophie, she was with him.'

'How she come to be there?'

'Kornblath, the one who was going to do New St James, hired her for him. She's a New York prostitute.'

'Well he can't come back. They'll lock him up.'

'Right.'

Alexander came in after knocking. Even he looked aroused.

'Bring us some tea, would you Alexander.'

'Yes, Mass Harry.' Before he left the room he even hesitated and was evidently about to speak, then thought better of it and withdrew.

'It's suddenly just like Christmas Eve,' said Harry dryly.

'I'm going to have a shower,' Paul said. 'Excuse me.'

He went quickly to his room in the positive manner of a man behaving normally because there is no reason not to. He had no plans in his mind nor any sense of the urgency of making plans. For a while, time at Norfolk had had meaning; now it had none. In a strange way he was more conscious of the hugeness of the house and the vastness of the estate than he had ever been. It was a minor empire which had been threatened and while the threat was there had been plainly limited; now it encompassed all that mattered. There was the ocean ahead and the Saddle behind and Palmira to the west and Pilotte to the east. And over there was St James, a shabby sort of town one went to about once a month and about an hour along the road was a place called Coral Gardens which wasn't really Cordoba anyway.

The incredible bedroom was cool and restful, the louvres closed, the twin double beds crisp with new sheets and coverlets turned down for a siesta. It was quite silent, only his steps ringing on the wooden floors. He went along opening louvres bringing light but not sun into the room for the room faced north as do all important bedrooms in the Caribbean. Except for a few vultures high in the sky, circling lazily, and a quick bird or two on the platform below him, nothing was moving. The sea was very calm, so calm that currents marked patterns on its surface. There was no vessel of any kind to be seen, not even a fisherman's canoe and the horizon merged with sky. There was no one cutting cane—there was no cane to cut. All the cane was in. The fields were brown with faint green lines which was the new cane planted. It would grow and there would be cutlasses flashing in the sun and the clink of them would reach the ears. And there would be small patches of colour which would be the women helping their men. And sometimes it would rain. But mostly it would be as it was today, blue with fluffy clouds. And the nights would be filled with stars. And cool after the unchanging heat.

He was swift in showering, swift enough for the tea to be enjoyable. It was strange taking tea on a day which was not a Sunday. But then it was Christmas Eve.

'You knew this man who found his body?' Sophie asked.

He told her what he knew of Hamilton. And he could see Hamilton with his stone eyes and his desperate manner. And he told her what he knew of Kornblath. And he could see Kornblath with his blue eyes and his well-founded manner. And so they progressed until the tea had been finished and the equipment removed. And they talked about Daniel, and Bertie Sasso, and Vernon Costa...they even talked about Foxwell and his two thousand acres of swamp. They talked the day away. And then Sophie called for Hesther and banged her wheel rims and sped away to be changed for dinner. So Paul and Uncle Harry went out on the platform. And it was as it almost always was at Norfolk on the nights when the moon rose over

Pilotte, and the breeze fell down the hills like water and apart from the town the only lights were their own buzz-off bulbs and the hard light of Copra Valley high up and to the right.

They saw the lights of the M.G. sift through the coconut palms along the shore road and through the citrus trees planted along the marl road leading to the house. They were in the white chairs with holes cut out in their arms to take the tumblers men who worked long hours in the tropic sun required. They heard the car door slam under Tom Long's cotton tree and Dorothea's quick steps up towards them. She was humming determinedly.

'Hallo, Dee,' Paul said.

'Hallo, Paul.' She kissed his cheek quickly. 'Hallo, Uncle Harry. Back early aren't you?'

And she bent to kiss him too but he stopped her with a movement of his hand.

'What did you say?'

'Uhm?' She was puzzled.

'Haven't you heard?'

'What?'

'The news?'

Paul saw the momentary hesitation, then the marvellous recovery. She laughed lightly: 'News? Really, Uncle Harry, I just don't know what you're talking about. Has something happened in St James? News doesn't travel very fast in Cordoba, you know.'

'This news does!' said Harry sharply. And he stood and Paul had never seen such hurt in his eyes. 'I'm going in to change,' he said; and left them.

Paul watched her. He saw her eyes following his uncle all the way along the platform until he turned into the house. She was absolutely still, her posture marvellous. She was wearing the same yellow slacks she had worn the first time she'd met Malcolm and a thin white fitting shirt which hugged the hips and showed the outline of her bra. Her coarse black hair was neat, tight to her neck, softened with its casual fringe, held firm for driving with a velvet band. Her skin was fresh and smooth and cool. But he saw the slacks and shirt discarded on a floor, the bra thrown anywhere, the hair unruly on a pillow, the skin wet with sweat. And behind the eyes he saw an agile mind, working quickly. The eyes caught his and for a moment hardened translating something of his thoughts and then were quizzical.

'What is this, Paul?' There was a half chuckle in her voice as if she knew someone was playing games with her but

297

didn't mind.

'New St James is off,' Paul answered brutally. 'So's Norfolk.' He stood abruptly, finished his whisky in a gulp. 'Have you got the key?' And when she didn't answer but looked at him with worried perplexity. 'Come on, come on. The car key!'

'I left it in the ignition.' She laid a hand on his arm. 'What's happened, Paul?'

He threw the hand off. 'Go and ask your friend Sophie. She's got all the details.'

Copra Valley was in darkness. The hard lights seen from Norfolk's platform had been switched off. But the moonlight was very bright and the house was quite clear, staring from its mound across the countless palm trees to the distant sea. Moonlight healed its shabbiness giving it with its archways and double staircase, fretworked balcony, louvred central door and windows, its simple roof, a cold nobility.

'Malcolm!' Paul shouted angrily, disbelieving the darkness, thinking his uncle had seen the car lights shafting through the trees and, not wanting to face him, or be bothered with him, had switched his own off. When there was no reply, he ran up the steps to the veranda.

But there was no one here, only a new length of rope, glowing at its tip which would burn for hours. Paul tried the door, rattling it. But the door was locked. He cursed, refusing to believe what commonsense told him. He was in that state of mind which will not be denied, which shuts out logic, which in impatience tramples reason underfoot. He ran down the stairs again and around the house to the back. Here there was a courtyard, high walled, with a stable for Malcolm's horse and a shabby little building where the woman, Aggie, slept. Here were no lights either, only the moonlight casting long shadows. He paused, momentarily hesitant. Ahead of him was a flight of broad stone steps, the only back entrance to the house. At his pause the cicadas, silenced by his movements, burst out again clamouring from every hand and in the distance a pottoo hooted mournfully. Then he heard other sounds: the whinny of Malcolm's horse and a strange bubbling sound, coarse, regular but interrupted which puzzled him for a moment, until he recognized it as the sound of a sleeping woman. Aggie, dismissed, had gone to bed.

Sanity told him Malcolm had gone out, down to the Alligator Club most likely. But anger refused to be denied. He went up the steep, wide, narrow steps and tried the door. It was locked. He put his shoulder to it, smashing the puny lock. He scrabbled for a light, found it and switched it on, surprising the big red ants, the beetles waving their antennae, the crawling lizard. Off the kitchen was a sort of space, too small to be called a hall, off which a twisting stair ran down to the bedroom floor. He hesitated then went through to the sitting-room, snapping on lights, into the long shabby room lined with the pitted greyish wood of coconut planks, ceilinged with white planks disfigured by the termite runs, furnished more with books than anything. On the table was an ash tray, filled with stubs. He picked it up and saw that many were stained with lipstick. In a paroxysm of rage he picked up the ashtray and hurled it with all his strength against a wall. The sound was curiously softened by the coconut wall and the ashtray, being tin, merely bounced away scattering stubs across the floor. He turned back to the space and ran down the stairs, so quickly as to lose his footing, only saving himself by grabbing at the handrail. At the bottom were two doors leading off a narrow passage. He hesitated, not knowing the geography of the lower floor, then opened one of them to find himself in a most extraordinary bedroom: large, one out of a collection of vaguely inter-connecting rooms with arches at their ends and its windows jammed, uncurtained casements, tiny, grilled with iron bars like prisoner's cells' and the walls and floor of stone. Like the walls the pitted ceiling joists were flaking with pink paint and from them bits of string which, presumably, once had held mosquito nets, hung limply. There were innumerable signs of insects; moths embalmed in dusty webs, with the spiders which had spun them dead as well, and lines of termite runs across the mouldering walls. For furniture there was an old ant-riddled dressing-table with a fly-blown mirror, a lumpy double bed devoid of counterpane, a wicker armchair, a dark wood wardrobe whose door had gone. For decoration there was a single sepia print framed in *passe-partout,* faded by time, runnelled by the lines which insects eating it had made. But none of this was remarkable compared with the books. Never in his life had Paul seen in what was, so-called, a bedroom, so many books. There were bookcases of bamboo, bookcases of white-painted wood, bookcases with glass fronts, bookcases carved and plain, bookcases in mahogany, oak and cedar, all of different heights and widths, butting up against each other and apart, spread through the line of what had been several rooms and was now converted into one, into a library. And still there were insufficient places for the books; in not one bookcase was a single space and in some of them the books were double depth and odd, higher volumes, could be seen peering over their lower fellows and in between the bookcases that didn't touch were piles of books and on their tops were more.

In the centre of the room was a table and on it more books, some carvings and a pair of human skulls, and on another table another skull, but this one long and thin which might have been an alligator's head, still more books, a half empty bottle of rum, dirty glasses and packets of cigarettes. On one glass there was lipstick and on one butt in an ashtray, lipstick. In the wicker armchair, furry with sprung fibre, was an arm seating for a glass containing dregs of rum and beside it stood a standard lamp with a rickety looking shade burned through in half a dozen places. There was also a large old-fashioned gramophone and in two corners yard-wide squares of plywood pierced by circles of orange webbing which were clearly speakers. And elsewhere, wherever there was space to fix them was the strangest collection of weird oddments: a swordfish's sword with missing teeth, a marlin's bill, an alligator's skin brown and opened out like an animal crushed by a massive weight.

Fascinated even out of anger, Paul looked about him, puzzled. There was something missing. And then he realized what it was, it was Malcolm's clothes—for the wardrobe was merely another store for books. There were two doors, the one obviously leading back to the narrow passage, the other a mystery. He opened it. It was a door hiding a fair-sized room in which was an iron bath, tidemarked with dirt, a corner basin with another fly-blown mirror and above it a dusty shelf holding a smeared toothbrush, a half squeezed tube of shaving cream, a lump of soap etched with scum. Beside it, on a rusty hook, hung a torn and ragged towel. But the remarkable thing was the floor which was so littered it would have been impossible to have stepped a straight course from one wall to the other for the shoes, the socks, the items of discarded clothes which booby-trapped it. And from the walls, on hangers hung on nails were coats, and trousers overhung with shirts and singlets. There was a chest of drawers with the drawers pulled out to different widths disclosing still more jumble. And as well there were everywhere all manner of objects which did not go by the name of clothes or what was normally found in bathrooms: more books, empty bottles, a stack of newspapers, a broken chair...

Paul stared at it bewildered, then, going back to the bedroom itself, sat down in the wicker chair sobered and amazed. This room, more than anything else ever could have, told him Malcolm's life. He put out a hand and picked up the nearest book, glanced at it, then, opening it, saw by the flyleaf a date was written. A fairly recent date. He opened another—and found another date. He got to his feet again and went round opening books at random. Every one had a date, most were worm-eaten. In one there was a dead worm caught between the cover and the flyleaf, as if it had travelled far but the cover had been too much—a pale, dead thing it looked and when he brushed it to the floor its going left a scar, an elliptically shaped hole which marked its grave. He turned a page or two. It was some sort of Court Room cases book and early on there was a drawing of what Paul took to be a policeman helping a jockey of a man up the steps of a witness box. Ahead was a judge. But the judge had no face, the worms had eaten it away. Slowly he put the book down where he had found it and went over to the bed. The sheets were soiled and creased. So were the pillows. And each pillow bore the imprint of a head. On the floor beside the bed, was the end stub of a cigarette. He picked it up. It was stained with lipstick.

He left the room and went up the stairs, through the sitting-room and, opening the door, went out on to the balcony and for a long time stood with his hands on the rotting balustrade, staring at the night and thinking. There was no anger left. He could not escape the comparison of the life which for thirty years Malcolm had led and the life he and Dorothea would have led if Errol Rose had not been murdered. As he stared at the silver night, with its clamorous insects, the thousand upon thousand intermittent sparks of fireflies, the stars lonely for all their number, the uncountable palm fronds silvered by the moonlight, overlapping, casting shadows, stretching down like spiders to the sea, he thought of town and cities, grand hotels, theatres, throngs of people and all the other innumerable facets of the life they thought of towns and cities, grand hotels, theatres, throngs of through books. He had guessed the meaning of the dates in Malcolm's books, the date when he had finished reading them. And he wondered if there were any books unread.

He went into the house and finding himself a glass and a bottle of whisky and a jug which he filled with water, settled himself on the balcony to wait for Malcolm to return. He put a cigarette in his mouth and reaching up beside him as Malcolm must have reached up a hundred thousand times, lit it from the glowing rope.

It was well into the night before Malcolm came back to Copra Valley. He wore white ducks stained with oil and the same blue string vest he had been wearing the evening Dorothea had first met him. His beard was heavy and contrasted strangely with the smoothness of the gold cross he always wore from the chain hung round his neck. He was drunk with the slowed up heaviness of the habitual drinker who does no more on returning home than throw himself upon his bed and go straight off into sleep.

He came slowly and carefully up the steps quite unaware of Paul's presence. In his hand he had a key which he held towards the door before discovering it was open. He swore and turned round with an air of slight affront. He saw Paul watching him.

'What the hell's all this?' He slurred.

Paul looked at him carefully in the light of what Uncle Harry had had to say and what he had discovered and been thinking about for hours. He noticed that for once the bright blue eyes had lost their brightness, that the lips were wet and loose. Yet for all that there was something about the man.

'I know all about what's happened here today,' he said.

'So?' The reply was challenging.

'And I expect you know what's happened

to Rose. And what it means.'

Malcolm raised a hand and vaguely waved in the approximate direction of Pilotte. 'Who doesn't?' he said.

'I've told Uncle Harry I lit that fire.'

'Crowing, eh?' sneered Malcolm.

'No. There's nothing to crow about.'

'I'm going to bed,' said Malcolm.

'I just wanted to tell you,' Paul said, 'that if you want some of Norfolk you can have as much as you care to take.'

'Piss off,' said Malcolm.

'It isn't that simple, Malcolm.'

'What's that supposed to mean?' The words were still slurred but there was something sharper in Malcolm's eyes. It was as if Paul had touched a chord so sensitive that even in his present state, Malcolm was alerted.

Paul stood and going to the veranda's edge pitched his cigarette over it. He watched its brief glowing parabola abruptly snuffed out by some vegetation.

'It's curious, isn't it,' he said, 'how totally unimportant all we've tried to do...you and me and Dorothea, I mean, has been. We might as well not have bothered.'

'You think we should...you think we should do something positive?'

Paul turned. There had been a curious cunning in the words, a threat even. He found Malcolm watching him.

307

'Yes,' he said. 'I think we should. I don't think we can spend the balance of our lives like three assassins who sacrificed everything decent and worthwhile to kill a man only to find he'd died on them in his sleep.'

'What's this,' sneered Malcolm. 'Death-bed repentance.'

'Something like that,' Paul agreed.

He realized he was wasting his time, that it would be more sensible at least to wait until Malcolm had slept off his drinking. But some instinct drove him into a final effort.

'Malcolm,' he said. 'There's something you don't know. Before Uncle Harry heard about Errol Rose, before he knew New St James was dead as mutton and after I'd told him I'd lit that fire, he volunteered to let Norfolk be developed for tourism. In effect he volunteered to make it over to me. And he won't change his mind just because the Kornblath thing is off. So really we're in just the same position as we would have been if we'd got control the way we planned.'

Malcolm was leaning against the door frame.

'You've forgotten my price,' he said.

Paul shook his head. 'Bog Pen and fifty thousand dollars.'

'Bog Pen, fifty thousand dollars...'

'I've told you. You can have as much of Norfolk as you want. And there won't be any restrictions against turning it into cash...'

'Don't interrupt.'

The words were slowly said, thickly spoken, but there was so much meaning, so much of contempt and menace in them that Paul was utterly silenced. He stared, frowning, uneasy, at the slouching figure in stained ducks and blue string vest, lit by the moonlight. He saw the glint of the small gold cross and he thought of the incredible library beneath his feet, every book read, some no doubt several times. He had come in anger but anger had died with understanding and deep disquiet had flowed into the vacuum anger's departure had left behind. He had wanted to make such amends as was in his power for Malcolm's wasted life, or at the very least, through the attempt, to expiate his own thoughts and actions. He had not been sanguine as to the likelihood of success but he knew he must make the effort. But this man, this huge, stinking, slouching, yet, for all that, exceptional and impressive man, was he realized beyond his reach. It was not the night's drinking which would defeat his efforts, it was something deep in the soul of a man who had nursed envy and frustration for too many years. There was nothing he could do. He would hear what Malcolm had to say, then go.

'Bog Pen, fifty thousand dollars and to get rid of Uncle Harry.' There was a loathsome satisfaction in his words.

'Are you quite sure,' Paul answered quietly, remembering what Dorothea had said, 'that it isn't yourself you hate?'

Malcolm raised his head a little, slowly, in the way men who have drunk too much often do. 'Oh,' he said. 'Wisdom.' He thrust himself away from the door frame by a movement of his back and made a pace or two towards Paul. Near enough to touch him, he swayed a little, yet not for a moment did his eyes leave Paul's. 'Fine fellow, my nephew,' he observed. 'Very wise. Very noble. Fine wife too. Best fuck I've had in years.' He waited for reaction and when there was none, folded his arms and nodded vaguely. 'Generous too. Willing to share it all.'

'Good night, Malcolm,' Paul said quietly and turned to go. But he felt a powerful hand suddenly on his shoulder. 'Well?' he said, turning back.

'Just one question.'

'Yes?'

'What you going to do about her?'

'I think that's my business, isn't it?'

'Going to turn the other cheek aren't you. Right?' Paul did not reply. 'Full to

310

the brim with good intentions. Right?' Still Paul would not reply. 'Very good,' Malcolm went on. 'Very good indeed. Noble. Very noble.' And after a moment. '"To be ashamed..."' He broke off, searching his befuddled memory, then found what he was seeking and resumed. '"To be ashamed with the noble shame, is the very germ and first upgrowth of virtue".' He dropped his hand from Paul and demanded. 'Agree?'

'Yes,' Paul said. 'I think I do agree. If it gives you any satisfaction, I'm certainly ashamed. And I'm going to do everything I can to make up for what I've done.'

'What have you done? Lit a silly little fire...'

'No, Malcolm. I've betrayed the trust Uncle Harry had in me. That's much more serious.'

'And you're going to make up for it. Be a decent fellow.'

'Yes.'

'Too late, my friend.'

'I don't think so.'

And abruptly, before Malcolm could have done anything to stop him, Paul turned and left him.

He lay awake for some time, assuming he wouldn't sleep at all. Beside him, in the other double bed, Dorothea was sometimes restless, sometimes silent. She had been awake on his return but they hadn't spoken. He was more conscious than perhaps he had ever been of the hugeness of the house and the vastness of Norfolk all around him. In effect it was all his now—its sugar, its citrus, its coconuts, cattle. The shacks where the workmen lived, the copra factory, Cuevas. Its marl tracks, river, reservoir. Its three mile white sand beach. The house itself.

Only the prospects had been denied him and as he lay listening to Dorothea's breathing and the tropic night sounds, reflecting on those prospects he found them no more substantial than the prospects of a very vivid dream wakefulness has banished. The problems of his life were very near ones and all to do with people—Dorothea, Sophie, Malcolm, Uncle Harry. All Blades. Kornblath, Tod, Hamilton, and for that matter Coral Gardens, were of another kind of life his own would scarcely touch. He would not be cut off from such people and such places, his outlook was not what Uncle Harry's had been—but he would see them from a different viewpoint. From now on his life would be bound almost totally to Norfolk just as the lives of all those to whom Norfolk gave a living would be bound up with his. It occurred to him with some surprise that for the first time in his life he had responsibility. From old Gran'paw at the gate to the youngest pickney they would look to him in trouble, pain or sickness, to settle quarrels, to advise—as up to now they had looked to Uncle Harry—and Uncle Harry's example would be a tremendous one to match. Well he would do his best and if, as he almost certainly would, he fell short of Uncle Harry's best, that could not be helped—the reflection did not overmuch trouble him. What troubled him more, what kept intruding into these easier musings, was what to do about the girl who slept, or pretended to sleep, beside him and the man he had left in the shabby little house up there, above him in the night. And it was more of Malcolm than of Dorothea he thought because there had been something menacing, something rather frightening in Malcolm's words. He could not shake off the nagging worry that none of them were finished with Malcolm yet. And against the background of such uneasy meditations the weariness of a long and emotionally exhausting day overcame him and he fell asleep.

In the modest room along the passage Harry had found sleep difficult to come by too. He had heard Paul come back and wondered, unhappily, on what might have taken place in Copra Valley between his brother and his nephew. But Harry was a patient and pragmatic man, content to wait till morning when Paul would tell him so much as he chose. His thoughts were more on Dorothea and what would be Paul's decision there. To Paul himself he gave little thought. Paul would manage. The boy had become a man. Sometimes manhood came slowly, as in his own case, through the change in Sophie; sometimes, as in Paul's, it came almost overnight. But Dorothea? There was a bigger problem.

But Harry too was weary, and an old man now—and eventually he fell asleep as well.

Only Sophie didn't sleep at all. Not sleeping did not disturb her. It was quite often that she passed whole nights without sleeping and then she would awaken Hesther and have her dress her and sometimes sit out on the platform, a shawl around her shoulders, waiting for the first glimmer of false dawn when she would go back to her room so as not to be caught out there by Harry over his cups of tea. Sometimes even, in the secrecy of the night, she would do something no one, not even Hesther ever watched her do, shuffle slowly and painfully round the house. Harry knew she did this, as he knew that in the privacy of her room Sophie would struggle from her wheelchair and shuffle round her room for a few minutes every day—but he took care never to let her know he knew. For he understood—at night, in a curious way, Sophie believed herself once again the mistress of Norfolk Hall.

Tonight she had much to think about and the hours flowed by causing her no concern and thus it was that she was, in that brooding mansion silvered by the moonlight, the only one to hear the car. It came very quietly as if the driver was anxious not to be discovered but the drive was gravelly, Sophie's room was on the ground floor and her hearing was acute. She knew the sound for what it was from a long way off. She reached for her stick and tapped it against the wall behind her, waking Hesther who came in sleepy-eyed but uncomplaining, helped her from bed to wheelchair, put the shawl around her shoulders, pushed her to the door, opened it, and was dismissed.

Sophie slowly turned the rims of her wheelchair. Not now the angry taps to speed her across the room, the night was a secret time, no one must be woken, no one must disturb her. Above all, no one but she must solve this mystery.

She made her way, a strange hunched figure in her nightdress, her hair wild and awry, the shawl about her shoulders and, propped in their special place, her sticks. The moonlight cast long shadows across the sitting-room, and the platform and Norfolk stretched below were cold and brilliant. Its mystery lay over everything and the lines it made were astonishingly sharp. There was the line where sky met sea and the gently shifting palms were crisply etched. The shadows of the citrus trees near at hand, and of Tom Long's cotton tree were painted black upon the ground.

Making her way to the very edge of the balcony the crippled woman peered into the night searching for the car which had brought her out and the man or woman who had driven it. At first she saw neither, she saw only what she had seen many times before, Norfolk by moonlight unchanging but for the trees which grew taller, died and were replaced. Or most of them. But not Tom Long's cotton tree spreading its branches far and wide as if to span eternity, as if it would never die. And looking at it she saw the car, half hidden by the branches but glinting back the moonlight. A sense of glee possessed her—it was intended to be hidden, that car, but she had seen it. There was someone out there. She listened but heard nothing but the night sounds—no crunch of gravel, no stealthy footstep on the stairs up to the platform. She was not afraid. The thought of intruders never troubled her, her fears were of another kind. But her curiosity was insatiable and her selfishness was absolute. She would find out who the intruder was. Unaided.

But the prospect was a daunting one. In twenty years she had never left the boundary of Norfolk's walls and to do so now was an almost inconceivable enterprise. But it must be done. Her curiosity was as overwhelming as her wish to keep this secret to herself. Slowly she turned her head to make sure no one was watching and then, with an enormous effort she forced her rigid body out of the chair, using her sticks, and hobbled with painful slowness along the platform to the place where the curving steps ran up to meet it. And there she stood a macabre witchlike figure bathed in moonlight leaning forward on her sticks.

She paused to recover strength and breath staring down the awesome flight of steps, seeing the shadow of their enclosing walls thrown by the brilliant light, trembling with excitement and trepidation. Dimly it came to her that she could never climb those steps unaided, that once she ventured down them, she would either have to call or wait for Harry coming out at dawn to drink his tea. But this did not shake her resolution and at last she risked her first stiff faltering step.

It was very difficult and very dangerous, the slightest error and she would stumble and, falling, possibly kill herself But somehow she managed first one step and then another. Already she had discovered the undertaking even more desperate than she had supposed but once started on it there could be no turning back. There was no way she could regain as much as a single step. So she went on, knowing no pain—pain had long since been burnt out from her body—but desperately perplexed. Her body could not be made to do the things she tried to force from it. The stiffness would not yield. She had to hump herself and fall, one foot then the other, then catch herself upon her sticks before she toppled. Each step was a victory and the flight of them, the triumph of her life—and so much so that at the bottom she turned to review them as might a climber review his mountain and lifting a stick she shook it at them exultantly.

By now she was bemused. The effort had been so huge as to dampen curiosity and muddle her thoughts. There was, she told herself, something...something to remember. What was it? She could not recall, She had quite forgotten the car glinting in the moonlight, forgotten the crunch of gravel. She had forgotten the intruder. What was it? Yes...that was what it was! Tom Long's tree. Something to do with Tom Long's tree. Of course! It's secret. It was being vouchshafed to her, to discover the secret of Tom Long's tree. She remembered the substance of her words to Paul, not that she had spoken, not the words, just the substance. Man was threefold—body, soul and shadow. And on the third day after death the shadow rose from the body and set on someone else alive. Tom Long, of course. Tom Long whose broken fingers had been mended in her own. Tom Long was in her, his tree was calling her. She must go to it. That was why she had come down those steps. To go to Tom Long's tree where the secret awaited her, waited with the ghosts of a hundred negroes who had kicked and twitched from it until they died.

She started to edge her way across the dewy grass the moonlight casting her shadow beside her, more bent, more stunted even than she was herself. Slowly the wretched woman made her way, watching her shadow and watching the tree. When my shadow meets the shadow of the tree, she told herself, then I shall know. Her eyes were bright, her mind exulting, her soaking nightdress trailing on the grass.

# Eighteen

'She's quite insane,' said Harry quietly.

'There isn't any hope?' said Paul.

'No. Apparently none at all.' And after a moment Harry said. 'I've known for years there was a possibility it might come to this, but I never imagined it would come so cruelly.'

It was mid afternoon—that time of a tropic day which has the least to offer. It was hot, still and very quiet. They were in the sitting-room. The doctor had just left.

'What will you do about her, Uncle Harry?'

'That's up to you, Paul, isn't it?' Harry answered quietly. 'I mean, she's not likely to become violent, nor would it matter if she did. Crippled as she is. And it's not likely she'll live all that many years.'

'You've forgotten Malcolm's note.'

'No.' He stood, and went to stand in the opening between the sitting-room and the platform. He was unused to sitting inside the house in the middle of the afternoon. But after a moment he came in and sat down again.

'Where's Dorothea?' he asked.

'In her room.'

'Have you spoken to her?'

'Not yet.'

'You can't put it off for ever.'

'No.'

'Have you made a decision?'

'No.' He came back to the note Malcolm had cunningly pinned inside his shirt so that when they cut him down they wouldn't find it. 'You seriously think Hastings won't do anything about that note?'

Harry shook his head. He looked older suddenly. One couldn't imagine him riding a horse through Norfolk's marl tracks again.

'No, Paul,' he said. 'I don't think he'll do anything. It's your land and that makes it your cane you fired. You can hardly arrest a man for arson for setting his own crops on fire unless he's after insurance money.'

'But it wasn't my cane,' Paul said. 'Only the land on which it grew.'

'You,'—there was a wry smile on Harry's face—'aren't remembering your *Merchant of Venice*, are you?' He shook his head. 'I don't think there's anything to worry about. At worst it would be a difficult legal point and they'd know I wasn't proffering charges. Anyway...with your father-in-law who he's going to be. No, they won't

321

trouble you.' And after a pause. 'I'm surprised Malcolm imagined that note of his would have the effect he hoped it would. What did happen between you two last night?'

Paul told him. Harry listened thoughtfully. When Paul had finished, he said: 'Whatever else you do, don't take all of the blame on yourself for what Malcolm did last night. He knows my habits; he wanted me to find him.'

'Dee said it wasn't so much that he hated you as that he hated himself.'

'That,' said Harry, 'is quite a wise remark. And a little comforting. But all the same he did hate me, you know. He had the Blades' trait, pride.'

'You're not proud?'

'No?' Harry smiled. 'Well I suppose pride takes different forms. What form is yours going to take?'

'Over Dorothea you mean?' Harry nodded. 'I'm surprised,' Paul said, 'you want me to stay with her. That you can bear the thought of her at Norfolk.'

'Look, Paul. I'm going to hold the fort a minute. Is that all right? Good. What's the girl done? Plotted with you and Malcolm to dispossess me of something that wasn't really mine in any case. Why should I hold it against her when I don't hold it against you...'

'You must.'

'It was agreed that I should hold the fort. But as you raise it... Lawks, man, what sort of fellow do you think I am? Do you think I haven't seen this coming? That I didn't realize there'd be a time when you'd get restive? Or a time when some girl or other mightn't put you up to trying to give me the boot? Matthew Blades might just as well have suggested swords or pistols in that bloody will of his. If anything was calculated to cause fratricide or...or whatever it's called when a nephew does in his uncle, that will was. No, since you ask, I can do more than accept Dorothea living here at Norfolk. I can hope she will.'

He got to his feet to fetch himself a small cigar, lit it unhurriedly and threw the match away.

'It hasn't occurred to you, has it,' he resumed, 'that, leaving aside what happened last night, I've not much to complain about so far as Dorothea's concerned? You think what you and she have been up to has been nothing but a disreputable waste of effort, don't you? Not so, Paul. Not so at all. You're different people from what you were. You particularly. She's what you needed—a Cordoban girl with fire in her blood. A girl who'd make you look into yourself, see what's in you, remember what you are. A Blades. You say I'm not proud? I'm the proudest man on Cordoba. Look at it... Come on.'

He went out to the platform.

'Look at all that lot, Paul.' He waved his arm across Norfolk's acres. 'That's all ours. Every last blamed acre of it. Why shouldn't I be proud? Why shouldn't you be proud? But you weren't. You were anybody's dogsbody at Coral Gardens. Until Dorothea Sasso came along and yanked you out of it. And the other thing? Sleeping with my brother; your uncle?' He shrugged. 'I don't know. Nothing like that's ever happened to me. Thank God. Maybe that's your cross. Maybe that's your punishment. But I tell you this, Paul...if you try to let yourself off the hook by blaming what happened to my brother, and what happened to my wife, on Dorothea letting Malcolm...'

'I wasn't,' Paul interrupted.

'Not now. But you might have got round to it. And that wouldn't be good enough. Not if you're going to go on living here. If you're going to go on living here, knowing Sophie's locked away in a world none of us can ever get into and every time you park your car under Tom Long's tree remembering Malcolm hanging from it and how we had to cut him down, if you're going to do that, then it mustn't be on the basis of excuses. And there mustn't be any sidling out of it. We're all to some degree or other responsible. All of us. Your friend Kornblath, that man Tod, Errol Rose. And me. Because I never found the way through to Malcolm. But most of all it's you and Dorothea who take the ultimate responsibility. Which is another good reason why she should go on living here.'

'Most likely she won't want to.' He thought of Kornblath's offer, of the airline ticket which had arrived in the same parcel as their wedding present.

'You were in love with her, weren't you?'

'I thought I was.'

Harry shook his head. 'You were in love with her. It was written all over you. You won't get her out of your system all that easily. Oh, now...yes. But it'll come back when all this lot's dulled. When maybe you've married someone else. Some nice dull girl who'll make you comfortable and bore you stiff. And you'll tell yourself that you were absolutely right to shake yourself free of Dorothea Sasso. But you won't believe it, Paul. No, man. You won't believe it. Or if you do I just hope I won't be around to see you become so smug.'

'You still like her, don't you?'

'Like her?' Harry chuckled. 'Let's say,' he said, 'I think she's quite a girl and between you you might produce some interesting Blades. And, as usual, I've talked too much.'

'No...' Paul began. But Harry was heading for the sitting-room.

'Seen that damned hat of mine?' he called.

Paul knew he knew exactly where his hat was.

'Where are you going?' he said, following him in.

'You won't believe it,' Harry answered, 'but I'm going to walk along that beach. Want to come?'

'What do you want to walk along the beach for?'

'You don't think,' said Harry, 'that just because Costa's going to be out on his ear any moment now and your friend Kornblath won't dare show his face in Cordoba again, there's not going to be a hotel on that beach before too long? You haven't changed your mind on that as well?'

'No,' said Paul.

'Then don't you think it might be a good idea if we decided on the kind of hotel we're prepared to put up with and the place to put it before Mr Tod gets here?' He put a warm hand, a sun-blotched hand, on his nephew's arm. 'Don't look so astonished, man,' he said. 'Life goes on. And you're going to need a project. And so is Dorothea—if she's agreeable to staying on here with you.' He reached for the hat which was where he always put it. 'Coming then?' he said.

'No,' said Paul. 'Not now.'

He waited out on the platform until Harry had driven out of sight in his battered old Ford—it occurred to him that perhaps Uncle Harry was feeling the need of a project too.

'We have to talk,' he said to Dorothea.

'Yes.'

'Uncle Harry wants you to stay.' And when she didn't answer. 'Aren't you surprised?'

'Very.'

He steeled himself. 'What are you thinking, Dee?' he said. And at her shrug: 'No. I want to know. What are you thinking?'

'I'm not thinking at all. I'm numb.'

'Is that true?'

'Yes.'

'Do you feel guilt?'

'Sleeping with Malcolm?' She shook her head. 'No. He attracted me. He was different. Even that room. No, I don't feel guilty over that.'

'I half expected you to be gone when I came back.'

She shrugged, but otherwise ignored the comment. 'What happened? Last night?'

'Nothing. I offered him as much of Norfolk as he wanted to take...'

'That was a waste of time.'

'Yes. But I did something else. Told him Uncle Harry had agreed to Norfolk being used for tourism. That he'd agreed I could do more or less anything I wanted with it.'

She raised her eyebrows. 'Really? Yes, well of course he wouldn't have liked that a bit.' She became brisker. 'I find it difficult to believe that Uncle Harry wants me to stay on here and you presumably don't. As for why I haven't gone already?' Again she shrugged. 'I don't know I've got an answer that makes sense.'

'You've got that ticket Kornblath sent you.'

'Well, yes,' she agreed. 'It's dated, of course, but I daresay I could change it. But I'd be going to him empty-handed, wouldn't I? You once told me if I went to him empty-handed he wouldn't give me house room.'

'And you'd want to make sure first.' The words were out before he could stop them.

'I'm sorry,' he said.

'Why should you be? You're absolutely right.'

'I'm sorry. It's easy to be cheap and gets us nowhere.' There was nothing to be gained by petty victories—either there was no purpose in talking to her at all or he had to speak to her as an equal. 'Uncle Harry wants us to go on together because he believes we have to use the mess we've made to make something of our lives.'

'He said that?'

'Not in those words. But, yes, he said it. And of course he's right. If we don't face the consequences of what we've done—Malcolm's suicide, Sophie's insanity—we'll spend the rest of our lives in a vacuum. We've got to live with those consequences, not run away from them. We've got to build our lives on a rotten foundation because otherwise they'll have no foundation at all.'

'That's not why I married you,' Dorothea said. 'To spend my life at Norfolk.' And, after a pause. 'I'm not a Blades, Paul, and times have changed. When Sophie married Uncle Harry to be mistress of Norfolk...well you couldn't look much higher, could you? Not if you we're Cordoban. But we know too much about the world these days.' She moved away, then turned. 'If you want to know I think there's something in what you say. But spending my days organizing a rambling house and my evenings sitting on a terrace looking at the fireflies—I'd go screaming mad.'

'It isn't what I've got in mind.'

'Oh?' She was puzzled. 'What have you got in mind?'

He studied her before answering. She was, for her, rather carelessly dressed with her shirt hanging outside her slacks. Yet it made little difference. She had the model's ability to look well in anything.

Yes, he told himself, she'd do very well.

'Norfolk Beach isn't going to happen,' he said. 'But something smaller... Coral Gardens works. Cordoba mayn't have the facilities to take big jets but people get to Coral Gardens just the same...'

'You're going to have a Coral Gardens here?'

'No. Coral Gardens is unreal. And too bloody self-important. But a small, quality hotel...to start with. To see how it goes. To feel one's way.' He looked at her directly. 'You can manage it. I'd play my part of course, but it'll be yours to manage.' He went to the window, one of the four tall windows in this, the most magnificent bedroom of Norfolk Hall, not to stare at his property from it, not to imagine where the hotel might be located, not to observe the brightness giving way to evening—but simply because he found making this suggestion peculiarly embarrassing.

He heard her answer, very quietly: 'You're a generous man.'

'A pragmatic one,' he said. But he was surprised to feel the beating of his heart. 'Does the idea appeal to you?'

'Yes.' Her voice was calm. 'As a matter of fact it does.'

Now he turned.

She regarded him in silence, visualizing him in her hotel, imagining him impressive in white tuxedo coming down for an evening drink after the business of Norfolk had been dealt with for the day. Mingling with the guests. Pausing to chat with one or two who had begged her to introduce them so that they could learn about sugar and things like that at first hand. From a real live planter. She even smiled.

'You're smiling,' he said.

'It's nothing. We'd live here though?'

'Yes.'

'And Uncle Harry. What about Sophie?'

'If the doctors advise it.'

'You think it would work?'

'I think it's worth trying. It's the only solution...'

He broke off, uncomfortable.

'No, it's a good word, man,' she said.

331

'A very good word.'

'We're going to have a problem,' he said. 'We can't run away from that. We've got to be busy, fill our lives with projects. We couldn't just...share a rambling house and spend our evenings together looking at the fireflies. We'd both end up drunks.'

'Malcolms.'

'If we both had separate interests. But we shared them with each other. Helped each other out...' It was too difficult. He felt a choking in his throat.

'You're a sentimental as well as a generous man, aren't you?' Dorothea said. And, practically: 'And what about sex?'

'I daresay we'd manage.' There was the first, faint touch of humour in his voice. 'If we didn't take it too seriously at the start.'

'Oh, I don't know about that,' she said. 'It's a very important thing to me. Could I have a shop?'

He could see her in her shop. It would be very chic. And everything in good taste. Dresses. Scarves. Perfumes. Practically all imported. Once or twice a year she would go to the States and Europe to buy for it. The guests would watch carefully what she wore herself.

'If you like,' he said. 'Is it agreed then?'

She looked at him thoughtfully and then she said:

332

'Give me a cigarette.'

'You've already got one.'

'I know.' She crossed to an ashtray and plunging her cigarette in it, ground it out. 'Give me a cigarette.'

He gave her one.

She went to a drawer and took something from it.

'Light?'

He came close to her. She held the something, an airline ticket, to his match. It did not catch easily but eventually it did. She lit her cigarette from it. 'If you'll excuse the corn,' she apologized.

She held the burning airline ticket in her hand, watching it, shifting it in her fingers until there was so little left she had to drop it to the floor. The ash was thick and flaky. Just one small corner remained unburned.

'That's that,' she said. 'What shall we do? Try a little not very serious sex? Or go down to the beach and decide where my hotel's going to be?'

'Uncle Harry's already down there doing that.'

She looked at him very steadily.

'Well then?' she said.

They stood a yard or so apart, looking at each other. Dorothea raised a hand up to a button on her shirt—then let it fall again.

He stood, quite still, for moments longer—then, very deliberately took the pace which pride told him not to take and undid the button for her.

This Large Print Book for the Partially sighted, who cannot read normal print, is published under the auspices of

**THE ULVERSCROFT FOUNDATION**